THE V̶ ̶ ̶ ̶ WARD

Francine Giles had d̶ ̶ ̶ ̶ ̶ ̶ ̶ ̶ her arrival in London. The fin̶ ̶ ̶ ̶ had made her the most fashio̶ ̶ the season. Her own wit and charm̶ ̶ the toast of the *ton* and the belle of ev̶ ̶ ̶

Yet the target of her campaign of conquest, th̶ Viscount Julian Whitehead, had remained seemingly untouched by her triumph. And the gentleman most struck by her success was the repulsive and relentless Charles Bottomley.

Somehow Francine had to find a way to defeat the designs of the indefatigable Bottomley while devising a weapon that would conquer the heart of the invincible viscount. . . .

IRENE SAUNDERS, a native of Yorkshire, England, spent a number of years exploring London while working for the U.S. Air Force there. A love of travel brought her to New York City, where she met her husband, Ray, then settled in Miami, Florida. She now lives in Port St. Lucie, Florida, dividing her time between writing, bookkeeping, gardening, needlepoint, and travel.

The Invincible Viscount

Irene Saunders

A SIGNET BOOK

NEW AMERICAN LIBRARY

A DIVISION OF PENGUIN BOOKS USA INC.

SIGNET TRADEMARK REG. U.S. PAT. OFF. AND FOREIGN COUNTRIES
REGISTERED TRADEMARK—MARCA REGISTRADA
HECHO EN DRESDEN, TN, U.S.A.

SIGNET, SIGNET CLASSIC, MENTOR, ONYX, PLUME,
MERIDIAN and NAL BOOKS are published by New American
Library, a division of Penguin Books USA Inc.,
1633 Broadway, New York, New York 10019.

First Printing, August, 1989

1 2 3 4 5 6 7 8 9

PRINTED IN THE UNITED STATES OF AMERICA

In the remote part of Yorkshire where Hawk Hall lay, newspapers were normally received up to a sennight after publication, but on April 1, 1814, word of the fall of Napoleon two days before, and the entry into Paris of the Allies, reached Hawk Hall almost before the ink had dried on the paper.

When the London Mail passed through Harrogate, gentlemen pressed sovereigns into the guard's hand for a copy of the *Times*, and word reached the surrounding countryside in a matter of hours.

Sir Godfrey Giles' friend and veterinarian, John Bierley, had walked up from the village to recount the good news that he, in turn, heard from a messenger waiting in Harrogate to pick up letters.

"The last letter I had from Kenneth was a month ago, Francine," Sir Godfrey remarked after John Bierley had left. "You can't have heard from him since then or you'd have told me."

"Of course I would have, Grandpapa, and it's been longer than that since I heard from Julian, though I've continued to write every week." Her green-hazel eyes widened in alarm as she realized they could not yet be certain that Kenneth and Julian were safe.

"Now don't put yourself in a taking over it. You'll get word any day now, I promise," he said to her, regretting that he had worried her needlessly. Though she had not told him in so many words, he knew she loved Julian, her brother's long-time friend and fellow officer, just as much as she did her brother, Kenneth, but in a very different way. "They may even now be on their way home," he suggested.

"I do indeed hope so, for these two years have seemed endless, and letters take so terribly long to get here," she said, turning away to try to hide the tears that threatened. "How did Mr. Bierley get word?"

"Someone must have had urgent need of a letter, for a messenger who had been waiting for the Mail to come in, rode through the village. There must not have been anything for us or it would be here by now," he murmured, then looked up as his housekeeper, Mrs. Parsons, entered the room, her starched skirts rustling.

"There's one for each of you," she said with a rare smile as she gave them their letters and quickly left the room.

Francine recognized Julian's writing at once, but she wished to open the letter in the privacy of her bedchamber, not beneath her grandpapa's eagle eyes, so she waited to hear what Kenneth had written, first.

"He says something about their being temporarily assigned as aides to some high-up colonel or other. I wish they'd taught him to write more clearly at Eton. They may be sent on a special assignment, he goes on to say, nothing dangerous, but it could be very interesting. They'll be home inside of two months if all goes well." The old man's eyes were moist, but his smile was one of profound relief. "I'm going to rest my eyes for a while now, perhaps take a little nap, so off you go. You can tell me what Julian has to say later."

Francine was a tall, slender young lady of some twenty-one years, though her deep-gold hair, fastened back in a long, thick braid, and her somewhat pixielike, lightly freckled face, made her appear considerably younger.

She walked slowly from the drawing room and up the broad staircase to her bedchamber. Seated at her inlaid cherry escritoire, she broke the seal and unfolded the single sheet of paper.

In all likelihood it was little different from the note Kenneth had sent her grandpapa, for there were no ardent words of love or even affection, unless one counted his telling her how very much he wanted to see her again. The salutation of "My dear Frankie," and "Your good friend, Julian" at the foot might have been penned to just about anyone.

But then, her letters to him were much the same, for she had kept a tight rein on her true feelings until the time when he would come to realize, as she had, that their love had changed from brother and sisterly to something much, much more. She believed that Julian had changed also, but that he was not yet aware of it. When he returned, she meant to make him see her as the lively, intelligent young lady she hoped she had become.

The very next morning, intensive preparations began for welcoming Kenneth home. Mrs. Parsons insisted that his bedchamber be completely cleaned from floor to ceiling, and for several days maids dashed back and forth from the room, taking out carpets to beat and air, washing every curtain and bedhanging, then ironing and replacing them. The local chimney sweep was called to make certain there would be no blockage when a fire was lit in the carved-oak fireplace.

After the first feelings of intense relief that the fighting was over, Francine and her grandpapa felt a decided letdown, for two months seemed far away. But as the house was made ready, their excitement mounted until they could hardly wait. Sir Godfrey had checked the wine cellar, and Francine the larder, to be sure sufficient food and wine was available at short notice.

Soon the young men would both be home, bringing their friends to visit, and giving and attending parties, for Julian had always run quite tame at Hawk Hall, as Kenneth had at the Whiteheads' home, some ten miles away.

There was only one disquieting problem as far as Francine was concerned, but it was quite a serious one.

Almost since the day Julian left for Spain, Squire Bottomley had been pushing his only son, Charlie, into dangling after Francine. The squire was a here-and-thereian, wealthy and overambitious, and bitterly disappointed in his son. Charlie was clumsy and slow-witted to the point that many thought him a little about in the head.

At first the young man's advances had seemed amusing, but once she realized the squire was most serious, Francine no longer thought it a laughing matter. However, her grandpapa had encouraged Charlie's visits, inviting him to luncheon or tea and generally making it impossible for Francine to avoid him.

Her opportunity to speak privately to Sir Godfrey about Charlie came the next morning at breakfast.

"I wonder if you realize, Grandpapa, how difficult it is for me to meet Charlie Bottomley every time I turn around in this house," she said quietly. "And I have been given to understand that he is here at your invitation."

"I don't see why it should be difficult, Francine," Sir Godfrey said with a serious expression. "He's had his eye on you for some time, and though his father leaves much to be desired, the young man seems harmless enough."

"Why give him encouragement when you know quite well that he will ultimately be disappointed?" Francine asked. "I don't wish Charlie ill, but I would die an old maid before I would wed him."

"You'll probably do just that if you wait until young Julian recognizes you as a desirable young woman," her grandpapa said shortly, knowing his words hurt but hoping to save her heartache later. "He was young and inexperienced when he left for Spain, but he'll not come back the same way. Chances are he'll have a Season in London and come home with a young bride."

"Perhaps you'll be proved right," Francine said shortly, "but I don't think he would be happy if that should happen, for deep down, I'm sure he loves me and will realize it one day. I believe it's just a matter of being patient, and eventually he'll feel as I do."

Sir Godfrey's tired blue eyes looked with love on his

granddaughter. He rose and put his still-muscular arms around her shoulders. "I may be an old man, but I know all about love, for I felt that way about your grandmama from a very early age. I just don't want you to get hurt and bitter. It wouldn't do any harm for him to see you go out occasionally with someone else. It's a pity that Charlie is the only young man around, but maybe there'll be a few others soon to give Julian some competition."

They both looked toward the door as the sound of running feet on the hard wood floors could be heard, and a lively little girl of five years burst into the room, closely followed by Francine's old nanny, who grabbed a small arm before the little Penelope could fling herself at Sir Godfrey.

"Want to see Grampa, want to see Grampa," the struggling child cried while Nanny held her firmly in check and finished buttoning her frilly dress and tightened the bow in her curly blond hair. Then she released the child, who sprang forward into Sir Godfrey's arms.

"You're getting soft, Nanny," Francine murmured. "If that had been I at her age, I would have received a sharp smack on my bottom, been taken back up to the nursery, and made to stand in the corner for the rest of the morning."

"It didn't do you much good, so I'm trying a different way with this one," was the tart reply, though the older woman eyed her former charge fondly. Then she nodded in the direction of Penelope and her great-grandpapa. "After two years it will be hard on both of them when her family decides to take her back."

"I don't know how my cousin can bear to be away from his child so long," Francine said quietly. "Despite the two of you spoiling her so much, she's a delight and it will be hard on me, too, if they suddenly come for her."

"We'll have to meet that when it happens, my lady, for she's not ours and we must be grateful for the time she's with us," Nanny said emphatically. "As for you, you should have been married long before now and having little ones of your own."

Francine tried to give Nanny a repressing frown, for not even Mrs. Parsons would dare be so forward, but she couldn't keep her face straight. She hurriedly left the room before she laughed outright, only to run into Charlie Bottomley, who had just arrived.

"Did you hear the news, Francine?" he asked. "My father just got his copy of the *Times*, and he said I should come right over to tell you all about it."

"We heard yesterday, by way of John Bierley, and we also got a letter from Kenneth. He said he should be home in a couple of months. Have you come to see Grandpapa?" she asked pointedly.

Charlie looked embarrassed. "I really came to see you while I have the chance, Francine, for Father says that you'll have no time for me when Hawk Hall is full of returning heroes. I have the gig outside if you'd like to take a ride with me."

It was just the kind of thing the squire would say, but for once, Francine had a good excuse. "I can't right now, Charlie, for I have to go out and see to the younger birds. I was delayed this morning, so I'd best do it at once."

She turned toward the back door, but Charlie was not so easily put off.

"I'll come with you, then," he said eagerly, "and perhaps I could give you a hand with them. Then, when you're finished, we could take a ride."

Francine sighed. "Very well, you may come and watch, but first I must ask Nanny to get Penelope ready. I'm sure she would love to go with us, for she hasn't had an outing for days."

Before he could think of a good excuse for leaving the child behind, she went back into the dining room and gave the necessary instructions, receiving a knowing look from Nanny.

For once Sir Godfrey took pity on Francine. "I'll join

you and Charlie outside in a few minutes," he said, "and take care of the older birds and peregrines while you're looking to the others."

There was a general exodus from the dining room, and a delay while Charlie greeted Sir Godfrey, then Francine led him out to the hawk houses. She was suspicious. Her instincts told her that Charlie had been ordered to propose marriage to her this morning, for he was not usually so persistent, but if she kept up a running conversation until her grandpapa came, she might be able to avoid it.

"Lord Julian is, of course, with my brother, and he also will be delayed for a couple of months, but when they both finally return, I'm sure they will be happy to tell you all about their exploits in both France and Spain," she lightly chattered. "It was unbelievably hot in Spain in the summers, and they wrote of being eaten alive by mosquitoes whose bites leave horrid bumps all over the skin that ooze and itch enormously. We in England complain of midges biting us, but think of how very much worse it could be.

"Of course, we do have horseflies, and they can give quite fearsome bites, but I should think that they are all over the world, both in hot and in cooler climates. Wherever there are horses, I suppose."

She took a quick breath, then went on. "And then, I recall, when they were on the march and arrived at some picturesque village, the staff officers were assigned to barns and bug-infested cottages where they had to keep their riding crops close by to kill the huge centipedes that crawled over the floors while they lay in their blankets." When Francine paused for breath, she glanced at Charlie, who was by now surreptitiously scratching himself as though he could actually feel the insects crawling upon him.

"Of course, they slept with their boots on so that no creatures could nibble on their toes during the night," she continued, then felt a firm hand upon her shoulder and turned around to find her grandpapa had caught up with them. By the grin on his face she surmised he had heard some, if not all, of her conversation.

"Makes you glad you weren't out there, and that it's all over now, my boy, doesn't it?" he said to Charlie, who was wriggling his shoulders as though something was biting his back.

"Yes, sir, it certainly does," Charlie said with feeling. "I came over to give you the good news but found that you already know about it."

Sir Godfrey smiled and nodded. "We heard yesterday, and though they say that bad news always travels fast, this time good news traveled faster. I am most eager to see our boys back home and settling into a quieter, more normal life once more."

He gave his granddaughter a light tap on her bottom. "You see to the little ones, and I'll show Charlie some of the beauties we have here. Come along, young man, and you can tell your father you've seen some of the finer representatives of a rapidly diminishing species. We'll let Francine get on with her work, for the sooner she finishes, the sooner the three of you can go on your outing."

If Charlie was disappointed, which Francine doubted, for she was sure his father was the one pushing the courtship, he bore it well. He listened patiently as Sir Godfrey described the finer points on the large birds, and he did not grumble when, in case she should fall out, Penelope had to sit between him and Francine in the gig, which was, of course, only intended to seat two.

"My father has promised to buy me a curricle as soon as he goes to London again, for he says that the best ones can only be found there. No one around here has one, but I'll bet your brother and Julian will each buy one as soon as they return," Charlie attested.

"I suppose they will," Francine agreed, "either a curricle or a high-perched phaeton, for both were very popular with the young men in London when I was there. Do you know who Phaëton was?"

"I've no idea," Charlie mumbled, "one of those Roman fellows, I've no doubt."

"He was Greek, actually," Francine told him. "He was the son of Helios, and he borrowed his father's chariot, the sun, for a day, and through reckless driving he would have burned up the earth if Zeus had not struck him dead with a thunderbolt."

"Mm. I'd better not get a phaeton then, or my father will swear I'm a reckless driver also. It's taken him two years to decide I'm careful enough for a curricle," Charlie remarked.

"I like this one the best." Penelope had been sitting quietly watching the women of the village hurrying along with their shopping baskets over their arms. "Can I drive it, please?"

"Not until you're a little bigger and your arms are stronger, my love," Francine said with a smile. Then she asked hopefully, "Are you getting hungry?"

"Oh, yes, Auntie Francine. Is it time for luncheon?" the child asked eagerly, for she always had a healthy appetite.

"It will be by the time we get back," Francine said with a note of satisfaction, and Charlie took the hint and headed back toward Hawk Hall. He knew his father would be angry, but he was quite relieved that there had been no chance to propose to Francine. It was a sort of reprieve.

Francine helped Penelope down from the gig and went into the drawing room while the little girl ran upstairs to find Nanny.

"Did Charlie go home to take a bath?" Sir Godfrey asked with a soft chuckle.

Francine tried to be serious, but her dancing eyes and quivering lips won out. "You knew exactly what I was doing, didn't you? And you certainly helped me by showing him the larger birds, but did you know why?" she asked.

"I don't believe you knew for certain, but I'm a big believer in feminine intuition. I imagine something told you he was going to propose to you," he suggested, watching the emotions flit over her expressive face, "for it would be like the squire to try to get his oar in first."

"I must have been right, for he looked most relieved when he dropped us off here for lunch. Poor Charlie! He doesn't want me, you know. He wants a nice, quiet young woman who will look up to him and make him feel more of a man," Francine declared. "That horrible father of his is behind it all, I'm sure."

"You can't blame him for wanting his son to make a good match, my dear. And with your title, the money your mother left you, and the money I shall leave you also, you are certainly that. I didn't think the squire would push for it so soon, but I'm sure you're right and he's afraid you'll be snatched up as soon as all the young men come back from the war." He looked thoughtful, then suggested, "Perhaps you should have a month or so in London again this year if Kenneth is there to look out for you."

"That's the last place I want to go, Grandpapa, and you know it," Francine said vehemently.

"I wonder," Sir Godfrey murmured, almost to himself. "I wonder if the lady doth protest too much."

"I would have to stay with Aunt Anastasia again," Francine continued, "and I doubt that she's any more aware of how to go on than she was the last time." She giggled. "Do you remember what she was wearing the day she arrived with Penelope?"

"I recall a green hat with swaying orange feathers, if that's what you mean," he said with a chuckle, "and how she berated me for not sending outriders to meet her when she had completely forgotten to let me know she was coming."

"And how she took me to one side and tried to tell me that I owed it to her to look after Penelope because she had brought me out, when it was you who had footed the bill for both me and your other two granddaughters," Francine said with a shake of her head.

"She wasn't unkind to you, was she?" he asked sharply.

"Oh no, of course not," Francine said, "but my

cousins made it clear that at nineteen and twenty they had no time for a seventeen-year-old up from the country."

"But all that is history," Sir Godfrey said. "It was four years ago, and surely you could now handle yourself with much more assurance?"

"Perhaps," Francine said rather haughtily, "if I felt it worthwhile."

2

"Frankie, I swear you've grown two inches since we left," Kenneth declared, swinging her around in his arms until she felt almost giddy.

"Nonsense, Ken, you've become accustomed to having your arms filled with more petite Spanish girls. I've always been tall, haven't I, Julian?" she asked, turning to gaze at the still-handsome young man, though his sun-burned face had a sterner look than it had worn two years before.

Then he laughed and for a moment seemed exactly the same. "There's only one way I can tell," he said, holding out his arms until she flew into them. He held her so closely, she could feel the brass buttons of his bright-scarlet uniform making an impression through her gown. It was as if time had stood still, for they embraced just as they had when saying good-bye two years ago. As Julian bent to kiss her cheek on that sad day, she had turned so that her lips touched his and lingered there long enough for her to feel the thrill of his response.

For a moment now he seemed to hesitate. This time as he bent to kiss her cheek, Francine's courage failed her and she could not turn her head to taste his lips, for he was somehow different, and she had to get to know him again.

"She's just as tall as when we left," he said to Kenneth, then murmured softly for her ears alone, "but she's not as brave."

Francine's cheeks went a rosy pink, and she said quickly, "You've not told us yet what kept you in France for two months longer than most other soldiers.

Were the French ladies so very lovely you couldn't leave them?"

Kenneth raised an eyebrow at Francine as their grand-papa asked, "Yes, what did keep the two of you so long in France, or is it still confidential?"

"Not at this late date, sir. Colonel Campbell had us assigned to his command," Kenneth began. "He was one of the four Allied commissioners who escorted Napoleon Bonaparte from Fontainebleau to Fréjus."

"You mean you were part of Napoleon's escort through France to the *Undaunted*?" Francine gazed at them in awe. "What was it like? You must tell us all about it."

"Ask Julian," Kenneth suggested. "I believe he could describe it better than I."

They turned to Julian, who frowned slightly as though wondering where to begin. "It was memorable, of course," he said, "and it also had its tragic moments. At first, as we left Fontainebleau, the crowds cheered him, but as we went farther south, the mood of the people became ugly. Napoleon was afraid, for you cannot imagine how fearsome an angry crowd can be. He had his own soldiers as well as us to protect him, but it would have taken only a little more animosity and they would have overpowered us all and torn him limb from limb. Any small incident could have triggered it.

"He was actually shaking, and left his carriage at times and rode beside it dressed as one of the commissioners—the Russian one, I believe. It doesn't mean that he wasn't a brave man. I think even the most fearless would have trembled. It was a relief when we reached Fréjus on April 28 and he boarded the comparative safety of the *Undaunted*. We were all strangely pleased to see that, once aboard, he recovered and was his usual pompous self again."

"That's very interesting," Francine remarked, "for you've made me, at least, think of him as human and not a monster. But why were the French people so angry with him?"

"He had taken their sons to war, and a great many of them had never returned," Julian explained. "The Grand Army was six hundred thousand strong in June of 1812, and by early December, when Napoleon issued a bulletin announcing its annihilation, there were fewer than one hundred thousand remaining. He placed the blame on the barbarity of the Russian winter, but on our journey through France, it was clear that the peasants blamed him."

"The two of you shared a unique experience," Sir Godfrey said. "It was certainly worth staying in the army for a little longer, I'm sure."

"We were grateful to Colonel Campbell for selecting us, although at one point I wondered if I might be one of the few British soldiers killed while we were at peace with France," Kenneth said quietly. "Napoleon was not the only man there who was scared."

Julian stayed at Hawk Hall for only an hour or so before going on to his own home some ten miles away. He and Kenneth knew that both their families were most anxious to have them home for a few days, and there would be time enough to see each other later.

Penelope was at first a little shy with the two young men, who were still wearing their uniforms because they had no other clothes with them. Julian was gone before she really got to know him, but when it was time to go to bed, she almost had to be dragged away from her Uncle Kenneth, for she loved the bright-red uniform and the gold braid and shiny buttons and hated to have to leave all the excitement for such an ordinary thing as sleeping.

"Does Cousin Phillip never come to see his little daughter?" Kenneth asked when Nanny had taken the child away. "You wrote that he married again some eighteen months ago, so I would have thought Penelope would have been sent for right away."

"According to Aunt Anastasia, he has been busy trying to beget a son and heir. He may finally have been successful, for his wife is in an interesting condition, I hear," Francine stated calmly, noting with some surprise the shocked expression on her brother's face.

"Perhaps I have been away too long, but surely single ladies do not make a habit of discussing such an intimate matter," Kenneth finally said.

"I discuss many things within the confines of my own home and family that I would not think of mentioning elsewhere, my dear brother," Francine said sharply. "It would seem that you have been away so long you have forgotten how close a family we always were."

"Now, children," Sir Godfrey broke in. "No quarreling on the first night home. She's right, though, Ken. We've always been able to talk freely about anything within these walls, and I hope it will always be so."

Kenneth smiled ruefully. "I have been away too long, much too long, and you must forgive me if it takes a while to get back into the way of things." His smile turned into a grin. "If I'm allowed to talk freely, may I ask a question that has puzzled me ever since I came home? Why is my lovely, intelligent sister still unmarried at twenty-one years of age? Is something wrong with the gentlemen around here, or have all of them been away in the wars?"

Francine flushed a deep pink and her grandpapa waited with some interest to hear what she would reply.

Her eyes flashed a pure green and her smile was a little fixed. "The only so-called gentleman around here appears to be Squire Bottomley's son, Charlie, whom you may remember," she said, a little too sweetly.

"You're joking surely, Frankie. You couldn't marry him, for I remember very well that he was a little slow and always on the outside of any of our activities," Kenneth said with a grin. "Of course there's no one in the village, but there are any number of young people within a distance of, say, twenty miles."

Sir Godfrey looked embarrassed. "That's my fault, I suppose, for it's been years since I've socialized with anyone who wasn't within walking distance. The only time we use a carriage is to take the occasional trip to Skipton market, or to the shops in Harrogate."

"Well, that's a thing of the past now, Grandpapa,"

Kenneth declared. "Julian and I are going to make up a little for what we've missed, and we'll make sure Frankie gets a chance to meet more people. Why, you're almost on the shelf, my love," he teased.

Francine laughed. "It's going to take a while for me to get used to having you here," she told him. "Who would have thought my brother would have turned into a matchmaker? But don't forget, I can play that game also."

"If you can find me a lovely, well-spoken, intelligent young woman, a little younger than I, with a medium-size dowry, who would love me for myself and not the idea of being a countess, I would be eternally grateful," Kenneth told her.

"It sounds to me as though you have been meeting the wrong kind of women." Francine was serious now, and when he nodded, she asked, "Does Julian feel the way you do?"

"I'm not sure how Julian feels. Don't tell him I told you, Frankie, but just after we arrived in Spain, Julian met a lovely, young *condesa*," he said quietly. "She refused to leave her parents when we had to retreat."

"What happened?" Francine's voice was barely a whisper, for she had guessed the answer.

"Her parents were still alive when we returned a few weeks later, but French soldiers had ill-used and then killed the *condesa*," he said quietly. "I don't know if Julian really loved her, or if he was just angry at such a senseless waste of life, but after that the women he frequented were mostly older than himself, yet not one could hold his attention for long. That was when the men started to call him the Invincible Viscount, for, unlike the rest of us who fell in and out of love every month, no female seemed to hold even a small piece of his heart for long."

Kenneth was obviously unwilling to reveal any more about his friend; he got up from his chair, stretching lazily. "It's been a long day and I'll be glad to sleep in my own comfortable bed tonight. It's good to be back, sir," he said to his grandpapa. He tousled Francine's hair and bent to kiss her cheek. "Good night, Frankie. Sweet dreams."

But Francine's dreams that night were far from sweet, for she saw a black-haired Spanish noblewoman in Julian's arms; she awoke as the *condesa* was dragged away from him into some strange, misty place. Julian was left standing with his arms wide open and empty, calling a name she could not remember.

She lay awake for an hour or more, wondering if she was mistaken and if the loss he had experienced had affected their burgeoning relationship more than she had thought possible. Then she recalled his greeting and could have kicked herself for not repeating her fond farewell.

Taking comfort from the fact that he remembered it despite all those women he had loved and left, Francine finally closed her eyes and fell into a less-troubled sleep.

It was three days before Julian returned to Hawk Hall, but when he did so, he brought with him a formal invitation from Lady Whitehead. She was giving a welcome-home ball for Julian and Kenneth, in ten days' time, and she wanted Sir Godfrey and Francine to be present at the intimate dinner that would precede the ball.

Although nothing would have stopped Francine attending, her first reaction was one of dismay. "I have nothing fashionable to wear," she moaned, "and everyone will be dressed in the latest styles."

"My mama uses Madame Eloise in Harrogate," Julian told her with an understanding smile, "and I'm sure she can be persuaded to make a gown in whatever style you wish within a matter of days."

Sir Godfrey carefully kept a straight face and waited to hear his granddaughter's next excuse, for she had not cared tuppence what she wore for the last couple of years.

"But what will I do with my hair?" she asked, pulling the single braid to the front and eyeing it distastefully.

"I can scarcely go with it this way, and Nanny has no aptitude where coiffures are concerned."

"There are at least fifteen maids in this house," her grandpapa said in feigned exasperation, "and I cannot believe that not one of them is adept at arranging hair. You can take the best one with you to Harrogate and let Madame Eloise recommend one of those Frenchmen I hear are all the rage, to cut and style it for you the same day. The maid can then learn how to do it for you at home. And you'd best keep her for your personal maid if she's any good. It's past time you had one."

With what would seem to be her problems solved, Francine still did not seem happy. She looked away from them, her fingers playing with the fringe on a pillow.

Julian walked over and sat beside her on the couch. "Don't you want to go to the ball, Frankie?" he asked softly. "What's really the matter?"

She looked embarrassed and finally confessed, "I can't dance, Julian. I listen to the music and want to move with it the way everyone else does, but when I get up, it's just as though I had two left legs. I stumble all over my partners' feet and then they don't ask me again."

"Now, Frankie, what kind of nonsense is this?" Kenneth asked disgustedly. "You've had a come-out in London, or part of one at least, so you should be able to cope with a country ball."

"Did your aunt not have a dancing master for you and your cousins?" Julian asked gently.

Francine shook her head. "They'd already had lessons from one, and were more than competent before they came to London," she explained.

"No wonder you didn't take, you little peagoose," Julian said with a laugh. "You should have told your aunt you needed a dancing master, or made your cousins show you how to go on."

"My cousins were not prepared to show me anything, for they were too busy securing husbands for themselves to bother with me, and you would have to know how vague my aunt is to realize that she'd never have remembered to hire one even if I had asked her," Francine said, silently appealing to her grandpapa for confirmation.

Sir Godfrey nodded. "That sounds just like Anastasia," he agreed. "She gets her mind set on one thing and worries it to death, and forgets everything else that should be taken care of."

"I'll give you lessons, Frankie," Julian told her, "and I promise that when I've finished, you will drift with the music every single dance, and your partners' toes will never be in danger again. Doesn't Nanny play the piano?" When Francine nodded, he rose. "There's no time like the present, then. Let's get her to play for us now and I'll give you your first lesson," he said, grasping her hand and pulling her toward the door. "Are you coming, Ken?"

"You can have that pleasure to yourself, Julian. I can think of many more edifying things to do than watching you teach my little sister to dance. I'll be either in the stables or at the hawk houses when you're finished." Kenneth glanced toward his grandpapa and saw the satisfied smile on his face. "Have I been missing something?" he asked when the others had left the room.

Sir Godfrey nodded. "Possibly," he said, his eyes twinkling merrily. "It's going to be a very interesting summer."

As they went out together, they heard the sound of a piano being played in the seldom-used conservatory, with emphasis more on keeping time than with feeling for the piece.

"You know how to do a cotillion, don't you, Frankie," Julian said, "for you must surely have danced it locally."

"You forget that I was just seventeen when my aunt insisted I join them for the Season in London," she told him. "Before that, I was too young to go to balls."

"I'd not realized that you'd had so little partying these years, but then my sister, Kathleen, has been in an even worse position. She's making her come-out this year, at the age of twenty, for one after another of our elderly relatives has died and she's not yet a month out of black gloves." He paused but did not utter a word of complaint as Francine stepped on his toe for the third time. "You two should get along well together, as I believe you've much in common."

"I'm looking forward to meeting all of your family." Francine was a little breathless, not with the dancing, but with her proximity to Julian. "It seems quite extraordinary that I've known you all these years and never once set eyes upon them."

"My mother was saying the same thing only yesterday. They're looking forward to meeting you also. There are not many young ladies who are expert in the care of falcons these days," he said, smiling warmly down on her, "and they cannot believe you're tall, slender, and graceful, but not an amazon."

Julian could not have been more patient had he been a trained dancing master, for he carefully explained the steps and movements while Nanny rested, then showed them to Francine and took her through them time after time until she could perform them perfectly.

It was almost three hours later and Nanny was becoming a little tired when Francine asked, "You are going to show me the waltz, aren't you?" She was in such high alt, just being with Julian, holding his hand and feeling his touch, that she did not really believe learning the waltz could make her any happier, but it would be fun to try.

For his part, Julian was becoming increasingly warm and uncomfortable, but had no desire to stop. He had never been so close to her before and was experiencing far-from-brotherly feelings, but telling himself that it was just the heat in the closed-up room that was making him perspire. For what must have been the tenth time, he slipped his fingers under his collar to try to ease the tightness.

"Of course," he agreed, turning to Nanny. "Can you play the infamous waltz, Nanny?" he asked.

She played a few lines, then asked, "Will it be too fast for you, or shall I try to go slower?"

"Go slower at first, then pick up the speed as her ladyship becomes accustomed to it," he instructed, taking Francine into his arms.

"Now, it's in three-four time, so you must just say to yourself, one, two, three, one, two, three, with emphasis on the one, until you can do it without counting," he murmured, starting to look quite flushed at her proximity.

How heavenly, Francine thought, to just float around in the arms of someone you love, and she closed her eyes to better enjoy the feeling, then suddenly realized that, though she had never done it before, she was dancing far too well. Quite deliberately, she missed a step, then another, almost tripping Julian also.

"Nanny, where are you?"

The small voice was coming closer and Francine and Julian drew apart as Nanny stopped playing and went to meet her young charge. Julian ran a finger inside his collar once more, then took out a kerchief to mop his brow.

"I woke and you weren't there," Penelope complained. "What are you doing?"

"Now, you were not alone, missy," Nanny scolded. "Mary was with you, I know." She turned to ask Julian, "Will that be all, my lord?"

"I think so, Nanny," he said, looking at Francine. "Do you think you'll be all right now, my dear?"

Francine looked worried. "Would you mind very much giving me just one more lesson on the waltz, Julian?" she asked, unaware of how appealing her green eyes, beneath their dark lashes, had become.

"Of course, if it will help. Will you be able to play for a half-hour or so tomorrow afternoon?" he asked Nanny, and when she nodded her assent and took Penelope off for tea, Julian added with an engaging smile, "Of course, I shall demand a reward for my services."

For just a moment, Francine thought he was going to do something most improper, such as kissing her, but her hopes were sadly dashed when he said, "Do you remember how you taught me to work with the hawks during the holidays the last summer we were here, calling the short-winged ones back and forth to exercise them?"

She nodded, remembering very well, for it had been the highlight of the summer for her.

"Do you think your grandpapa would allow you to show me again? I found their training most interesting and would like to keep a few hawks of my own now that I'm home for good."

"Grandpapa won't mind. In fact, he'll help you all he can if you are really interested. Why don't you come over at about eleven tomorrow morning. We don't do it much later, for it must be done while they're hungry, and it's not good to leave them that way for long."

He gave her a mock salute. "I'll be here promptly at eleven, then, and afterward we'll practice the waltz so that you can do it without looking at your toes." His eyes sparkled as he added, "Or treading on mine."

They had walked out of the conservatory as they talked and were in the hall when Kenneth entered the front door and came toward them. He glanced suspiciously at Julian's shoes.

"Do you still have all ten toes?" he asked his friend as Francine made a face at him. "Well, since Julian was decorated twice for bravery, he was the best candidate for the job. Which reminds me. When are you going to Harrogate, Frankie? You'll have to be quick about it if this Madame Eloise is to finish a gown for you in time for the ball."

"I know," she said. "I thought I'd go the day after tomorrow, and tonight I'll interview the maids, as Grandpapa suggested."

"Would you like Julian and me to go along with you and take you out to dinner at one of the inns there afterward?" he suggested. "While you're with the modiste, we could go to see a mare I'm interested in at a stable just outside of Harrogate. She has an excellent pedigree, and I may buy her, if the price is right. Are you free that day, Julian, for I'd like your opinion of her?"

"Of course I am, and I'd be glad to see it. But I must be off now or my mother will be wondering where I got to. They've worried so much about me these last two years that they can't get out of the habit," he said with a smile that showed he understood. "I'll see you tomorrow at eleven sharp, Frankie."

With a wave of a hand he went off in the direction of the stables and Kenneth looked curiously at his sister. "He's continuing the lessons tomorrow?" he asked, his eyes crinkling with amusement.

"As a matter of fact, he is, tomorrow afternoon," Francine answered. "But at eleven he wants me to show him again how to exercise the hawks by calling them. If you recall, he was always interested in them and he's thinking of keeping some himself."

Kenneth nodded. "I do remember, now that you mention it. That's how he first met you, and he couldn't get over a young girl handling hawks. You'll practice dancing afterward, I suppose. Have you graduated to the waltz yet?" he asked with a sly grin.

Francine blushed. "Yes, I have, if it's any concern of yours," she snapped. "I didn't notice you volunteering to teach me."

Kenneth laughed and hugged her to him. "You'd have been very disappointed if I had, Frankie. Now, admit it."

"All right," she said softly, "but please don't tease Julian, or you might put him off."

He shrugged. "If you say so, I won't, but I'm not at all sure you're right. Let's go and join Grandpapa for tea. He's been waiting at least fifteen minutes already."

3

"I see you are punctual as ever," Francine said as she and Julian walked over to the hawk houses. "What a pity it did not rub off from you onto my dear brother."

"Ken's too much of a dreamer to remember the time of day. Why else do you think he studied astronomy at Cambridge?" Julian asked. "Whenever he was late for supper, I could always find him with his eye to a telescope."

Francine changed the subject. "How much do you remember about calling off the hawks?" she asked.

"That short-winged hawks will not willingly keep on the wing without going to perch," Julian said slowly. "And that two trainers stand at a distance from each other and alternately bring the hawk from one to the other by showing the lure or the outstretched fist."

Nodding her approval, Francine handed him a gauntlet and a bag of treats. "You give it just a few each time," she said.

Taking a sparrow-hawk on her gauntleted fist, she led the way to the back of the hawk house and out onto the gaunt, windswept moorland behind. It was still too early for the heather to be in bloom, but in a month or so it would change from a brown-gray to a glorious purple. The day was perfect, fresh but not too windy as they went toward one of the low dry-stone walls.

"You see the wall over there that's tumbling down?" Francine asked. "Stand about halfway along it, Julian, and hold your fist out for her. Then when she comes to it, give her a few treats from your bag."

The hawk was a young female, with a body about a

foot long, and her plumage was dark brown on the top, with dull white underneath, while her legs and feet were a soft gold color.

Her sharp eyes soon spotted Julian's proffered fist and when she quivered with excitement, Francine raised her arm and threw her off toward him. Spreading her shorter wings, the hawk did not soar high aloft, but made directly for the outstretched fist.

Francine watched Julian, tensed as he waited to receive the hawk, and she could not recall ever feeling as happy as she did at this moment. The air was almost crisp and the sky was an exact match to the blue of his eyes. His dark brown hair, caught by the wind, was no longer quite so neat, and though she was too far away to see it clearly, she knew that his face held an expression of eagerness that softened his strong, handsome features.

She watched him reach into his bag for the treats the hungry hawk awaited, then look in her direction for her signal that she was ready to receive her again.

They spent almost two hours, Francine carefully selecting the different hawks for the combined exercising and feeding practice, and then they returned to the house, where Sir Godfrey was sipping a glass of sherry before luncheon.

"I hear your interest in hawks has not diminished, Julian," Sir Godfrey said as he filled and handed him a glass. "When you're ready to start on your own, I'll help you get set up and pick out some of my own partially trained hawks for you. After that, you'll probably wish to capture and train your own from the wild state. How did it go this morning?"

Francine spoke up. "It went well, except that I believe he was giving them bigger treats, for the hawks seemed reluctant to leave his fist for mine," she said, smiling happily.

"That will teach you to be more specific in your instruction, young Frankie. My idea of a few was four, then I saw that you gave them only three," Julian told her. "I did enjoy myself, though, for the birds are in magnificent form. You must work very hard to keep them that way, sir."

"It's really a matter of constantly checking to make sure they are eating properly, for some of them are like spoiled pets and will not eat unless they get their favorite food, and they lose the pink of their condition very quickly," the older man said. "And speaking of food, why don't we go into the dining room and find out what we are to have today for luncheon?"

Kenneth was already there, and when the three men declined a sweet after the meal, Francine did also and excused herself, for she wanted to wash as thoroughly as possible and change into the gown she had set out, the only one she owned with a low neckline.

Dora, the local girl who would from now on be her personal maid, was already upstairs, waiting to help her into the gown and comb her hair into a softer style than the serviceable braid.

"A little rosewater would be nice, my lady," Dora suggested, and Francine agreed, applying it generously on her arms and neck.

When she went into the nursery to see if Nanny was ready, that good woman took a look at her former charge, then gave a nod of satisfaction. The two of them went down to the conservatory and Nanny began to play a lilting waltz, which soon brought Julian hurrying into the room.

Still unaccustomed to the dance, Francine genuinely stumbled the first time, but then she gave herself to the dance and the feel of Julian's arm. He seemed unusually quiet, so she stopped concentrating on her feet, lifted her head high, and was delighted to see his blue eyes straying with a most unbrotherly frequency to her bosom.

When they paused for breath, he appeared once again to be having a problem with the tightness of either his collar or his neckcloth. She would have liked to suggest he loosen it, but knew this would be going beyond the bounds of propriety.

They resumed the waltz, and Julian seemed at first to be more comfortable, though Francine trod on his feet twice, which meant practicing a little longer. When he started tugging futilely at his neckcloth once more, she decided she had gone far enough, took pity on him, and suggested that she was as good at the waltz as she was ever going to be.

He grinned and quickened the pace until they were spinning wildly across the floor; then, still holding her hand, he removed his other one from her waist and she dropped into a graceful curtsy while he bowed low to an imaginary audience.

"You are now the best partner I have ever had, Frankie," he told her as she was recovering her breath, "and I shall insist the waltz be one of the two dances you save for me at the ball. You do know that you may not dance more than twice with the same gentleman, don't you?"

Francine's face fell. "I was aware that one could not do so at Almack's and at balls in London, but surely here one does not have to comply with such strict rules?" she suggested hopefully.

"I'm afraid so, my dear, and I am indeed much more disappointed about it than you," he said gently. "But now that you need not be ashamed to stand up with anyone, I'm sure you will enjoy yourself immensely."

"It was very kind of you to spend so much of your time teaching me, Julian, and I really do appreciate it," Francine said quite sincerely. "Kenneth would, if pushed, have taught me a few steps, but he would not have been as kind and patient as you have."

She smiled so sweetly up at him that Julian was immediately smitten with remorse for the desires that had passed through his head while they had been dancing. Most unbrotherly desires that would have shocked the little innocent, he thought, had she but known.

"It was my pleasure, and I will get my reward in seeing you enjoying the ball," he told her, but he was not being quite truthful in this, for he decided there and then to make sure she danced only with young men of whom he approved.

Francine's gown, of green satin with an overskirt of gold lace, was the most beautiful one she had ever seen. Her hair, which had caused her genuine concern when she had seen Monsieur Maurice snipping an alarming amount of it onto the floor, framed her face and fell to her shoulders in a cascade of deep gold curls. He had gone to great pains to explain to her that, "My lady has her own elegant height and does not need the hair pouffed on the head to make her appear taller."

When Kenneth and Julian had seen her, they had exclaimed in delight and told her that she looked so lovely they were going to the best inn for dinner—instead of the lesser one they had planned to take her to. She had not believed their flattery, of course, but after a few heads had turned to look at her as they entered the inn, she began to feel that perhaps they had only exaggerated a little.

Of course, they would have taken her to the best inn whether she had looked different or not, but there was a new look in Julian's eyes as he watched her sip her wine and raised his glass in a silent toast. And it was he who helped her into and out of the carriage each time.

Was it her imagination, or did his hand linger longer than usual about her waist as he guided her in and out of the inn, and into Hawk Hall? She sighed. If it did, he was probably completely unaware of it.

Her grandpapa had sent to her bedchamber a beautiful necklace and earrings of gold and emeralds, and when she went a little shyly down the stairs to join him and her brother in the drawing room, they both came to the foot of the stairs to watch her descend.

She gave an embarrassed little laugh. "You'll make me so nervous, if you're not careful, that I shall break my own record of five falls down these stairs," she said, but her eyes rivaled the emeralds for sparkle, and for the first time in her life she knew that she looked lovely.

"We have a little time to spare if you would like a glass of sherry before leaving, my dear," her grandpapa told her. "But you may not need it, for your eyes tell me you're already excited enough."

Francine declined. "No, thank you, Grandpapa, for, the way I feel tonight, it might easily go to my head."

"How do you feel, little sister?" Kenneth asked. "If it's anything like the way you look, it must be quite wonderful. What a difference dressing like a grown woman makes!"

"You don't look exactly unhandsome yourself, Ken," Francine told him, glancing at the elaborate folds of his cravat and his jacket and breeches, newly arrived from Weston of Bond Street.

"Feels good to be out of uniform, doesn't it?" Sir Godrey said. "I notice you've filled out quite a bit these last two years. Your old jackets were looking decidedly skimpy."

"We stopped off in London for a couple of days to order quite a few outfits, but I knew I'd need evening wear before anything else, or I'd not dare to show my face after dark," Kenneth remarked with a grin, "in case those old breeches should split."

The two men teased and flattered Francine by turn, all the way to the Whiteheads' residence; then, once there, they handed her over to a rather stupefied Julian, who took her to greet his mother and father.

"We're so happy to meet you at last, my dear," Lady Whitehead said graciously. "We've heard so much about you that we hardly believed you were real, did we, darling?"

As Lord Whitehead, Earl of Whitby, grasped Francine's hand and was about to reply to his wife, a pretty, brown-haired young lady came hurriedly over to the countess and asked, "What on earth is the matter with Julian, Mama? If I didn't know him better, I would say he was in a nervous state, but Julian never gets nervous."

"Perhaps this young woman had something to do

with it," the earl suggested. "This is Kenneth's little sister, Lady Francine Truesdale, Kathleen. And as you must have guessed, Francine, this outspoken minx is our only daughter, Kathleen."

Kathleen started to laugh, then took Francine's arm and led her to a couch. "You're the little sister who helps train hawks? I'm truly delighted to meet you, and please do forgive me, but you're not a bit the way Julian described you. Has he ever seen you dressed like this before?"

It was impossible to take offense at anything this charming young lady said, and Francine replied honestly. "No one has ever seen me dressed like this before, for I've never owned such a beautiful gown. Nor did I know there was any jewelry in the house until Grandpapa sent these to my chamber." Her hand went up a little self-consciously to the lovely necklace.

Kathleen was wearing a simple gown of cream satin, banded with coffee-colored satin ribbons at the hem and at the high waist, where the ribbons were tied in a flat bow in front, with the ends hanging almost to the floor. She wore creamy pearls at her throat, and smaller ones were woven through her dark-brown hair.

"It's just a family dinner party, really," Kathleen chattered, "a few aunts and uncles, but Mama felt it was high time we got together with Kenneth's family. We haven't been able to do anything social for years because several relatives, all incredibly old, have passed away one after the other these last few years. I live in daily dread that the last two will stick their spoons in the wall before I even get to London for my late Season come-out."

Francine could not help but laugh at Kathleen's irreverent expression. "I know that it's not really funny, but I can understand how you feel," she said. "However, a London Season is not always as enjoyable as you might think. There are so many rules and regulations, and even such a silly thing as the color of your hair or eyes can decide whether you will be popular or not."

"Oh, dear." Kathleen looked alarmed and beckoned her brother over. "Julian, do you know if blondes or brunettes are popular in London this year, for if it's not brunettes, perhaps I should wait for the little Season before I come out."

Julian eyed her with amusement. "Has this scamp been telling you about her own abbreviated stay there?" he asked. Then he said kindly, "You need have no fear, for since his quarrel with Prinny last year, the Beau is not quite so popular as he once was, and with fewer gentlemen aping him, I don't believe he is able to exert as much influence. Now, even ladies with unusual shades of hair, like deep gold"—he smiled warmly at Francine as he spoke—"can become Incomparables."

Kathleen sighed thankfully. "What a relief that is, anyway. It would have been just my bad luck to find that no one would look at brown hair. Do you get to take Francine in to dinner, Julian, or did Mama put her with one of our old uncles?"

"Don't worry, I wouldn't let that happen. I take our guest, and Kenneth takes you in," he assured his sister. "You seem to be getting along famously with my extremely outspoken little sister," he said to Francine. "I don't recall her being so direct in her remarks before I went to Spain."

"Perhaps it's the frustration of not being able to come out," Francine said softly as Kenneth came over and Kathleen turned to speak to him. "It must have been very upsetting, and she's still worried that something else will stop her going to London."

"I do understand," Julian said, "and, of course, there was little for her to do here when the family was in mourning."

"Had you introduced us before you left for Spain, you might now have a hawk house all set up here," Francine said with a mischievous grin.

"You're right, of course. It's just one of the many opportunities I missed." He offered his arm. "May I? I believe we are now ready to go in to dinner."

Julian was on Francine's right, and as had been

expected, one of his elderly uncles was on her left. Though he was introduced to her at the start of the meal, by the time the first course was finished and she turned to converse with him during the second, he had by then forgotten.

"And who might you be, young lady?" the old man asked. "One of young Julian's country flirts I'll be bound, ha, ha, ha."

"Not at all. I'm Kenneth Truesdale's sister, Francine, my lord," she told him quietly.

"What's that? You'll have to learn to speak up a bit, missy. I can't abide young chits that talk in whispers. Now, what was it you said?" he asked so loudly that Francine was sure the whole table must be eagerly awaiting her answer.

"That young chit's my granddaughter, you old rogue," Sir Godfrey called from across the table, ignoring protocol. "And she doesn't speak in whispers; it's you that's deaf as a doorpost."

The older man leaned forward to peer across the table at the speaker. "Why, it's Godfrey Giles," he said in surprise. "I thought you were dead long since, for I've not seen you in years. Where've you been hiding yourself?"

"I've been at Hawk Hall, as always," Sir Godfrey replied, "busy bringing up Francine and her brother. I've had no time for gadding about the countryside."

When the conversation between the older men first started, Francine and Julian had exchanged grins, and she had breathed a sigh of relief that she did not have to shout at the deaf old man. Now she realized to her horror that he was looking her up and down.

"You've done a fine job of it, Godfrey. Going with my nevvy, are you, my dear?" he asked Francine, giving her a familiar nudge that nearly knocked her off her chair.

"No, sir," she almost shouted, to make sure he heard her. "I'm just a guest here like you."

"You don't like him, you say? Nonsense! All the girls

like Julian. Always have and always will," the old man grunted.

"I think I'm going to leave the room," Francine murmured, making as though to stand up.

Julian's hand came around her shoulder and pinned her firmly to the chair. He leaned across and spoke to his uncle. "I am a friend of her brother's, Uncle John. We fought together in Spain and France, and this party is in his honor and mine," he said loudly and firmly.

"Why didn't you say so right away, Julian? Thought you were finally getting yourself leg-shackled. It's time, you know, and you could do worse, for she's a beauty." He smiled and nodded at Francine, then, as the course was being removed, he turned to the lady on his left.

Francine did not dare look at Julian, so she concentrated on the pattern of the dinner fork until he said softly, "Everyone knows him, and no one at the table will think anything at all of his remarks, so stop looking as though you're planning to steal the silver, and have something to eat. You'll need all your strength for the dancing later."

She turned a flushed face toward him and he chuckled.

"We'll have to see that you go out more often, for half the fun of a dinner is listening to people like Uncle John." He paused, then ordered, "Say something, or else everyone will really think you don't like me."

"You heard your uncle. If the girls always like you, and always will, they'd not believe that I didn't, anyway," she said with a hint of a giggle. "Did you really think I would have left the room?"

"It certainly looked that way," Julian said, "and I wasn't going to take any chances. What does it feel like to be the most beautiful young lady here?"

"I'm not at all. Your sister is much prettier than I am, for I have a great many freckles, and there is a cousin at the end of the table who is quite lovely," Francine whispered.

"One day I must try to count just how many freckles

you have," he murmured. "But I said beautiful, my dear, and tonight you really are. I'm going to have to fight the young men off just to get my two dances," he said, "and just think what Uncle John will say to that."

"He'll probably never notice, for I have a feeling he and Grandpapa mean to head for the card room as soon as supper ends, and we won't see them again until it's time to leave." Francine smiled up at him. "Would you like to make a wager on it?"

"You're too sure of yourself," Julian avowed. "I only bet on certainties."

Although Francine knew he was paying her an unusual amount of attention to try to make her feel better, she was still very grateful to him, for she would never know for sure if she really would have left the room in embarrassment.

They were almost at the end of the meal, and as soon as Lady Whitehead gave the signal for the ladies to withdraw, Kathleen hurried toward Francine.

Sure that her newfound friend was going to make some remark about her Uncle John's words, Francine was quite surprised when she seemed to be completely unaware of them and spoke instead of her brother, Kenneth.

"Kenneth was telling me all about the movement of the planets, and the way he explained it I found it quite fascinating," she said a little breathlessly. "I never realized that was his real interest. I always thought he would go in for hawking as a hobby, like you."

"He knows how to handle the hawks and helps out willingly when needed, but it's not Ken's principal interest," Francine agreed. "Why don't we arrange for you and Julian to come to tea one day, and . . ." She shook her head. "That's no good. It would have to be dinner, for I was going to suggest going up to his room, but you can only see the stars at night."

Kathleen sighed. "It wouldn't be proper for me to go to his room, though I'd love to see the things he described through his telescope."

"We would all go up, of course," Francine said, "and then it would be quite proper. I'll find out what night would be best for stargazing and then send you an invitation."

"Would you, Francine?" Kathleen was delighted. "I'm so glad I finally met you, for we have so much in common."

Yes, Francine thought, each other's brothers, if nothing else. She could hear the faint sounds of violinists tuning their instruments in the ballroom, and she just couldn't wait to waltz with Julian again.

As if she had transmitted her thoughts, Julian was suddenly at her side, requesting her program. "Mama has asked that the four of us, Ken and Kathleen and you and I, start off the dancing, and then she and Papa will signal the others to join us. Aren't you glad now you had those lessons, Frankie?" he asked with a grin.

"What if I tread on your toes?" she asked nervously.

"I won't say a word, I promise." He laughed. "They already have so many bruises that a few more won't make any difference."

She looked as if she was going to hit him, and he held up his hands as though to shield himself. "I'll tell Uncle John you don't like me anymore," he threatened.

He handed her program back to her and she could not resist peeking at it. A cotillion in the first part of the ball and a waltz after supper had been marked off. "The leading-off dance does not count, for Mama and Papa will split us up after we've been around twice," he explained.

Taking her arm, he led her to where the orchestra was ready to start. Kenneth and Kathleen were just behind them. Suddenly her nervousness passed, and Francine danced as though in a dream until she found herself in the arms of the earl. After that she never sat down except for just a few moments between dances, and then she was swept away by some other strange young man.

Only when she danced with Julian was she aware of her partner, and those dances passed far too swiftly.

What she did not notice was that Julian spent most of his time, when not dancing with her or with someone he was obliged to dance with, standing in an alcove of the ballroom watching her float around the room.

He would afterward say that he was a little tired and had enjoyed just watching the others, but Lady Whitehead seldom took her eyes off her son that night, and there was a smile of satisfaction on her face. He might not yet know it, but his mother was quite sure that he had fallen in love with his friend's young sister, and she wholeheartedly approved his choice.

4

———————

"**H**ow would you like to be our guest for the balance of the Season in London, Kenneth?" Lady Whitehead asked when he joined them for luncheon the day after the ball. "We have plenty of bedchambers in our London town house, so one more person would be no imposition, and I think both Julian and Kathleen would enjoy your company."

"That's most generous of you, my lady," Kenneth told her, "and providing my grandpapa's health remains good, I will accept with pleasure."

Julian was, of course, delighted, for he and Kenneth had been together so long it would seem strange for them to be more than two hundred miles apart. One thing did concern him, however, and he mentioned it to Kenneth when they were alone later that afternoon.

"You know, Ken," he said with a frown, "it seems most odd for the three of us to go to London and for Frankie to stay here in Yorkshire, but I feel that she would decline if my mother asked her to join us."

Kenneth nodded. "She can be a touchy little thing at times," he agreed, "and I'm sure you're right."

"But what if your Aunt Anastasia were to be persuaded to invite her?" Julian asked. "After all, Frankie and your grandfather have looked after her grandchild, little Penelope, for more than two years now. Surely she should put Francine up in town, and we could do the rest, see that she goes to the right places, meets the right people and such."

"That's a good idea. I'll drop her a note today, and I'll ask her to send Frankie an invitation immediately, for the Season is now in full swing but will be over before you know it," Kenneth agreed.

"It certainly will. Let's see if we can find some writing materials in my father's study and do it now," Julian said, rising. He was most aware of Kenneth's tendency to put things off, and he did not intend that this should be delayed for a moment.

The two young men left the room and an hour later they emerged from the study. Julian was carrying the letter for his father to frank and send off right away.

It came as a surprise to him, however, when, some days later, he heard that Francine had received the invitation from her aunt and was not inclined to accept. His family was leaving the next day for London, and there was little he could do, but he felt strangely disconsolate at the thought of her not being there.

He had not reckoned, however, on Sir Godfrey. When the older man heard of the invitation and Francine brought her reply to be franked, he glared at her.

"I assume you are making arrangements to leave for London as soon as possible, and this is to tell my daughter when you will be there," he said sternly, knowing it was nothing of the sort, for she would have discussed her plans with him before replying.

"Grandpapa, you know I cannot go and leave you and Penelope here alone," she said in an exasperated tone. "Who would keep her entertained and plan her meals? And who would help with the hawks?"

"Penelope will be cared for by the same good woman who kept you entertained and planned your meals whenever I had to go away. Nanny, of course," he snorted. "And we have a score or more men, under George Millman, who is himself as capable as any falconer I've ever met. You've looked downpin ever since Kenneth left, though I know he's not the one you're missing most."

He ripped the letter in half and threw it on the fire. "Now," he said, "you will go back up those stairs and write your aunt a letter telling her you're coming, and then get started on your packing. If you mean to have young Whitehead, then it would be not at all the thing to leave him alone in London with all those pretty young things just eager to get their hands upon him.''

"Whatever do you mean, Grandpapa?" Francine asked in her starchiest voice.

Sir Godfrey chuckled. "You can get down off that high horse, young lady, for he may be a little short-sighted, but I'm not. Now, off you go. I want to see that letter of acceptance before you seal it.''

As she flounced out of the room, he called, "And don't forget to pack that low-necked gown. You may need some extra dancing lessons."

He was still chuckling to himself when she returned, pouting a little, with her short letter of acceptance, but when she saw his face, she had to break down and laugh.

"I've known you a lot longer than he has, my love, and if you just be yourself, you'll win him in the end. I'm giving you a very generous draft on a London bank that should cover all your needs and to spare, but if you run short, don't hesitate to write me for more. And don't skimp. Go to the best modiste in town and get the finest she has. You can show the *beau monde* a thing or two if you try," he said confidently.

"Penelope and I will get along just fine. We'll miss you, and you know it, but I could not be more proud of you. Lady Francine Truesdale is not just seventeen anymore, and she's going to set the *ton* back on its heels." The pride he felt shone in his old eyes, and there was a tear or two there as well.

Before she left the next day, Francine asked for further reassurance about funds, for she did not want to spend money her grandpapa could ill afford.

"There's nothing to worry about in that direction, my dear," he assured her. "I have more than enough for all of us right now, and it will all go to you anyway, for Kenneth inherits the rest of his father's estate next year. So spend as much as you need and don't skimp. My bones are too old for traipsing around London, or I'd go with you and put a fire under that young man's breeches.''

"Oh, no, Grandpapa, that would never do. It's a good thing you're not coming with me,'' she said with a laugh, then became serious. "I've loved him for so long and so very much that no one else will do. And if I thought he did not feel the same way about me, deep down, I'd leave him alone and be content to live here and just be a falconer. But I'm so sure that he truly loves me that I have to try to make him see it. You do understand, don't you?''

"Yes, my dear, I do. And when I see the way he looks at you sometimes, there's little doubt about it, whether he's aware of it or not,'' the old man said. "I remember how I felt about your grandmama after I'd met her three or four times. I wasn't ready to get married, I thought, but if I ever did, I'd want someone just like her.'' He paused, smiling as he reminisced. "Then some of the other young men started to see what I saw in her, and ready or not, I knew I'd have to do something about it. I never regretted it, and though she's been gone a long time, I still talk to her sometimes when I'm on my own.

"Now be on your way, take care, and have a wonderful time.'' He clasped her in his arms as if she were still his little girl, his face against hers, then she kissed his cheek, wiped her tears, and went quickly out to the waiting carriage.

With a feeling of renewed confidence, she commenced the long journey, made more arduous because she had promised her grandpapa that she would not travel after dark, but she arrived in London at last and drove directly to Lord and Lady Withers' large town house at 24 Dover Street, off Piccadilly.

As soon as she set foot in the hall, all the old feelings of distaste came flooding back.

It was not the house itself, for though the dark floral wallcovering had been there since her aunt was a newlywed, and the horses' heads had topped the newel posts at the foot of the stairs since Lord Withers was a boy, she knew it was much the same as most of the London homes.

She could almost see her two cousins, their pale blond curls tossing as they ran lightly down those stairs and into the drawing room to greet their latest gentlemen callers. If she listened carefully, she could hear again their tinkling laughter in the drawing room, so different from the strident, raucous sounds that emanated from their bedchambers when they talked over the activities or the evening's entertainments on their return.

It had been made only too clear from the outset that she was not welcome in either bedchamber at any time, and Francine was not one to trespass where she was not wanted.

This time, however, everything would be different. Her cousins were not in town, and she was no longer a timid seventeen-year-old. All she had to do was be firm with her aunt.

"Where are all your clothes, my dear?" Aunt Anastasia asked, striding into the hall and seeing only the one piece of luggage. "Whatever are you going to do?"

"Have them made, of course," Francine told her. "I recall hearing that Madame LaGrange is now the best modiste in town, and I shall go there first thing in the morning."

"You'll do nothing of the sort," her aunt retorted, "for she charges three times as much as my woman does, just because she's in a better location. I'll give you her direction before you leave."

Francine had no intention of using her aunt's modiste, but there was little point in telling her so, so she smiled, kissed her cheek, and conveyed her grandpapa's best wishes, together with a round of the local Yorkshire cheese she liked, a York ham, and some of his cook's best fruit cakes.

"How thoughtful of Papa," Lady Withers murmured. "I have plans for this evening, but it's quite informal so they won't mind my taking you with me.''

"It's very kind of you, Aunt Anastasia, but I'm afraid I am quite travel-weary and have decided to stay home and have an early night. Please don't worry about anything, for my maid will take good care of me,'' Francine said, quite determined not to attend any function until she had been outfitted properly for the occasion.

Her aunt seemed surprised, but gave a small shrug. "You can have supper with Lord Withers, then, for he seldom accompanies me these days, but eats at home before going to his club for the evening.''

Francine had heard part of her aunt's story from older women when she was in town before, and part from her grandpapa, and knew that Aunt Anastasia had been rather jealous of her beautiful younger sister, Francine's mother, but devastated when she and her husband died in a tragic boating accident.

She had few beaus of her own until she met Lord Withers, and when he offered for her, she had felt very grateful and determined that her first duty would always be toward him. By what Anastasia thought was her own good management, her first child had been a son, and after that she had two daughters.

Her achievement in giving her husband a son and heir had, however, been somewhat diminished when their son's wife produced a daughter, little Penelope, and then died. Although the people involved would have denied her part in their plans, Lady Withers felt she had been instrumental in persuading her son to remarry and was now anxiously awaiting the arrival of her first grandson.

Francine sincerely hoped her aunt's wish would be granted, for she seemed to be in a very nervous state, as evidenced by the bonnet she had obviously forgotten to take off when she came indoors, and her shoes, which were both black but not quite the same style.

After sending a note to her brother at the Whiteheads' residence, Francine, like a dutiful niece, dined with her uncle.

The next morning, while her aunt was still abed, she had her own coach brought around and took Dora, her maid, with her to visit Madame LaGrange in her exclusive establishment just off Bond Street.

Leaving the coachman to walk the horses, Francine went up to the door of the house, which looked more like a private home than a place of business, and rang the doorbell.

When a maid opened it, Francine walked directly inside, then said, "I am Lady Francine Truesdale. Please inform Madame LaGrange that I wish to see her." She noticed a salon to the left, furnished with gilt chairs and small tables. "I will wait in here," she informed the girl, entering and taking a seat, but leaving her maid in the hall to await instructions.

Some five minutes later, an older lady, obviously French and dressed elegantly in black, entered the room. Her expression was one of polite curiosity.

"What can I do for you, my lady?" she asked with a trace of a French accent. "I do not believe we have met."

"My brother, the Earl of Exeter, and his close friend, Viscount Whitehead, informed me that you are the finest modiste in London today. They suggested I call upon you. I will be frank with you, Madame. I came out some four years ago with no one capable of advising me as to attire suitable to my height and coloring. I did not take, and I do not mean to repeat that mistake this time.

"I want you to outfit me in the kind of clothes that will make me, if not an Incomparable, at least a most attractive young lady of fashion. If you will be so kind, I would like you to complete each outfit for me down to the last glove and kerchief, for I do not pretend to know anything about such matters, never having had anyone to advise me on them. You will, of course, be well-paid for your services if you undertake this task."

A softening appeared in Madame LaGrange's eyes, and her mouth looked somewhat less grim. "You know, I am sure, that with the victory celebration all the *beau monde* are crying out for more and more new outfits, my lady?''

"I had assumed as much," Francine replied calmly.

"Would you mind standing, my lady, so that I can see just how great this height is that you speak about?''

Francine complied, turning around slowly so that the modiste could estimate her task.

"Ah, yes," Madame said thoughtfully. "The height is a challenge, but with the excellent carriage and slender bones you could indeed be most striking. I imagine, also, you want the first outfit by tomorrow.''

"I would like it by tonight, actually, though I know that is impossible," Francine said with a smile.

Madame LaGrange pulled a bell rope and the clanging could be heard echoing through the house. "Inform your coachman that you will not need him for three, maybe four hours," she instructed Francine. "If your maid is useful, she can be of help, and I might, just might, have a gown that could be altered to fit you tonight.''

Two assistants hurried into the room, and Madame spoke to them in rapid French as she swept out. Francine and Dora were taken down a hallway and into a large fitting room; her gown, hat, and gloves were quickly removed and she stood in her undergarments while measurements were taken by the assistants.

Before they finished, Madame was back with a cream lace gown over a satin slip in a warm gold, a shade deeper than her hair. "This is an evening dress that was being made for someone who had to leave town before it was completed. I believe the color will be good for you, and the length also, but it must be taken in considerably.''

Madame held it up in front of her unusually tall customer and gave a quick nod of satisfaction. Before Francine realized what was happening, she had stepped into the dress and a pin was being placed here and a tuck there until Madame stepped away and gave it an appraising look.

"Turn around and let me see the back," she ordered, and when Francine did so, she saw herself full-length in the mirror.

It was an exquisite garment with a tiny bodice of the deep gold, quite tight so as to display the bust, and a row of cream lace arranged to spill over the top edge. Short full sleeves in the gold satin were edged in the same lace, and the skirt was completely plain to about twenty-four inches from the hem. Here the skirt was trimmed with a drapery of cream lace entwined with pearls and ornamented with full-blown golden roses spaced at regular intervals. A rouleaux of cream satin was placed above and below the ornamentation, making the skirt stand out in an elegant circle.

"You have a pearl necklace and earrings, my lady?" Madame asked, and when Francine nodded, she said, "Then you will need a hair ornament in ivory, cream kid gloves, an ivory fan, cream satin shoes, and a gold beaded reticule."

As she spoke, one assistant wrote each item down in a little book while the other carefully removed the dress so as to leave the pins and tucks in place.

"You would like a carriage dress today also?" Madame asked with a wry expression on her face. And when Francine nodded, she muttered, "As I thought, but Madame LaGrange can do the impossible."

Now the process was repeated, but this time the dress was in deep-green bombazine trimmed with green and cream silk. A bonnet in the same shade trimmed with cream crepe roses and lighter green leaves was found to suit her to perfection.

Francine could not help but speculate on what happened to the lady for whom the garments had been made. Was there a death in her family, or did she perhaps run out of funds? she wondered.

"There is one more walking dress that we will fit. It cannot be finished by this evening, but will be delivered before noon tomorrow." The Frenchwoman waved a hand and an assistant went out and returned with a round dress in thin jaconet muslin over a blue sarcenet slip, the bottom of the skirt flounced with rich cut-out embroidery. The spencer to be worn with the dress was of striped lutestring, and the fronts were richly ornamented with braiding.

The other assistant carried a leghorn hat with a large brim turned up in the front and slightly in the back, and the crown trimmed with rouleaux of blue satin.

Then bolt after bolt of fabric was cut, draped, and pinned upon her. Francine had not realized how tiring it could be to stand and be poked, pinned, and prodded for three hours, and was relieved when Madame told Dora to help her mistress dress.

"That will suffice for today, my lady. The gold gown will be delivered late this afternoon, and the green carriage dress also, so that when you come back tomorrow at the same time, for further fittings, you will look like a customer of Madame LaGrange instead of . . ." The twinkle reappeared in Madame's eyes, and with it the semblance of a smile.

"Instead of a chit just up from the country, Madame?" Francine asked with a grin.

The pale, thin lips twitched. "Those were your words, not mine, my lady. And now you must go home and rest so that you will properly display my gown this evening."

"Thank you, Madame, for you are doing far more for me than I could possibly have expected," Francine said graciously.

The Frenchwoman shrugged. "You will do justice to my work. I would not have made such a grand effort had that not been so."

Francine knew this to be more than flattery, for the modiste was in a position to select or reject her clients, and she had come to her without a personal recommendation. She sent Dora outside to see if the carriage was there and, when she returned, hurried into it and went directly home.

Although she had requested a gown for this evening,

she had no idea if she would be attending a function where she might wear it. She had told Kenneth, in her note, that she would be out most of the morning, and she was secretly hoping that he might call this afternoon or send her an invitation to some affair he and the Whiteheads were attending tonight. Her alternative was to accompany her aunt, and it would be a crime to waste her new gown on an evening spent playing cards.

As she entered the hall of the Withers' house, she looked anxiously at Vernon, their butler, hoping for a message of some sort, but when none was forthcoming, she continued up the stairs and to her bedchamber, where she sank onto a chaise and started to remove her shoes.

She wiggled her toes and had just begun to stretch out for a well-earned nap when, after the briefest of knocks, the door opened and Lady Withers came in.

"My dear Francine, you must let someone know when you go out," she lightly scolded. "Lord White-head was here with his sister only moments ago, but as I had no idea where you had gone, I did not know what to do."

"Did they not leave me a note or tell you when they would return?" Francine asked hopefully.

Her aunt fumbled in the reticule she was carrying and produced an envelope, and Francine, resisting the temptation to snatch it from her fingers, held out her hand.

"Such a handsome young gentleman," Lady Withers said archly, "but you have not told me where you went."

Francine leaned forward and took the envelope, then said, "I went to see Madame LaGrange, of course."

"Unless you were recommended by a duchess, she must have sent you packing, I'm sure, for I hear she is in a position to pick and choose her clients," Lady Withers asserted. "Where else did you go?"

Francine could not resist a naughty smile. "I was there all morning, Aunt Anastasia. And she will be delivering the first two gowns and accessories later this afternoon.''

"And how much are they going to cost you? A pretty penny, I'll be bound. Papa will be horrified when I tell him the kind of bills you are already incurring,'' Lady Withers said with a sniff, clearly insulted that her niece had not taken her advice.

To upset her aunt on her first day in town was the very last thing Francine wished, so she took that lady's hands in both of hers and said soothingly, "Please don't worry your head about it, Auntie dear. It was Grandpapa who told me to go to the best modiste. I'm twenty-one already, you know, and need to be well-dressed if I am to find myself a husband.''

"I suppose you're right,'' Lady Withers said, somewhat appeased. "My daughters didn't take my advice when they came out and they still landed themselves good husbands, so you'll probably do the same. You'd best rest now, for Lord Whitehead said something about calling for you this evening.''

As the door closed behind her aunt, Francine opened the envelope and her eyes lit up. There was a ball they were all going to, and Lady Whitehead was, at this moment, procuring an invitation for her. She would be called for at seven o'clock, taken to their home for dinner and from there to the ball.

Silently blessing Madame LaGrange for her efforts, Francine put away the note and fell into a sound sleep.

5

Madame LaGrange was true to her word; she had even added a beautifully embroidered shawl to the garments delivered in the late afternoon. When Francine awoke, the evening gown and its accessories were spread out on her bed, Dora had a tub of hot water waiting, and she was putting away the green carriage gown.

Two hours later, as she floated noiselessly down the curved staircase of her aunt's house, she heard both Kenneth's and Julian's voices, and the higher-pitched one of Lady Withers, coming from the drawing room. Vernon was passing through the hall, and on an impulse, she beckoned to him and whispered with a mischievous grin, "Announce me, Vernon. I want to make an entrance."

There was a gleam in his eye as he walked to the door and in stentorian tones announced, "Lady Francine Truesdale," then stepped back as she swept into the room and dropped an elaborate curtsy.

Julian stepped forward to take her hand, whispering, "What a gorgeous gown. Madame LaGrange, I'm sure," as his lips brushed her cheek.

"Thank you, Julian, you are right, of course. It's good to see you," she murmured, then she held her cheek up for her brother's kiss.

"Most impressive, little sister," Kenneth said softly.

"Which, the gown or my entrance?" she asked with a delighted laugh, then twirled around so that they could see it properly.

"You certainly look different than when you were here a year or so ago," Lord Withers remarked kindly, and his wife gave him a little nudge.

"It's been four years, George, and we've all changed since then," she said, then added rather grudgingly, "And I must admit, Francine, if that's one of the garments that was delivered this afternoon, Madame LaGrange has worked miracles."

Francine was unsure whether to take the remark as a compliment or an insult, but gave her aunt the benefit of the doubt. She declined the sherry, and a few minutes later the two young men escorted her to their waiting carriage.

"Was the journey very tiring?" Julian inquired. "Not that one would think it from the look of you."

"It was terribly slow," she told him, "for Grandpapa made me promise not to drive at night and I could not go back on my word."

"I should think not," Kenneth said, frowning a little, "for the roads are dangerous for a woman traveling alone at the best of times, and treacherous after dark."

"I was not exactly alone, Ken," Francine protested, "for there were two coachmen taking turns, and four outriders with me, all armed, of course, as well as my maid."

"Mm, an armed maid must have indeed been formidable. Is she French, by any chance?" Julian asked with a grin, and quickly moved his feet out of range as Francine tried to kick him. "No matter, for the main thing is that you did arrive safely, if a little slower than you would have liked. My mother was on pins until she heard you were finally here, and your aunt must have been also."

"I don't really know, for she was so horrified because I arrived with only one piece of luggage that she did not even inquire about my journey. Aunt Anastasia is a little vague at the best of times," she informed them, "as I well recall. Now tell me whose ball we are attending this evening, and how Lady Whitehead managed to procure an invitation for me at such short notice."

"It's at the house of one of my mother's old

acquaintances, Lady Jersey, and she assured us that she remembers you well, but she may be thinking of someone else," Julian told her. "Mama did not press the matter once she secured the invitation for you."

"I remember her very well, but I am sure she has no recollection whatsoever of the scraggy mop-headed female I appeared," Francine said firmly, "nor will anyone else have, or at least that is my earnest hope. Do you think she might be mistaking me for my mama?"

Julian shook his head. "I doubt it, but it is unimportant as long as you have an invitation, for this time you will be noticed and remembered. You will be the loveliest and best-dressed young lady there, I can assure you."

"I say, Julian," Kenneth interjected, "don't you think you're doing it a bit too brown? I'm going to have to squire her about most of the time, and her head will be as big as Brummell's if you keep that up."

Francine was just about to give her brother a generous piece of her mind when she noticed the twitch at the corner of his mouth as he tried to conceal a grin.

"It's a good thing we've arrived, Truesdale," Julian told him, "for I have a feeling you would have received one of the severest set-downs you've ever experienced." He stepped out of the coach and offered his arm to Francine. "Come, my dear, let's leave your boorish brother to dwell upon his own shortcomings."

As they started up the steps to the town house, Francine held out her other hand to her brother. "Be grateful that you can never quite keep a straight face, or you might have found yourself in deepest trouble," she told him with an affectionate smile, then she stepped inside the house and into the warm embrace of Lady Whitehead.

"Oh, my dear," she said as she stepped back and took a good look at Francine's gown. "How exquisite! You'll put everyone to shame in that beautiful gown."

Francine dropped a curtsy. "Thank you, my lady. I'm so glad you like it. I cannot help but wonder for whom it was made, for it was, of course, altered to fit me today.''

"No matter who should have worn it, I can assure you she could not have looked as well in it as you do, Frankie,'' Kathleen said as she came running down the stairs.

"Let's not stand on ceremony,'' Lady Whitehead said. "Come into the drawing room for a sherry before dinner. There'll just be the six of us, for I thought that you'd prefer a quiet family dinner before going to Sally Jersey's ball.''

Perhaps it was Julian's flattery, or Lady Whitehead's kind, motherly attention, or Kathleen's unspoken offer of friendship, or her brother's teasing, or probably a combination of all these things, for Francine felt a sense of well-being that she had never felt so far away from home.

By the time they had finished their sherry, dinner was announced, and they conversed informally throughout the simple meal as though Francine was a part of their warm, happy family.

Afterward, the carriage was brought around and they rode to Lord and Lady Jersey's home, and Francine had her first glimpse of streets lit by gas lights.

"They're the thing of the future,'' her brother told her, "though a few years ago they weren't at all well-received. As the gas lines are extended, they will make the streets much safer at night and put the ruffians where they belong.''

There was the usual wait while carriages ahead disgorged their passengers, but at last their turn came and they entered the house and stood waiting to go through the receiving line.

Francine felt a momentary panic as she recalled how scared she had been before of tripping on the hem of her skirt, or making a clown of herself in some other way. If anything of the sort were to happen, she would not dare face Madame LaGrange tomorrow morning, she realized, so she held her head high and turned to smile at

Julian, who waited at her elbow to present her to her hosts.

"Julian," Lady Jersey said, "how delightful that you are in town again. I hope we will see more of you now that those dreadful wars are at an end."

She smiled, questioningly, at Francine, and Julian said, "This is Lady Francine Truesdale, Sally. She's Kenneth's sister, and—"

"And almost the image of her dear mama," Lady Jersey said wonderingly. "I'm most happy to meet you, my dear. But this is your first Season? I don't recall . . ." she murmured, and Francine decided an explanation was in order.

"I was brought out four years ago by my mother's sister, Lady Withers, my lady, but my grandpapa was ill and I had to return home," she told her, smiling confidently.

"You must have been a child at the time, my dear, and now you're all grown up. I look forward to seeing you at Almack's and will make sure you receive a voucher. Enjoy yourselves," she told them, and turned to the next guests.

"That's the first dragon slain," Julian murmured in Francine's ear. "Now we can do as she suggests."

Lady Whitehead took her duty to Francine just as seriously as to her own daughter, and their cards were quickly filled with only the most trustworthy of gentlemen, including, of course, her brother and Julian, who once again took two of Francine's waltzes.

"How are you getting along?" Julian asked when he claimed his second waltz before taking her in to supper.

"Splendidly," Francine told him. "If I believed everything these young men say about me, my head most certainly would be as large as, who was it Ken said, Brummell's?"

Julian smiled fondly at her. "Your grandpapa instilled far too much common sense into you for that to happen, Frankie," he assured her. "There's a big difference between knowing you look lovely and getting a swelled head, and you're in no danger of the latter."

"I haven't said so as yet, but you gentlemen look rather dashing, too," Francine teased. "The Whitehead party stands out even in this crowded ballroom, don't you think?"

"Of course I do, and that reminds me, do you have a riding habit with you?" he asked hopefully.

"Not yet, unfortunately, but I will have one within a couple of days. I do have a carriage dress, though, which I have to wear to Madame LaGrange's establishment tomorrow so that I will look like one of her customers."

"Is that what she said?" he asked, and when she nodded, added, "She must be quite a character, for I hear she declines more customers than she accepts, even when they're highly recommended. How did you get her to make your clothes?"

"I brazened my way in, for I had nothing to lose, and she took a liking to me, I suppose." She smiled happily at him. "Today has been one of the most interesting and sucessful ones of my life, thus far."

"There'll be many more like it, Frankie, just you see," Julian said confidently. "As soon as your habit is ready, let us know, and we'll take you riding in the park before breakfast. You'll have to make do with Ken and me, for Kathleen is not an early riser as a rule."

"I don't have a horse yet, for Ken was going to buy a mare for me to use and then send it to his stables in Sussex when we leave for the north," she said thoughtfully. "Has he been to Tattersall's yet?"

"I believe we're going there tomorrow, and I'll most certainly remind him," he promised. "And now let's join the others in the supper room. Sally usually provides plenty of food, and that's one of the things you have to remember in London—which hostesses feed you well and which do not. Of course, Almack's is the worst of all for providing the most tasteless of refreshments."

They went through to the attractively decorated supper room, where they found the rest of their party sitting at a table between a pair of orange trees festooned with garlands of white and yellow daisies.

"You look as if you're having a lovely time, Frankie," Kathleen said, "as I most certainly am. Isn't it fun meeting so many people who don't remember you from when you were in the cradle, as is always the case at home?"

"It makes a refreshing change," Francine agreed, "though there's something very comfortable about being with people who have known you all your life. They're less critical somehow."

"Lady Jersey's balls are always a highlight of the Season," Lady Whitehead told them. "As a patroness of Almack's, she's very careful to ensure that no unsuitable people get in, which is very reassuring for us mothers with young daughters."

"What time were you planning to leave, Mama?" Julian asked as he came back bearing plates piled high with food.

"After about two more dances, I think, for it's already one o'clock in the morning, and I know that Francine has had a very busy day, haven't you, my dear?" Lady Whitehead was not guessing; she had seen her try to conceal a surreptitious yawn.

"Please don't leave on my account," Francine begged.

"We wouldn't think of doing so," Julian assured her. "If you fall asleep we'll just prop you up in a corner and then Ken and I will carry you out as we leave."

"Julian," Lady Whitehead laughingly scolded, "treat our guest with a little more respect, please."

"I think you had the right of it when you said after two more dances, my dear," Lord Whitehead said gruffly. "If the boys wish to stay on a bit longer, we can send the carriage back for them."

Kathleen was about to make a loud protest, but Kenneth assured his hosts that he would prefer to depart with them, leaving Julian little option but to do the same, which had, in any case, been his intention.

"Tell the coachman to go first to the Withers' house on Dover Street," Lady Whitehead asked Julian when they had said their good-byes to Lady Jersey, "for I know Francine is tired and needs to be in her bed as quickly as possible."

Francine opened her mouth to deny it, but Julian only laughed at her. "You need your bed, sleepyhead," he whispered, "for those lovely, long lashes are becoming too heavy to hold up."

She turned her head to hide a yawn. "Oh, dear, I'm afraid you're right. This is most embarrassing," she murmured. "I'm quite unused to such a late night."

Julian stepped out of the carriage at Dover Street, reaching inside to lift her down after she had offered her apologies and her thanks to her hosts, then he took her on his arm up the steps to the front door.

"Will you be home tomorrow afternoon if we call?" he asked, and when, for a moment, she looked blank and blinked in some confusion, he told her, "Don't worry about it, we'll come by and see for ourselves."

He squeezed her hand while Vernon stood holding the door open, then he gave her a gentle push inside, waiting until she crossed the hall and started up the stairs before turning on his heel and returning to the carriage.

Dora had waited up for her, and within what seemed only a few minutes she was tucked into bed. She fell at once into a deep sleep, from which she did not waken until morning, when the maid brought in hot chocolate and started to get out her new carriage dress for their visit to Madame LaGrange.

"I have already heard that my gown was the talk of the ball, my lady," the modiste told her as she came into the room followed by assistants laden with garments in various stages of completion, "and I'm delighted to find you so unfashionably punctual."

"I have a grandpapa who would scold me severely if I were anything else," Madame," Francine said, wondering who had told her of the ball. "I was wondering how quickly you could have that blue riding habit for me. I had to turn down an invitation last night for lack of anything suitable to wear."

"It is already finished, my lady, and among the garments you are about to try on," the modiste informed her triumphantly. "Now we must get to work on some others."

At the end of an hour, Francine felt that she did not want to try on another gown, but she knew she would never be able to properly express her gratitude to the French modiste for all that she had done toward making this visit an outstanding success. With these clothes she could not help being the talk of the *ton*, but what Francine did not realize was that the clothes would not have been anything had she not possessed the flair to wear them.

When they left, with several boxes of complete outfits, Francine would have liked to drive in the park, but her carriage was closed and not really suitable, then she remembered people had talked last night of some kind of a peace proclamation that was to take place today. Perhaps the coachman would know something about it, she decided, and she tapped on the roof for him to stop.

"I believe it's to be at St. James's Palace, milady," he said. "I don't know 'ow close I could get, but we might as well try if you've a mind to see it. Then the 'ole procession goes to Charing Cross and Temple Gate, wherever they might be."

"Let's go to St. James's Palace, for you do know how to get there, I'm sure, and if there are people waiting, we'll know it hasn't started yet," Francine suggested, looking forward to watching a little of London's famous pageantry.

When they came close, they saw some carriages strategically placed, and drew alongside to await the ceremonies. Outside the palace gate a party of Horse Guards was drawn up, and there were several official-looking gentlemen just standing talking.

Before long a contingent of what looked to Francine like officers, among them a drum major and drummers, and a sergeant with several trumpets, marched over from the St. James's stable yard and they all formed a procession outside the palace gates.

Then two of the officers stepped forward, one of them holding a scroll of parchment, there was a drumroll and the sound of trumpets, and when it was quiet once more, the officers read aloud His Majesty's Official Proclamation of Peace.

Once more the trumpets sounded, after which there was much ado while the procession reformed, and then, with the Horse Guards leading the way, flanking the procession and bringing up the rear, they all moved on, presumably to Charing Cross.

Francine was as excited as a little girl, for she had never seen anything like this before, but when the coachman asked her if she would like to go along behind them, as some of the other carriages were preparing to do, she decided against it.

"We'd best go back to Dover Street now," she told him, "for it must be close to time for luncheon."

But before he whipped up the horses, a voice called them to halt, and peering out of the window, she saw Kenneth and Julian approaching on horseback.

"I thought there was something familiar about the carriage," Kenneth said. "What on earth are you doing here on your own?"

"I'm not exactly on my own, Ken," she told him, "but I had a little time before luncheon so thought we might be able to catch a glimpse of the parade, but I didn't notice you watching it."

"We arrived too late," Julian said regretfully. "Spent too long at Tattersall's. Was it worth watching?"

"Oh, yes. I thought it was great fun, for I've never seen anything like that before," she told him, her face quite radiant with the excitement of something new. "Just listening to the drumrolls and the trumpets would have been enough, but when that officer unrolled the parchment and started to read the actual royal proclamation, I felt as though I was a part of history."

"If you had told me you wanted to see it, I would have brought you here myself, Frankie," Julian told her gently. "It's not a good idea to go to this kind of event on your own, you know."

"I'll say it's not," Kenneth said sharply. "You can't just go driving all over London alone, Frankie. It isn't done. For a start, no lady ever drives alone down St. James's Street past the gentlemen's clubs, you know. I hope you didn't come that way."

Francine was shocked. "I didn't, as a matter of fact, but I was about to take that route back to Piccadilly. What is so special about driving past the clubs?"

"The members, some of whom stand in the windows watching the street, have the effrontery to think that any lady who does so is trying to seek their attention," Julian replied wryly. "And though we know that is something you would never intend, please return via Pall Mall, my dear, to please me."

"But of course, I will, for I have no desire to do anything that might offend the *beau monde*. I only wish there was a list that was handed to you, perhaps, at the turnpike when you enter, so that you could not make these dreadful faux pas by mistake." Francine looked a little rebellious, then smiled warmly at Julian.

"You forget, Frankie, that anything you do wrong reflects on Lady Whitehead, for she has quite openly taken you under her wing," Kenneth snapped, appearing a little angry that Julian was taking the whole thing too calmly. "I'm sure you would not wish to put Kathleen's come-out in jeopardy."

"My goodness," Francine said, her green eyes flashing angrily at her brother's tone, "what a fuss you are making about a simple mistake that I almost made. And as I do not drive around with my head sticking out of the window as a rule, it is almost impossible to believe that any of the so-called gentlemen would have known whose carriage it was." She was becoming quite upset, for it was unusual for Kenneth to take her to task this way.

Julian looked across at Kenneth with eyebrows raised, and the latter flushed. "I'm sorry, Frankie. I did come across a bit heavy-handed, didn't I? You were feeling so excited at having seen your first formal procession, and I had to go and cast a damper over it." He nudged his horse close and touched her cheek. "Shall I tell her what we bought this morning, Julian, and bring back her smiles?"

"You owe her that at least," his friend said firmly.

Francine looked from one to the other, remembering where they had been. "You bought a mare for me?" she asked eagerly.

Kenneth nodded. "I found a lively chestnut mare that you'll really enjoy, for she's beautiful, with excellent lines, and I'll be able to breed from her later."

"How soon will she be delivered?" Francine asked, her face alight with excitement once more.

"How soon will she be delivered?" Francine asked, her face alight with excitement once more.

"They're delivering her to the Whiteheads' stables this afternoon, then I'll go over her carefully once more, and we'll bring her for you to try out in the park at eight o'clock tomorrow morning. That is, of course, if you have a riding habit in one of those boxes I can see inside," he said. "Now, am I forgiven?"

"Of course, Ken. We're never mad at each other for long, thank goodness. Was that all you bought?" she asked.

"It was all I bought, but Julian here bought a high-perch phaeton and a matched pair of chestnuts, a shade darker than yours, to draw it," Kenneth told her.

Julian saw the delight on Francine's face. "The phaeton needs a few extra touches of paint before it's delivered, but as soon as I've tried them out myself, I'll take you driving in the park," he promised, noting the warmth that came into her eyes at his words.

"I'd best get back to Dover Street, or Aunt Anastasia will scold me for being late for luncheon. You can tell the coachman yourself, Ken, what route he is to take."

As her brother moved to the front of the coach, Julian came closer and took Francine's hand, raising it to his lips. "Until later," he said, then backed away as the coach began to turn around.

T he mare was exactly what Francine would have chosen for herself had she been able to do so, but unfortunately ladies were not permitted to enter the premises let alone bid in Tattersall's auctions.

She had been in London a week already, and each afternoon she had either been riding in the park with Kathleen and her brother or Julian, or the latter had taken her up in his phaeton so that she could show off more of Madame LaGrange's outfits.

Today, however, it was Lady Withers' day for receiving, and Francine had agreed to stay home and help with her aunt's guests. Kathleen would be coming, but neither Kenneth nor Julian cared to pay such calls, so she doubted that they would put in an appearance.

She had just replaced her aunt at the tea urn when she heard an only-too-familiar voice asking for her. What on earth could he be doing in town, and why did her grandpapa give him her direction? she asked herself while quietly seething.

"Here she is, Mr. Bottomley." Lady Withers was always happy to see men come to her teas, no matter what they were like. "One of your beaux from Yorkshire is here, Francine."

She finished pouring the cup she had started, and handed it to a maid to take over to a guest, before looking up to greet the young man she had come to regard as her nemesis.

"What on earth are you doing in town, Charlie?" Francine asked unsmilingly, noting the country cut of his jacket and the badly tied cravat.

"My father decided it was time I saw something of

London once he knew that you were here," the young man explained artlessly. "But I'm not sure that I like it very much. It's too big and there's too much bustle for me."

"I don't imagine you do, and if you mean to stay for long, you should find yourself a good tailor, for you'll not do well with the ladies, dressed as you are in country clothes." Francine was being candid, but she counted it as a kindness.

"You certainly have a way of taking the starch out of a fellow, Francine," he complained, "but if you can tell me where to find a tailor, I'll go tomorrow."

Francine sighed. "Charlie, I have not the slighest idea where you can find a tailor. Your father should have given you the name of his when he ordered you to come to town."

Kathleen, who was passing out tea, overheard Francine's remark, and said, "I'm sure that Julian or Kenneth will be glad to give the young man the name of theirs, Francine."

Quite exasperated with Charlie for making her appear rude, Francine performed the introduction and listened while Kathleen arranged to get the name of Julian's tailor for him.

When Kathleen went away to hand out more tea, Charlie said, "My riding habit is quite new, so I'm sure it can't be very much out of style. Will you come riding with me in the park tomorrow afternoon?"

Because it was always so crowded, Francine did not ride her mare in the park on an afternoon, but picked the quieter morning hours to do so. She did not, however, wish to ride at any time with Charlie Bottomley, so she shook her head and was about to give him an excuse when he asked, "Will you come with me to Vauxhall Gardens one evening, then? My father said it is a most interesting place where they have firework displays and lovely gardens."

An elderly lady sitting nearby heard Charlie's request and glared at Francine in disgust, then turned away.

"Nice couples do not go to Vauxhall Gardens alone, Charlie. It would be most improper," Francine said in a loud voice, hoping that the eavesdropper was still listening, "and, in any case, I have evening engagements with my brother and his friends for the next two weeks or more."

"Would Kenneth let me come, too?" Charlie asked eagerly.

Not while I live and breathe, Francine thought, then forced a smile, for now several other people seemed to be looking their way. She suddenly decided what she must do. "Look, Charlie, if you really want to ride in the park, I'll go with you the morning after next, at eight o'clock. Be here at that time, and I'll be ready and waiting," she said. "And now you have to learn the first rule for gentlemen paying calls. Twenty minutes is the longest they may stay, and you have already exceeded that time, so make your regrets to Kathleen and Lady Withers and go wherever you had planned to go next."

Charlie looked amazed. "I never heard of such a silly rule. I came to spend the afternoon with you," he said plaintively.

"If you wish to stay in London, you must comply with the rules. Do as I say, Charlie, or I won't come riding with you," Francine said desperately.

With obvious reluctance, he rose to his feet. "Eight o'clock on Thursday, then," he said, then went to say his good-byes to his hostess.

"You don't look very pleased," Kathleen remarked as Charlie departed. "Did I do the wrong thing in offering him the name of Julian's tailor?"

"No, not at all," Francine told her friend. "I'm just a little cross that Grandpapa gave him my direction, for he knows I don't want to see Charlie. He was speaking so loudly, however, that people were beginning to stare, so I consented to ride with him in the park early Thursday morning. It will be quiet and I will be able to tell him to stop bothering me, without drawing the attention of my aunt's friends."

"Can't Kenneth speak to him if he is disturbing you so much?" Kathleen asked.

"Not when my grandpapa has allowed him to visit Hawk Hall at any time. Charlie is not a bad person, but his father is quite ruthless in his efforts to find him a suitable wife, and it seems his sights have been set on me." Francine noticed Kathleen's worried expression. "Don't be so concerned about it, for I'll just make myself very clear and then perhaps he'll return to Yorkshire."

They started to talk about their latest gowns and what they would wear to the musical event they were attending that evening, and soon Charlie was forgotten.

"Has Madame LaGrange made you something very special for the fete on Friday?" Kathleen asked. "It will be my first time at Carlton House, and Mama said I should wear something that doesn't crease easily, for gowns go limp in such crushes."

"Mine will not, for there is so much scalloping and ornamentation on the bottom of the skirt that it could stand up on its own," Francine said dreamily, for the gown was in a blue-green lace over white satin and was very lovely. "And the top is cut very low and square, and scalloped also, as are the tiny sleeves." She was looking forward to the occasion very much, as were Kenneth and Julian, for it was in honor of their former commander, the Duke of Wellington.

"It sounds beautiful, and Mama was only remarking the other day how very many shades you can wear with your unusual color of hair," Kathleen told her. "As she said, everyone notices you the minute you enter a room."

Francine nodded. "I know, and some of that is due to my height, but it would have been hopeless once more had I not persuaded Madame to dress me. Her clothes give me a new confidence in my appearance, and she seems to much enjoy the challenge." With her wardrobe increasing daily, Francine was able to hold her own against any young lady in society.

As soon as the last of the afternoon visitors left, Kathleen went with Francine to her bedchamber and positively drooled over her friend's wardrobe. Her mother, Lady Whitehead, made sure that her gowns always suited her, but they lacked the little touches that made Francine's clothes so outstanding.

It was with a feeling of great reluctance that Francine rose at seven-thirty on Thursday morning and allowed Dora to help her into her new riding habit in a soft shade of tan. She ate nothing, but did sip a cup of hot chocolate before leaving, for she would have breakfast when she returned, and the sooner that was, the happier she would be.

Charlie was, unfortunately, on time, for she had every intention of returning to the house if he was so much as five minutes late, so they started for the park, avoiding the more heavily trafficked Piccadilly and going past Berkeley Square and along Charles Street to Park Lane.

"Best keep your horse under a tight rein until we reach the park, Charlie, for there are a surprising number of carriages on the road even at this hour." Francine advised, being more familiar with the area than her escort. Her groom accompanied her but stayed at a distance as Francine had instructed him to do.

They rode without conversing most of the way, often in single file, until they reached the entrance, and Francine could hear, but ignored, Charlie's constant complaints to himself about how close the carriages came, the discourtesy of other riders, and the dirt underfoot. Once inside the park, Francine picked a quiet path and then turned toward Charlie.

Before she could speak, however, he asked plaintively, "You're not still mad with me for staying too long the other day, are you, Francine? It's a silly rule, like most things seem to be in London, and I don't think old friends should need abide by it."

"Perhaps not," Francine allowed, "but we can't

change the rules overnight, and what is more to the point, we are old friends and neighbors, but nothing more than that, as I have told you time and time again. I know that your father is pushing you to visit me and try to court me, Charlie, but it's no good. You're wasting your time pursuing me. You might just as well spend it in seeing the sights if you do not wish to return north just yet.''

The unhappiness was plain to see on the young man's face, and Francine looked away for a moment, sorry that she had to be the cause of it. Her soft heart was her undoing, however, for in looking away she failed to see Charlie raise his whip and inflict cruel blows first on her mare's rump and then on that of his own horse.

Unused to such harsh treatment, the mare took off as though the devil were after her. Francine let her have her head for a moment before attempting to control her, and out of the corner of her eye she saw Charlie go flying past her, clinging to his horse's mane.

It was several minutes before she felt the mare even try to respond to her attempts to slow her down, but she was well-trained, and as the hurt diminished, she started to obey her mistress. Talking to her soothingly and stroking her mane, Francine managed to calm the frightened animal, then turned around to look at the nasty wheal beyond the saddle.

Swearing to get even with Charlie Bottomley, Francine started back, meeting her groom near the entrance to the park and then proceeding with him through the streets and back to her aunt's house. She had no idea where Charlie was, and at the moment it was a good thing, for she felt a strong inclination to give him a taste of what he had given her mare.

She dismounted at the door, leaving the groom to take the horse back to where it was stabled and instructing him on a soothing ointment to prepare and put on the mare's rump.

After washing the smell of horse from herself, Francine joined her aunt for breakfast in the dining room, listening with only half an ear to the latter's meaningless chatter and excusing herself as soon as she had partaken of sufficient sustenance.

As she passed through the hall, she gave Vernon instructions that she was, in the future, not at home if Mr. Charles Bottomley should call to see her.

To let out some of her anger, she started to write a letter to her grandpapa; she was halfway through it when Vernon came to tell her that Lord Julian Whitehead was here and asking to speak with her.

Suddenly, the unpleasant events of the morning were forgotten. She rose eagerly, checking on her appearance before going to join him in the drawing room.

"How nice to see you, Julian," she exclaimed as she entered the room, holding up her cheek for the kiss he usually gave her, but this time he ignored it. She shrugged lightly. "I've had such a horrid day up to now, which makes it twice the pleasure. I'm afraid my aunt is out visiting this afternoon, but if we leave the door open, I'm sure it will be all right."

"I doubt that you'll wish the servants to hear what I have to say," Julian said grimly, walking over and closing the door.

Francine looked mystified. What on earth could have put Julian in such a stern mood and how did it concern her? she wondered.

"This morning you risked your entire reputation for a foolish whim. Has it ever occurred to you that here you cannot do exactly whatever you want to all the time, as you do at Hawk Hall? Sometimes you have to think of the risks involved not only to yourself, but to your family and to the people who have befriended you, like my mother and my sister," he said angrily, his eyes glaring at her in a way they had never done before.

This was a new Julian, and though she was quaking inside just at his tone, she determined she would not let him know it. She forced a smile that did not reach her eyes. "Just what horrendous crime have I committed, my lord?" she asked lightly. "I don't recall having stolen the crown jewels recently, nor have I offended any of the dragons who guard Almack's so jealously."

"Put a curb on that sarcastic tongue of yours," he ordered. "How quickly you forget! I hope you'll not try to deny that you were sapskulled enough to gallop at an extremely rapid pace through the park this morning, for I saw you with my own eyes."

So that was it. He must have seen her after Charlie was out of sight, probably while she was trying to bring her mare under control. "As you say you saw what happened, why should I try to deny it, Julian?" she asked quietly, but he was not yet finished with his tirade.

"No wonder your come-out was a failure if you insisted on behaving in such a way. It's a good thing for you that people have forgotten your misdemeanors from four years ago. But they'll not forget what you do this time, young lady. They might forgive a seventeen-year-old, but not a female past twenty-one, and particularly one who has made a point of always being more exquisitely and expensively gowned than their own daughters," he said scornfully.

Francine was close to tears, but she would not let Julian realize this.

"I saw no one, other than my groom, who came to meet me, and I very much doubt that anyone except you saw the gallop you so obviously deplore. If the word gets around, therefore, I must assume that it has been spread by you," she told him coldly.

"Or by the man I saw galloping with you in the distance," he thundered. "The park in the early morning is a very foolish place to have an assignation, Francine."

His accusation was the last straw. "What I do or do not do in the park or anywhere else is none of your concern, Julian Whitehead," she said angrily, her green eyes flashing. "You're not my brother and it is high time you realized that. Even Kenneth would not dare speak to me the way you have today."

Francine turned quickly, determined to get out of the room before the tears started.

Julian was still not finished, however. Grasping her arm, he swung her around, but Francine was stronger than he realized. The sharp sting as the palm of her hand met his cheek with force was enough to make him let go of her, and she was out of the room and halfway up the stairs before he realized she was gone.

He left the house even more angry than when he had entered it, and when Lady Whitehead informed him early that evening that she had just got word that Francine was indisposed and would not be joining them, he was even more furious with her for not having the good manners to send word earlier to his mama.

He had no way of knowing that she was completely shocked by his anger, and when the tears that had puffed her eyes and made it impossible for her to go out that evening had finally stopped, she still could not believe that he had spoken to her that way.

What was even worse, for the first time in years she began to doubt that he did love her, as she had believed.

She spent an almost sleepless night, but rose at the same time as usual. However, Aunt Anastasia took one look at her and decided she must be coming down with something.

"I'm sure I'm not," Francine told her, "but I've probably been doing a little too much after the quiet life I live in Yorkshire."

"It will be quite a crush at the prince's fete tonight, you know," her aunt said in a worried tone. "Do you think that perhaps you should not go, for it takes strength just to get from one room to another in such a crowd?"

Francine smiled. "I think Madame LaGrange would refuse to make another gown for me if I stayed away, for she designed my dress just for the occasion. How could I disappoint her so? And Kathleen is to be presented to the prince."

Just then Vernon announced her brother and Lady Kathleen, and Francine rose to greet them.

"You do look a trifle jaded, Frankie," Kenneth said rather undiplomatically. "You're just not used to all this dashing from one ball to another every night."

Kathleen said nothing, but was much more concerned. Though she knew her brother had a temper when roused, it was most unlike Julian to be as ill-tempered as he had been since early the previous morning. He had been even more furious when he found that Francine was indisposed and could not be with them last night, and she had a strange suspicion that he was the cause of her friend's absence.

"You will be coming to the fete tonight, won't you?" she asked, and was relieved when Francine smiled and nodded.

"I was just telling Aunt Anastasia that I wouldn't miss it for anything. I only wish Grandpapa could see me in that gown, for he would be so very proud." She looked a little sad, for she missed the old gentleman at this moment more than usual; he would, she knew, have made her put the incident in its proper perspective.

"Do you know who we ran into just now, Frankie? Charlie Bottomley, and he was coming from this direction, but it was a little early for him to call. After all, he's not family," Kenneth said with some surprise.

"But we would not have refused to see him," Lady Withers said, "for he is a friend of Francine's and from her own village, I believe. He must have been going somewhere else."

"I gave instructions to Vernon that I was not at home if he should call, Aunt Anastasia," Francine said, "so he may very well have been here."

Lady Withers did not look at all pleased. "I hardly think it is your place to refuse entry to any guests who call, Francine. You are, after all, only a guest here yourself."

"I am aware of that, my lady," Francine said evenly, "but I did not refuse him entry. I simply said that I was not at home to him. I am sure that had he asked for you, he would have been admitted."

"There's not much difference, to my way of

thinking," her aunt retorted, "but I'd like to know why you no longer want one of your beaux around."

"He is not now, and never has been, one of my beaux, as you put it, my lady. He is just the son of one of my grandpapa's neighbors," Francine said, becoming more and more embarrassed by the inquisition.

Much to Francine's chagrin, Lady Withers gave an angry snort and marched out of the room.

"I'm sorry," Francine said. "I didn't mean for you two to witness such a scene, but I didn't know how to stop it once it started."

"You could have stopped it by telling her what he did, you little widgeon," Kenneth said, "but if you had, then by tonight half of London would have been aware of it. Can you tell us?"

"Perhaps I should wait in the hall?" Kathleen suggested.

"There's no need, for I trust you completely," Francine assured her. "I consented to ride in the park with him early yesterday morning, only so that I could explain to him that I am not and never will be interested in his suit. I tried to be kind, but he didn't even seem to be li'tening; then he suddenly gave my horse a cruel blow and sent her off wildly, and for some reason did the same to his own horse."

"What on earth did you do?" Kathleen asked, full of concern.

"I let her run for a few minutes, then brought her gradually under control, but she was hurting and I had to let her run some of it off. The groom was, of course, left far behind, but I turned back, joined him, and came home."

"What happened to Bottomley?" Kenneth asked.

"I really don't know, and to be honest, I really don't care. The last I saw of him he was clinging to his mount as it passed me. He might very well have been thrown or brushed off. If you had seen the wheal on my mare's rump, you wouldn't have cared either," she said feelingly.

"I hope no one saw you galloping," Kathleen exclaimed, "for they would never understand what had happened."

"At the moment I don't care about that either, but I'd like to ring Charlie Bottomley's neck. Because of him I have just quarreled with two people very close to me. And I will be unable to stay here if Aunt Anastasia remains angry," she said sadly.

"Then you can come to us," Kathleen assured her. "We've got lots of room and Mama would love to have you, I'm sure."

"You are a dear, Kathleen, but I hope it does not come to that, or my grandpapa would be most upset."

"He certainly would," Kenneth agreed. "I believe we had best leave, Kathleen, and let my sister make her peace, if she possibly can. I'll check on the mare later, Frankie, for I want to make sure she's getting the care you ordered in that stable."

7

After Kenneth and Kathleen left, Francine made her way reluctantly to her aunt's bedchamber, to which the latter had retired with a megrim.

When there was no answer to her knock on the door, she opened it quietly and put her head around to see if her aunt was sleeping. A pair of hurt, angry eyes glared at her from the huge four-poster bed, and unwilling to stay at odds with her aunt, Francine stepped inside and closed the door behind her.

"Go away, I don't want to talk to you," Lady Withers said petulantly. "You're just like your mother was—always had to have her own way and take over everything."

Francine sat on the edge of the bed and placed her own cool hand on her aunt's forehead soothingly. "I truly didn't mean to take advantage of your hospitality, my lady," she said softly. "You see, Charlie Bottomley is the son of a very ambitious, wealthy country squire who thinks that because I'm now twenty-one I should be willing to marry his son."

"I found him a nicely mannered young man, if a little countrified," her aunt muttered.

"In the normal way he is," Francine agreed gently, "but he hates his father to be angry with him, and so he does things his father wants, rather than what he himself would like to do."

"You don't trust me because you think if you told me what he did to annoy you, I'd tell everyone, but I do know when to hold my tongue," Lady Withers asserted.

Francine realized that if she told her aunt the whole story, and she spread it around, she would have to leave town. But if she didn't tell her and she remained at odds with her, she could hardly continue to live here and would have to leave town also, for she could not stay with the Whiteheads no matter what Kathleen said.

If she could lose either way, it would be better to keep at least one person happy, her aunt, so she quietly told her what had happened in the park, omitting only the fact that Julian had seen her.

Halfway through the story, her aunt sat up in bed, and by the time Francine finished she had made a miraculous recovery.

"You did the right thing in refusing to see that young man, for it was a very deceitful, nasty thing he did, whether on his own account or because his father told him to do so," Lady Withers said. "I'll tell Vernon that I am not at home to him also and then you'll run no risk of seeing him here. I may not have as much town bronze as most ladies of my age, for I never wanted to be in London except when necessary to help my family. But you're my family, too, though I was too busy watching my own girls to look to you when you were here before."

"I know, and I was very young, and very naive, and very lonely away from Grandpapa," Francine admitted.

"No one can accuse you of being naive now," her aunt said. "What I'm looking forward to is seeing you in that gown you've had made for tonight. Don't leave without letting me see it, will you?"

Francine smiled with relief and promised she would not do so, and then went to rest for a while. It had been an exhausting morning, and if she did not sleep a little this afternoon, she would be too tired to enjoy herself this evening—or to face up to Julian, as she knew she must.

She stretched out on her bed and was asleep almost before her head touched the pillow, not waking until Dora aroused her to take her bath.

The water, perfumed with oil of lavender, felt soothing, and she stayed in it as long as she could, then

Dora toweled her dry, helped her into a dressing gown, and arranged her hair in an elegant froth of curls.

The blue-green of the lace over the white satin gave a cool, refreshing appearance, and the scalloped lace edges of the low-cut bodice exposed a great expanse of creamy white skin. A double row of scallops at the bottom of the skirt was outlined in a deeper aqua crepe, and inside each scallop deep-pink roses, purple thistles, and green shamrocks were heavily embroidered, as a tribute to the occasion, and this added weight made the skirt hang in a bell-like circle.

A matching lace hair ornament, aquamarine necklace, and earrings, white kid gloves, reticule, slippers, and a deep-aqua silk shawl, richly embroidered with the rose, thistle, and shamrock motif, completed the outfit.

As she turned around to make sure the gown looked perfect from the back, Lady Withers knocked and came into her bedchamber. "Very beautiful, my dear Francine. Your mama would have been so proud of you," she said. "Lord Withers and I will be along later, but I doubt that we will find each other in the terrible crush at these affairs." She leaned forward and, for the first time, kissed Francine's cheek. "Try to make up with your brother's friend, for the woman always has to make the first move, you know."

She was gone before Francine could ask her what she was talking about—or how she knew.

Her carriage was waiting to take her to the White-heads' house, for there had been no suggestion that anyone would come for her this evening, and she felt a moment of sadness as she was conveyed the short distance. When she reached the house, however, she stepped from the carriage with her head held high and a bright smile on her face.

"How lovely you look, Francine," Lady Whitehead said, "and how fitting your gown is to the occasion. I am sure the prince will be quite impressed."

"Not too impressed, I hope, my lady," Francine said

with a laugh, "for I've heard it can be a little difficult if he takes a sudden liking to a young woman."

"Who can blame him for thinking her willing if the young woman in question has a gown designed especially for him?" Julian's voice came from somewhere behind her, and Francine would not turn around, but his mother saw the look of anguish on the girl's face.

"Julian, what a nasty thing to say," Kathleen scolded angrily. "If Francine should decide not to attend because of your remark, I shall not go either."

"Children, stop this at once." Lady Whitehead sounded quite shocked at the outburst. "We have accepted the invitation and we are attending the fete. If the prince has the cards checked to see who did not show up at his parties, I am sure he will be quickly made aware of any young lady who was to be presented to him and did not come or send an acceptable apology. The carriage is waiting and we'll be late if we don't leave at once." Lady Whitehead hurried the girls into the coach, telling them to take the center seats on each side so that their gowns would not be creased.

As she took her seat, Francine did not know which would be worse, for Julian to take a seat next to her or across from her, where he would glare at her the whole time.

They had hurried for nothing, it seemed, for as they turned from Piccadilly into St. James's Street, they became part of a long line of carriages, all presumably waiting for the ones ahead to discharge their passengers at Carlton House.

Julian, resplendent in his scarlet uniform, worn to honor the Duke of Wellington, had taken the seat across and to her left, so that Francine, in order to avoid looking at him, spent the whole time with her head averted, gazing at Kenneth, also in uniform in the other corner, who kept giving her puzzled glances.

After what seemed an age, the carriage doors were finally opened and they emerged, but they had to

proceed slowly up the steps of the portico and into the
house itself, for they found themselves behind what
looked like fifty or more others waiting to show their
invitations at the entrance to the great hall.

"Once we get inside, we must be sure not to lose sight
of each other," Lady Whitehead admonished, "for in
this crush we might never see one of you again."

Francine offered up a tiny prayer that Julian might
suffer that fate, then took it back quickly, for she knew
she didn't really mean it.

"Best give the boys two each of the place cards so that
if we do get separated, we'll find each other at the
supper table," Lord Whitehead decided, handing the
cards to Kenneth and Julian. "Give Francine your arm,
Julian, and you take Kenneth's, Kathleen," he said,
taking a quick look to his right to be sure that it really
was Lady Whitehead who was clinging tightly to his
own.

Although this was the first time she had been to
Carlton House, Francine had been presented four years
ago, and now Kathleen was to be presented to the
prince, and though she did not say so, of course, she did
not at all envy her friend. Kathleen, wearing white for
the occasion, clung nervously to Kenneth as the party
made their way to the throne room, where the prince
would be holding court.

As they passed along into the octagonal vestibule,
Julian pointed out the four bust portraits above the
scarlet-and-gold upholstered benches, telling Kenneth,
"They're the prince's Whig heroes, Fox, Devonshire,
Bedford, and Lake."

Francine's arm was becoming stiff, for she held her
hand so as to barely touch Julian's arm. She had no
intention of clinging to him, or even of keeping her arm
there all evening, but was waiting until Kathleen had
been presented and would then move along at a distance
from him.

They had reached the rose satin drawing room, the
walls of which were hung with satin damask, making a
rich background for a collection of paintings. Francine

would have liked to have seen them closer, but it was impossible in the crush of people. All she could see at close range was the carpet beneath her feet, which had gold fleurs-de-lis on a blue ground.

"Just one more room and we'll be in the throne room," Francine heard Julian tell Kathleen and Kenneth, for he had not addressed a single word to her since they had left home. She looked up as they passed through into the next room, and saw an elaborate gold stuccoed and painted ceiling, and on her left she could see the tops of French windows heavily draped in crimson satin, but she doubted that they were ever opened, for the prince was known to have an abhorrence of drafts.

Lord Whitehead presented his daughter, when called to do so, while the others watched from the side of the room, and though she was nervous, Kathleen made a faultless curtsy, spoke a few words with the prince, then stepped backward until she had rejoined her family.

Before the next young girl could be presented, the prince held up a hand and murmured something to one of his attendants who, to Francine's horror, came over to Julian and spoke softly to him. Julian replied and the attendant went back to the prince.

"He wishes to speak to me, and to meet the beautiful young lady with me," Julian said briefly. "Now is your chance, so you'd better make the most of it."

Wishing she was wearing boots, Francine kicked Julian's ankle and almost succeeded in causing him to trip, for he had taken a step forward at the same time. Only she noticed, to her horror, the slight jerk before he recovered his balance. Now she would be even deeper in trouble, she thought, but she put on a bright smile and went forward on Julian's arm to meet the Prince Regent once more.

"The Duke of Wellington speaks highly of you," the prince said, "and told me he misses his Invincible Viscount very much. Quite a reputation you have." Julian murmured a response and stepped back, leaving Francine facing his royal highness.

She made her curtsy, and the prince extended his hand to assist her, then told her, "I remember your mother and father, my dear, and what a loss their tragic death was to us all. They would have been very proud of their beautiful daughter."

He asked her age and nodded approvingly when she told him, then Julian offered his arm once more and they backed away from the prince, joining the party edging their way out of the room.

Julian was wearing an extremely angry expression on his face, and Francine decided she'd had as much as she could take from him this evening. She would stay by his side, but was not going to touch him anymore if she could help it.

A few moments later, a group of people brushed past, and when they had gone, Francine realized she could not see Julian or any of her party. She must try to find them before they missed her, or he would be quite justified in being furious.

Retracing her steps, she wandered through the various rooms, trying to get a glimpse of them. Then she went down a staircase that led to the dining room and conservatory on the lower level, where dinner would be served later in the evening.

Waiters were serving drinks in the lower vestibule, and Francine tried to hide behind a huge urn while she looked for the white gown or deep-blue one of Kathleen and Lady Whitehead, but both colors were very popular here tonight, and each time she thought she had found them, it turned out to be someone else. It was no use looking for the scarlet uniforms either, for there were a great many officers wearing them, as it had been requested on the invitation.

At first she felt secure in the knowledge that she would eventually find them, but as time went by, she became increasingly worried. Then a slurred voice said, "Ah, just look what we have here, Bertie," and her arm was held in a hard grasp as she was pulled toward a door through which she could see a dark staircase.

"Unhand me, you fools," she said angrily, struggling

to free herself from them, but the two men were in their cups and thought they had found a prize for themselves.

"Take your hands off the lady at once, or you'll be sorry," came a familiar commanding voice.

"The army's after us, Bertie," one of the drunks said fearfully. "Let's get out of here."

Francine was released as the men staggered down a passage as fast as their shaky legs would permit, stumbling over each other in their haste.

Francine rubbed the arm they had held, where deep red marks were already visible, and waited for Julian's outburst. He had turned back and was glaring fiercely at her, about to release his anger at her for tripping him, then disappearing and giving him the trouble of finding her, in a torrent of scathing words. Then he saw her white, frightened face and her hand trembling as she tried to cover the bruises with her shawl.

Gentle now, he helped her arrange the shawl and held both of her hands in his when he felt them shaking. "We'd best go outside into the gardens until you're recovered," he said quietly. "I believe I saw an open door over there."

Placing an arm comfortingly around her, he guided her through the door and out onto a curving footpath where he could see a secluded bench. After brushing the seat with a kerchief in case it should be grimy, he helped her sit and arrange her gown, then sank down beside her, holding her against him until her trembling ceased.

"I really should scold you for causing me all this worry, but I haven't the heart to do so," he said, a note of tender exasperation in his voice, "for I did more than enough of that yesterday. You didn't deliberately get yourself lost, I'm sure."

"No, of course not." Francine was feeling a little better now. "I just did not want to hold your arm any longer, but I meant to stay close by. Then, suddenly, some people pushed past me and you were gone."

"But you did deliberately try to trip me in front of the prince, didn't you?" He sounded a little grim, but not in a rage, as she had expected.

She shook her head. "That was not deliberate either, for I tried to kick you for what you had just said to me, but my slipper was soft and slid farther forward than I intended."

"I should not have insulted you just at that moment," he admitted, "but there are far more effective ways a lady may show her displeasure than that. One day I may teach you some of them. Was holding my arm such an unpleasant thing to do?"

"Not really, but you were so awful and unfair that I didn't want to touch any part of you. You've never been like that before."

"Like what?" His face was close to hers and she was suddenly aware of a warm, aching feeling deep inside, and her heart began to strangely flutter.

"Unwilling to listen to my side of the story," she murmured less accusingly than she had intended for she was experiencing an odd shortness of breath.

"If I listen now, will you tell me what really happened?" he asked, his voice deep with understanding.

Leaning against his strong chest, with his arms holding her comfortingly close, Francine told Julian all that had transpired in the park that morning, leaving nothing out, and when she had finished, he sighed deeply.

"It seems I owe you an abject apology for jumping to a completely wrong conclusion. Will you forgive me, Frankie, and forget the terrible things I said to you?" he begged, his lip temptingly close to hers.

"Of course I'll forgive you. You don't know how awful it felt to be so at odds with you. It's never happened before, and I hope it will never happen again." As she spoke he seemed to become aware of his nearness and moved back a little. Francine sighed in frustration.

"I'm sure it will," he warned, regretfully, "for, as your brother could tell you, I have quite a miserable temper when I'm aroused, but I promise to always listen to your side in the future."

She could feel the muscles of his arm as she nestled

closer, his warm breath caressing her cheek as he murmured, "You gave me such a scare when I couldn't find you, Frankie. I don't know what I would have done had those drunks harmed you. Then I became angry and frightened you, which is the very last thing I want to do to you, my love."

Francine gasped, for his lips were tracing a pattern from her cheek to the corner of her mouth, and she felt an urge to throw her arms around his neck in a most unladylike way, and pull him closer. She turned her head toward him, anticipating his kiss.

The sound of giggles close by made them spring apart guiltily, and Julian realized to his dismay that his behavior was little better than that of either the drunks or of her would-be friend Charlie.

"This is neither the time nor the place for a meaningful conversation," he said, glancing around and seeing a couple disappear into a darker area of the gardens. "We'd best go inside and find your brother and my family, for it must be almost time for dinner to be served."

He rose and helped Francine to her feet, placing her shawl carefully around her shoulders. Then he led a very disappointed young lady back inside and to the area where the tables were set for dinner.

They found that their places were at a long dining table in the conservatory, and the rest of their party breathed an audible sigh of relief when they saw that Julian had found the lost sheep.

"It would have served you right if we had gone home without you, Francine," Kenneth said, playing the part of the big brother for once, but behind Francine's back Julian shook his head in warning and Kenneth softened his tone. "What happened?" he asked quietly as she took her place next to him, with Julian on her other side.

"A mass of people separated me from Julian, and when I looked around, you were nowhere in sight. Fortunately, Julian found me down here in the vestibule," Francine told him.

"You were lucky no one tried to take advantage of you, wandering alone like that," Lady Whitehead said gently, "but I knew that if anyone could find you, Julian would."

The shawl had slipped, and Kathleen was gazing in horror at the dark bruises forming on Francine's arm.

"Don't look at me like that, Kathleen," Julian admonished. "I got there just in time as it happened. Another five minutes and she would have made mincemeat of the two drunks who thought to accost her."

Everyone laughed with relief, and the subject was dropped in favor of a discussion on the number and variation in uniforms to be seen. Both Kenneth and Julian had spoken with Wellington at some time during the evening, and both reported that the duke was in the best of spirits and eager to get back to Paris.

For Francine the rest of the evening passed in a dream. From the depths of despair earlier in the day, her spirits had risen to heights she had never before experienced, and she was imagining what Julian would say to her when next they were alone together.

Soon it would be Kathleen's come-out ball, and she imagined Julian making an announcement of his own afterward. Telling the guests that he had finally given his heart away, he would bring her forward to place an emerald betrothal ring upon her finger.

He would kiss her, in front of everyone, of course, but by then she would be used to his kisses and would not want to swoon just at the thought of his lips coming nearer to hers, as she had tonight.

Before that, of course, he would have been in touch with her grandpapa, by special messenger, and received his permission and his blessing, for he had known about her feelings for a long time.

She just couldn't wait until tomorrow for all this to start happening.

8

The Whiteheads' home had become a hive of activity as preparations intensified for Kathleen's coming-out ball. Lady Whitehead wandered around, muttering vaguely and consulting long lists that she carried most of the time. The two young men decided they were in the way and spent less time there and more time at the Withers' home with Francine.

Although glad to see them, Francine had come to realize that her brother was always with Julian these days, because Julian wanted it that way. She had not had one moment alone with him since the night of the fete, and though he was friendly and kind to her, the special feeling that existed between them that night was no longer present.

It occurred to her that he might have said, and almost done, a little more than he intended, and was now regretting it. Though she was disappointed, they were at least no longer at odds. For the time being, she must be content with this.

As was bound to eventually happen, on one early-morning ride with the two young men, Francine encountered Charlie Bottomley again, riding alone, and he latched on to them at once, trying to tell them that the previous incident had been a simple misunderstanding and that she had not allowed him to explain.

"There was a bee on your horse, Francine," he said earnestly, "and when I tried to swat it with my whip, it stung the mare and set her off in a gallop."

"And then the bee jumped onto your horse and stung it also, I suppose," Francine suggested dryly.

"That's right," Charlie said eagerly. "I knew you

would understand. I had the devil's own time getting him under control, you know, for he ran under some trees and I was swept off. It's a wonder I wasn't killed.''

He looked around for sympathy, but when none was forthcoming, he continued, "You must be constantly on the go, Francine, for I've called at your aunt's house time and time again and always found you both out. Don't you ever stay home? It must be awfully tiring for someone of Lady Withers' age to be out so much.''

"Charlie," Kenneth said kindly, "when ladies are not at home, it does not always mean that they are out. Quite often they are in the house but do not want to be disturbed by visitors just then. They might be still sleeping after a very late night, or resting in the afternoon so as to be fresh for the evening activities, or just want to be alone for a while.''

"That's not the way things are done in Yorkshire," Charlie countered almost angrily. "It sounds to me like another of those silly things people only do here in London, like not staying more than twenty minutes when they come to visit. What can you say in twenty minutes?''

"As you are so obviously uncomfortable here, Charlie, why don't you go back to Yorkshire? Surely there's little point in remaining in a place you don't like," Francine suggested, trying to make it sound as kindly as possible, but fast losing patience with him.

Charlie shook his head vehemently. "Can't do that. Father said I was not to show my face again until I . . .'' He stopped just in time and flushed in embarrassment at the blunder he had almost made.

Julian listened as his two friends conversed with one he considered a congenital idiot, and realized how kind Francine was in comparison to most of the young ladies he had met. Even though the fellow had, quite deliberately he was sure, put her in what might easily have been a disgraceful position, she still spoke quite gently to him.

He had given a great deal of thought these last few

days to his feelings on the night of the fete. There was no question but that, had there not been the sound of someone giggling nearby, he would have kissed Francine in a most unbrotherly fashion. He was grateful for the interruption, for he felt sure she did not see him yet in the light of a lover and he wanted to give her time to get used to the idea.

There had, of course, been that one occasion when she had accidentally turned her head as he was kissing her good-bye. It was a couple of years ago, but he still remembered the softness of her lips and the feeling in his guts. She would have been chagrined if she'd known what she had done to him!

But would she now? After all, she was twenty-one already, not a chit straight from the schoolroom. In the gowns Madame LaGrange had designed for her she looked most sophisticated, and he had been quite infuriated when Prinny showed an interest in her, but he knew that underneath was the girl in a pigtail whose gentle hands and soothing voice coaxed the falcons to do her bidding.

"I'm sorry, Charlie, but we will be going home in a week or so, and have more engagements than we can possibly attend as it is," Francine was saying. "Have you taken yourself off to the Tower of London or been to see the firework displays in Vauxhall Gardens?"

"You'd like to go there?" Charlie asked eagerly.

"Good heavens, no! I've already seen them, and as I explained, I don't have the time, but you might find them interesting and might even run into some acquaintances while there," she suggested with little hope and a great deal of exasperation.

"Couldn't do that, for you're the only one I know in London and you don't want to go," Charlie said glumly, then brightened up as he had an idea. "I know you like to ride in the park. Will you ride with me here tomorrow morning?"

"After her last experience, my sister will not go riding with you again," Kenneth said firmly. "And it's time we headed for home now, so we'll wish you a good day and be on our way."

As they rode off, Francine said, "I hate to be nasty to him, for he's not an unpleasant person deep down. It's only when he tries to do his father's bidding that he becomes obnoxious."

"Just the same, he almost ruined your reputation, Frankie, and it's possible his father told him to do that also, for I doubt he would get such an idea on his own," Julian said in a warning tone. "You'd better watch yourself when you get home, for there's no knowing what he'll try there."

"I don't think he really knew what he was doing, Julian. I just can't believe he realized to what extent he could damage my reputation. He's a little slow, but harmless, I think," she tried to assure him.

"I'm not so sure about that, for if he's willing to do whatever his father tells him, and if the man is ruthless, you can expect strange happenings when you return, mark my words," he asserted.

"I think you're being a little hard on him, Julian," Francine said softly. "But I will talk to Grandpapa about his behavior here in town, for he's been letting Charlie have the run of the house lately," she said. "At one point, every time I turned around he was there. I don't know where Grandpapa got the idea from that any young man around was better than none at all."

"He's always liked young people, or he'd never have let Aunt Anastasia leave Penelope with him," Kenneth asserted. "And, by the way, how are you and my aunt getting along now? Did you succeed in making your peace with her?"

"Of course I did, Ken, for I couldn't have stayed had she still been angry with me. She's rather dear, really, and I hated upsetting her so, but we're closer now than we've ever been."

They rode back toward the Withers' home in a companionable silence.

"We'll see you this evening for dinner, Frankie, and

you'll need to be ready to calm down both Mama and Kathleen, for you'd think no one else ever had a come-out ball, the way they're behaving," Julian said with a grin. "Kenneth and I are going to see if there is anything we can do to help them, and if not, we plan to retire to the club for the afternoon and keep out of their way."

"Shall I come and get you?" Kenneth asked her, and for a moment Julian was annoyed with himself for not having offered first.

"No, don't, for you may be needed for something at the last minute. I'll come in Grandpapa's carriage and send it back for Lord and Lady Withers. If they should wish to leave before I'm ready, then you can bring me back here later, Ken," Francine said, then added, "If I can, I will come a little early and at least take Kathleen off of her mama's hands, for I'm sure she'll be worrying that her gown is not quite right, or her hair might come down, or something."

"Better you than me," Julian said with a laugh. "I've never understood women fussing so."

"You haven't?" There was a mischievous twinkle in Francine's eyes. "Now, be honest with me, Julian. How long did it take you or your valet to tie that cravat? And how many were spoiled before you were satisfied that it was a perfect waterfall?" She looked down at his boots. "Of course you did not put that shine on your boots yourself, but did you or did you not examine every inch of them to make sure there was not the minutest mark upon them? And though it cannot be seen beneath your hat, did you not spend at least fifteen minutes or more waiting until every hair on your head was arranged in a perfect windswept style?"

By the time she finished, Julian was laughing heartily and crying, "No more. I'm sorry. I give in."

They arrived at the Withers' home still laughing, and though Francine invited them inside for breakfast, they declined, for Kenneth wanted to go and look at a stallion they had heard was for sale and could take home with him if it was as good as it was supposed to be. He was gradually buying outstanding horses for the day when he would return to his father's family estate permanently and set up a first-class stable.

Her Aunt Anastasia was in the dining room when Francine entered a few minutes later, still chuckling softly at the fun it had been to tease Julian once more. Since the upset over the galloping incident, the two had been much more friendly. She greeted her niece with a questioning smile.

"I hope you were laughing with the young men and not at them," she remarked, then, when Francine only nodded, she asked, "What are you wearing tonight, my dear? Something new, I'm sure, for this will be one of the last big balls before everyone starts leaving for the country."

"I selected my gown for this evening very carefully, and compared with some of my others, it is extremely simple," Francine told her. "It is a pale-lavender silk, embroidered around the hem, the sleeves, and the neckline in the same shade and also a slightly deeper tone, with just a few seed pearls for contrast. It is quite elegant, but I did not want to wear anything showy that might take away from Kathleen's gown, for we will be togethe   ite a lot tonight."

"But what about you?" her aunt asked. "Are you not just as anxious to make an impression on the gentlemen as your friend?"

Francine shrugged. "Not quite, for I can always go back to Grandpapa and the hawks," she said aloud while thinking sadly that that would be her fate if Julian did not want her, after all.

"Even Charlie Bottomley would be better than that." Lady Withers snorted. "And I won't believe that you spent so much money and time becoming the most elegant young lady in town just to go home to Papa's pastime."

"It's a lot more than just a pastime, Aunt, for he and quite a lot of his friends throughout England and Scotland are keeping alive an ancient practice,"

Francine tried to explain, knowing full well, however, that her aunt would never be able to appreciate it. "To rear the hawks from babies, or catch wild ones, and train them to be the finest peregrines around is quite an achievement. You know, Julian is most interested and is planning to build a hawk house of his own. Grandpapa will supply him with the birds at first, of course."

"Julian should be married and raising babies of his own," the older lady asserted. "I thought at one time that you and he might make a match of it, but it would seem you're no more than friends, after all."

Francine carefully schooled her features, for she had no intention of allowing her aunt to realize her true feelings in this regard.

"He and Kenneth have been friends since Eton, and I suppose they always will be," she said lightly, then changed the subject. "I'm going early to see if I can help tonight, and I wondered if you would like me to send my carriage back for you and Uncle George."

"That would be nice, but you'll not want to leave when we do, I'll warrant, for we'll not play more than a few hands of cards before George will be asleep," Lady Withers said with a dry chuckle. "He never was much of a drinker, I'm thankful to say. But he's never loud and obnoxious. Just a few glasses of wine, and if I'm not there to tell him he should go home, he finds himself a comfortable chair and will sleep till morning if he's not disturbed."

Francine laughed. "So I've noticed. But you needn't worry about me tonight. Take my carriage home whenever you wish, and either Kenneth or Julian will bring me back," she said, then got up. "If you'll excuse me, I must change. I'm promised for a ride to Kew Gardens with Lord Hardcastle and his sister. We're to have a picnic luncheon, and they're taking everything so I need not disturb Cook."

"Isn't Lord Hardcastle a little long in the tooth for you, my dear?" Lady Withers asked with raised, doubtful eyebrows. "He must be at least thirty-five and has been looking for a mother for his two children for the last five years.''

"I know, but I have refused so many of his invitations that I felt I must accept one for politeness' sake. A picnic in the gardens is quite harmless, I believe.''

"It is, as long as you don't let him take you for a stroll in the woods," Lady Withers warned, "and don't tire yourself out too much for tonight.''

"I'll not do either one," Francine said merrily, and hurried from the room and upstairs.

Dora was waiting for her in her bedchamber with the gown she was to wear for the picnic hanging ready. The girl had proved to be invaluable, and Francine was quick to show her appreciation both in words and in small gifts on occasion, for Sir Godfrey paid her wages.

"We'll be going home soon now, Dora," Francine said as she slipped into the gown and stood while the maid fastened the hooks up the side. "Will you be as happy as I will be to see the rugged Yorkshire moors again?''

"Oh, yes, milady." A bright smile came over Dora's face. "And I'll be that glad to see my Tommie again.''

"Tommie?" Francine raised her eyebrows in surprise.

"He's been with Sir Godfrey since he was a boy, milady, and we're to be wed just as soon as my brother Davie starts work," Dora told her.

"I'm afraid I don't understand what your brother, Davie, has to do with your getting married," Francine said, quite obviously confused.

"It's the money, milady. Once I'm wed, my wages will be my 'usbands, not going to feed my little brothers and sisters. So I 'ave to wait until Davie starts working, or the others will starve," the maid explained as best she could.

"And does Davie have a job to go to?" Francine asked very quietly, for she had never realized this young girl was helping support her family.

"Not yet, but he's ten now, and big for 'is age. Squire Bottomley said as he might use 'im in a month or two, but he'd 'ave to work for nothing until he learned the job." She sounded a little dubious about this, then smiled softly. "He can read and write and he was teaching me until we came to London."

"That's good, Dora, for you can sit right down and write to Davie this afternoon and tell him he now has a job with my grandfather. And he'll be paid from the first day he works," Francine said, disgusted at the squire's mean ways. "I'll put your letter in with mine to Sir Godrey, and it will go out first thing in the morning."

Dora did not know what to say. "I didn't mean to be forward, milady, truly I didn't. But if you've got a job for young Davie, I'd be so grateful, and so will 'e. Ma said that if 'e didn't get something soon e'd 'ave to go lodge with Auntie Gertie near Wakefield and go down the mines." She paused. "You see, I've been telling 'im 'e mustn't work for the squire, 'cos 'e's mean to them that work for 'im, 'specially real young lads and lasses."

Despite her own concern, Francine noticed that Dora, in her confusion, started to drop the aitches she'd been trying so hard to use.

"I didn't know that about the squire, but I'm not at all surprised," she remarked. "Now, while I'm gone, just you be sure to write that letter. You may use the writing materials in my desk drawer, and I'll want to see what you've written when I return."

She hurried downstairs to greet Lord Hardcastle and his party, and for once Francine was quiet as the others chattered, for her conversation with Dora had given her much to think about. All who were employed, both inside and outside at Hawk Hall, were well-paid, well-fed, and well-clothed. It had never occurred to her that a little boy of ten would have to go out to work to help feed his family, or that a girl could not get married because her wages were so very necessary at home.

"Have you been to Kew Gardens before, my dear?"
Lord Hardcastle asked Francine.

He was sitting across from her in the open landau,
and beside him was his sister, Miss Ellen Hardcastle,
while at Francine's side was a young female cousin of
theirs, just up from the country for a few days.

"Yes, I was there a few years ago, but I understand
that it has been enlarged since then," she told him,
smiling brightly to make up for her unusual silence. "I
do hope the weather stays fair, for on my last visit we
had hardly stepped out of the carriages when there was
the most dreadful downpour."

"Oh, dear," Miss Hardcastle said in some alarm.
"What would we do if that should happen today?"

"Get wet, I'm afraid," Francine said dryly, "as we
did on the last occasion, or shelter in the Orangery, for I
believe it would take some time to put the hoods up on
this vehicle. So let us hope for fine weather."

Regrettably, Miss Hardcastle's day was spoiled by
this interchange, for from that moment on she worried
constantly that it might rain, kept looking at the sky for
the slightest sign of a low cloud, and refused to stray far
from any structure solid enough to give shelter.

She was a birdlike, spinster lady who had spent the
last few years looking after her brother and his children,
worrying over their slightest cough or chill. Lord
Hardcastle had become accustomed to this and fully
expected her to take care of him until he acquired a new
wife.

Francine was surprised and amused by the way his
sister fussed over him and then finally persuaded him,
when the sky became overcast, that the wind had too
much chill in it and that they should leave before the
rains came down and they all caught their deaths of
cold.

"We must have the hood put up before we get
inside," Miss Hardcastle insisted, to Francine's chagrin,
for she was not feeling at all chilled.

Once inside the landau, however, Francine did begin

to feel ill, for it was quite dark and the leather of the hood had the most awful smell. Her three companions seemed accustomed to traveling in such a dismal manner, so she made herself suffer in silence, vowing, however, never to venture forth with any of these people again.

She was so relieved when they reached the Withers' home that she thanked them effusively, insisted that Lord Hardcastle not get out lest he should catch a chill, then scurried indoors and up to her chamber in case that awful smell of soot, grease, and leather should still be about her person.

Dora confirmed her suspicions by taking sniffs at her garments as she removed them, then asking, "Where did you go today, milady?"

"Oh, dear," Francine groaned. "Order a bath at once, Dora, or Lady Kathleen's guests will most certainly shun me. I think I know now how a poor polecat must feel."

Trying in vain to conceal a giggle and at the same time turn her head away from the offending garments finally became too much for the maid. "Oh, milady," she said between laughs, "I'm so sorry to laugh, but I can't help it."

"It was the carriage, Dora, when they put up the hood in case it rained," she said, joining in the laughter, "and I had to ride all the way home from Kew Gardens in the dimmest of light and surrounded by that awful smell. I just knew it would penetrate my clothing, and you'll have to wash my hair or no one will dance with me."

She gave a sigh of relief when a knock came on the door and maids entered with hot water for her bath.

"Have them take those garments out of the room, Dora, before the whole chamber smells of it," she called as she went behind the screen to remove the rest of her clothes.

As Dora brushed her hair dry an hour later, Francine asked, "Did you write that letter to your brother?"

"I did, and here it is. I'm not good at spelling yet, so I hope you can read it," Dora said a little shyly.

"It's perfectly legible, Dora," Francine said a few minutes later. "Leave it with me and I'll write Grandpapa in the morning and have him send this one to your brother. Now help me into my gown, or I won't get there in time to give Lady Kathleen a hand."

The pale lavender looked lovely against Francine's dark-gold hair, and with pearls in the embroidery, she decided to wear just a simple pearl necklace and earrings and a lavender comb. She took a final look in the mirror, noting how the color seemed to bring out the blond in her hair, then she turned toward the door.

"Put a cloak around your shoulders, for you'd best accompany me as the carriage is coming back for Lord and Lady Withers. I shall probably be quite late, Dora, so you needn't wait up if you start to feel tired," she said as she swept out and down the stairs, the maid at her heels.

But Dora didn't reply, for she would have waited until five in the morning if need be. She'd always liked Lady Francine, but now she was her idol, and nothing was too good for such a kind and generous lady.

9

"Francine, you angel." Kathleen threw her arms around her friend's shoulders and drew her into her bedchamber, where everything was in a state of chaos. "You look so beautiful and I know I'm going to look absolutely awful."

Lady Whitehead smiled distractedly at Francine. "Do you think I could leave you to help my daughter?" she asked on a note a fraction short of desperation. "You see, the caterers have left one-third of the sweets behind and have had to go back for them, and one of the violinists has fallen and broken his arm. How could he have been so inconsiderate?"

Francine steered the older lady to the door, knowing full well that Kathleen would be much calmer without her mother's problems added to her own.

"Now, my love," Francine said as she closed the door behind her hostess and came back into the room, "let's just sit down and you can tell me why you will look absolutely awful, then I'll see what I can do to make it not quite so absolute."

Kathleen allowed herself to be drawn to the chaise longue, and once she was stretched out upon it, she took a deep breath and began, "Mama swears she'll not patronize Madame Louise anymore. Can you believe that my gown arrived just a half-hour ago in creases? Millie has gone down to the laundry room to press it out herself, for she cannot trust anyone else to touch it."

"I should think not," Francine said with a sly grin, "for, of course, there's nothing else in your wardrobe that you could possibly wear, is there? As this gown was the third that was made especially for tonight, you'll really not need to appear in your birthday suit, will you?''

Kathleen started to giggle. ''Wouldn't that cause some excitement?'' she said. ''But the waltz would not be the same without a full skirt to float and sway around.''

''You're right.'' Francine nodded, frowning slightly and appearing to consider the matter. ''You'll have to wear a full skirt at least. Which of the posies are you going to carry? The largest one, I should hope, if you're only going to wear a skirt.''

''Kenneth's, of course, you tease. It's the pink rosebuds on the left side of the dresser,'' she told her friend, then asked shyly, ''Do you think he'll notice?''

''Of course he will, widgeon. A man always looks to see if his flowers are being worn or carried, and then he gets madly jealous if they have been passed over.'' Her face suddenly wore a puzzled expression. ''You know, I simply can't imagine Ken ever being madly jealous,'' she remarked in a very sisterly voice. ''Why don't you carry one of the others, and let's see what he looks like? I'll explain later that it was my idea,'' she said with an impish grin.

''I'll not take that chance, for I don't want to make him jealous tonight, whether his sister takes the blame or not,'' Kathleen said, laughing, then looked at Francine in surprise. ''Do you know, I'm perfectly calm now and looking forward to everything, and just before you arrived I was almost shaking with fear? You really are a dear to come early like this and help me. I suppose you knew how I'd feel because of your own come-out ball.''

Francine chuckled. ''In a way I did, but let me tell you a little about my come-out while we wait for your gown. You see, my come-out was combined with that of my two cousins, and I had to dress myself, for, as usual, they had all the maids running in every direction. My gown did not suit me in the slightest; my hair was long and all I knew to do with it was to pile it high on top. I was very thin, and when I stood in a corner, I'm sure everyone mistook me for a mop that had been leaned against the wall and forgotten."

Kathleen giggled at the description.

"I did not receive a single posy, for the young men flocked around my bright, vivacious, older cousins and never even noticed the skinny girl, just seventeen years old, who was supposed to be with them," Francine said with a grin.

"So that's why you insisted on Madame LaGrange and no one else for your gowns, and your hair had to be cut by a French hairdresser. You must have been most unhappy when you did not take," Kathleen said softly.

Francine smiled ruefully. "To say I did not take is an understatement, and I was miserably unhappy away from Grandpapa, for there was no one to talk or to laugh about it with. At balls I took to sitting in any quiet corner I could find and listened to everyone complaining about the terrible crushes at each successful party and how exhausted they felt and simply had to sleep until noon. Then Grandpapa was ill and wanted me home, so I left right away. I have hoped ever since that I did not cause his illness by wishing something would happen to take me away from London."

"But what was wrong with Lady Withers?" Kathleen asked. "She must have seen what was happening and should have done something about it! But I suppose she was too busy with her own daughters."

"You've met her on occasion," Francine said. "She was not deliberately unkind, but she has not the slightest idea of how to go on or how to dress herself, and all she thought about was that my cousins must get husbands. She need not have worried, for they were most astute in this regard. They knew how to dress, and the gentlemen who called would gaze at them in wide-eyed bedazzlement. I predicted that they would both be betrothed before the end of the Season, and I was right."

A little maid came scurrying in, her arms filled with

white lace and satin, and within minutes Kathleen was dressed, looking very lovely as she waited for a hair ornament of pink rosebuds and white net to be put in place.

Francine reached for her brother's posy and placed it in Kathleen's hands, then slipped an arm through hers. "Shall we make our entrance now?" she asked, and the two young ladies went out and down the staircase together to greet the waiting dinner guests.

Kenneth and Julian came toward them, offering their arms to take them in to dinner, and when Julian bent his head to say, "You look more lovely than ever this evening," Francine gazed up into his bright-blue eyes and murmured her thanks.

As he seated her, he asked, "May I have the first waltz and the waltz before supper? Mama is positive that the orchestra will play out of time because one of them had an accident, but I don't mind if they do, do you?"

Francine shook her head. "We don't need them, for we can dance without music, can't we? All I have to do is listen to you saying, 'one, two-three, one, two-three, one, two-three,' and my feet automatically follow yours."

"As long as they don't follow so close they get on top," Julian said with a grin. "You have done wonders with my sister. Before you came, she had been making no end of a fuss about every little thing, until Mama had to go try to calm her down. Who would have thought that my little sister would be so nervous about a ball? How did you do it?"

Francine laughed lightly. "I just told her how my come-out ball had been, with my two cousins, and it quietened her down completely."

"Well, if you couldn't dance, I suppose it would be difficult. But you're certainly making up for it now. I like to watch you dance almost as much as dancing with you, for you enjoy it so much. I'm very glad you waited for me to teach you how," he said, his voice warm and soothing.

"I could not have had a finer teacher," Francine told him, her green eyes twinkling merrily, "nor one with more patience. And your poor feet, they must have been sore for days!"

"Well, not exactly for days, my dear, but certainly for an hour or two. In fact, I began to wonder if you were perhaps taking a fine revenge for some injustice I had unwittingly done you," he teased, "for every time I thought you had finally got the knack of it, you would trip again and confound me."

To cover her own embarrassment that he had guessed her ploy, Francine leaned toward him and whispered, "Who is the gentleman on my right?"

"You've not met him?" Julian asked unnecessarily. "He's a second cousin of Mama's and I suppose I'd best introduce you before the next course. Don't go and feel sorry about his lisp, for it is not a birth defect but simply a nonsensical affectation."

"Hush, Julian. You don't want him to hear you," she warned, wondering how it was that she was always seated beside some rather strange relative of the Whiteheads.

"I don't very much care if he does, for he knows how I feel about it, but I'll not embarrass you if that's what you're worried about. Cuthbert," he said a little louder, grinning widely, "I want you to meet Kenneth's sister, Lady Francine. This is Sir Cuthbert Childs, Frankie. She's all yours, Cuthbert, through the fish course, then I want her back for the main course."

Before turning to talk to the young man, Francine delivered a well-aimed kick at Julian's ankle and felt gratified when she heard a distinct "Ouch."

She had just placed a small piece of salmon in her mouth when Sir Cuthbert spoke.

"I thuppothe you come from Yorkshire, if Kenneth ith your brother," he ventured.

A nod and a smile from Francine was his reward for such a brilliant deduction. Then, when she was able, she asked, "Do you live in London, or are you here for the Season as we are?"

"I don't really live anywhere," he told her. "I jutht flit from one family member to another ath the mood taketh me. I heard of the ball, and tho I dethided to vithit my couthin for a week or two," he lisped slowly.

"That's nice," Francine said with a faint smile, and took another mouthful of food so that she would not need to say anything further for a while.

"I think I mutht be a little in the way, though, for she wathn't ath pleathed to thee me ath uthual," he continued. "Perhapth when the ball ith over she and I can have a long cothe about old timeth."

"Of course, you must have much to talk about," was all Francine could think of to say, while feeling sympathy in advance for Lady Whitehead, whose much-needed rest would be disturbed tomorrow by this young cousin.

She felt a foot pressing lightly against her left one and resisted the temptation to kick Julian once more. Had she known that he had deliberately placed Sir Cuthbert next to her, instead of a rather dashing young Corinthian on his father's side of the family, she might not have restrained herself.

"Did your foot slip a little while ago, my dear?" Julian smiled, but there was a devilish glint in his eyes as Francine looked up at him.

"Slip?" she asked, looking her most innocent. "I don't recall, but it might very well have done, I suppose. I didn't hurt you, did I?"

"I doubt that my ankle will ever be the same again, but I will grin and bear it and just hope it suffers no further damage, or else I may be unable to execute the waltz later in the evening," he countered with only the merest hint of a threat.

"I'd hate that to happen," Francine said sweetly, "and I'll cross my ankles to be sure my foot cannot wander away. Are you sure you didn't bang it on a leg of the table?"

"Very sure, minx," he murmured. "Behave yourself and don't forget that I'm bigger than you are."

"What are you two whithpering about?" Cuthbert leaned toward Francine. "I wath going to athk if you heard about the fun they had at the fireworkth in Kenthington Gardenth. Eight-foot-long thtickth from the rocketh came raining down on the people watching, and they ran in all directionth, thome of them under threeth, and thome under tableth. Two of the rocketh went off thidewayth and hit one man in the leg, and another right in hith middle." He laughed heartily as he told of the misfortune.

"He'th dithguthting," Francine muttered to Julian, who heartily concurred.

"I believe my mama is about to signal the ladies, Frankie. Don't you feel ashamed leaving me to talk to such a bore?" he asked.

"Come with us, then," she suggested, "if you can forgo your port and cigars. I, for one, would love to have you join us."

"My courage deserts me, I'm afraid, but I will move over and join Kenneth as soon as you go," Julian told her. "And there is the signal now. We'll not stay here long, I promise."

He got up to help her, giving her hand a warm squeeze before releasing it.

"A most delicious dinner, Lady Whitehead," Francine said as she and Kathleen walked with the other ladies to the drawing room. "Everything was perfect and it went without a single hitch."

"Thank you, my dear, I thought the beef was a little underdone, but then so many people prefer it that way. But I don't know how Cousin Cuthbert came to be sitting next to you. He should have been sitting at the other end of the table, and that handsome Lord Morrison should have been on your right." Lady Whitehead frowned, then suddenly chuckled to herself.

"What is so funny, Mama?" Kathleen asked.

"I just remembered seeing Julian in the dining room before dinner. I'll bet anything he changed them for a joke, the rascal,'' she said, smiling and shaking her head.

Francine said nothing, but she became very thoughtful and wished she could be sure of Julian's motives. Could he have wanted her all to himself?

They had barely settled in the drawing room and sipped a cup of tea before the musicians could be heard tuning up. Lady Whitehead excused herself, her daughter, and Francine, so that they could give the ballroom and refreshment room a final check before the other guests started to arrive.

The receiving line formed hurriedly, and as Francine started to walk away, Lady Whitehead came after her. ''My daughter and my son both insist that you be part of the receiving line, Francine. Now don't give me an argument, my dear,'' she said as Francine started to protest. ''There's no time for that with the first guests already coming through the hall. You stand here next to Julian, and your brother can stand next to you to make sure you stay in place.''

''I've never done this before, Julian. What do I have to do?'' she asked in sudden panic.

''Just take each person's hand very lightly by the fingertips, or you'll not be able to use yours for a week, then smile and murmur 'So nice to see you' and 'So nice of you to come,' alternately,'' he said with a grin. ''And afterward Papa will take Kathleen around once, and then, as Kenneth and Mama split them up, you and I will join them on the floor.''

He saw her startled look and added, ''It's just our way of saying you're family, don't look so scared.''

After that, everything was a blur to Francine, and she smiled and murmured a greeting until her face seemed frozen that way. Then, all of a sudden, there was no more receiving line, Kathleen and Lord Whitehead were dancing, she and Julian were out on the floor, and she was drifting dreamily around in a waltz.

''You must have had a strange come-out if you've never been in a receiving line before,'' Julian said as he whirled her around the floor.

"There was no one to help me dress and fix my hair, so I was late and they were already in line when I came down. I just went and sat behind a potted palm until the dancing started," Francine told him, glad that she could now laugh about it.

"What did Sir Godfrey say when you told him about it?" he asked. "Surely he'd not have sent you to London if he thought that might happen?"

"I was home a little while before he began to be suspicious, and then he was furious with Aunt Anastasia," she said, smiling as she remembered some of the things he had said, which she could not repeat. "You see, Uncle George had to pay some gambling debt or other, which left them short of funds for their daughters' come-out. My aunt then had the brilliant idea that, as I was just seventeen, she would bring me out at the same time."

"And your grandpapa was to foot the bill?"

Francine smiled ruefully and nodded. "He wasn't really taken in. He would have paid for it anyway if she'd asked, but this way she made it seem as though she was doing us a favor."

"If I recall, there was nothing timid about you at seventeen years of age," Julian remarked, frowning in puzzlement.

"Not when I was at home, working with the hawks and doing the things I knew best," Francine agreed. "But when I was sent to a place as big as London, into a life I knew nothing about, it was simply awful. It took a month before my sense of humor came to the surface."

"Well, you certainly pushed it all behind you. I doubt if anyone can remember you having been in town before. Madame LaGrange has made you the best-dressed young lady in town, and your delightful disposition has made you the most popular. A little too popular sometimes, to my way of thinking," he said a little ruefully. "How many proposals have you received?"

"Only three of the proper kind, but I've lost count of the other kind, more than a dozen I think," she said, laughing. "And the proper ones thought I had lots of money, of course."

Julian looked at her in mock horror. "You mean you haven't? What am I doing dancing with you, then? I must drop you off behind a potted palm and find myself an heiress."

She smiled a little sadly as she recalled how earnest the young men had been, and how disappointed at her refusal. It was fun to be popular this time, and to be surrounded by good-looking, charming young men vying for her attention everywhere she went. But it was nothing more than fun, for none of them ever measured up to Julian in her estimation.

The opening dance was over and they had wandered to the side of the room as they talked. Now several young men were hovering at a distance, and Julian, noticing them, said a little abruptly, "I'll leave you to your suitors, but don't forget my two waltzes."

Although her card was quickly filled, for Francine time stood still until Julian came to claim his next waltz. However, after circling the floor once, she felt uncomfortably warm. "Do you think we could go out into the garden for a few minutes, Julian?" she asked, and after one look at her flushed face, he steered her toward one of the open doors.

They found a seat a little away from a lantern where a light breeze cooled Francine's hot cheeks. "Is that better, my dear?" he asked considerately.

"Much better," she murmured, wondering what she could do now she had him out here. If it was daylight, she could ask him to see if she had something in her eye, but what did one do in the darkness to attract the attention of an unromantic man? "Do I still look so flushed?" she asked, leaning toward him.

"To be honest, I can't see whether you're flushed or not out here," he told her, putting up a hand to feel her cheeks. "And if you've been bringing gentlemen into gardens at night like this, I don't wonder you've received so many improper proposals."

Francine stamped her foot in frustration, but only succeeded in hurting it with only thin slippers for protection. "You're the only man who has ever been in a garden with me at night, Julian Whitehead, and you've not even held my hand. How dare you say such things to me!"

She was almost in tears, for everything was going wrong, when she suddenly felt his arm around her shoulders. His other hand raised her chin so that he could look into her eyes, and he drew her closer.

His lips were cool from the night air, but when they touched hers, parting them slightly, they felt as though they were on fire. She gave herself up completely to the most exciting sensation she had ever known, then felt bereft when he drew away from her.

"I just wanted to know if your lips would taste as wonderful as they did once, long ago, when they touched mine by accident," he murmured softly.

"And did they?" she breathed, completely unaware that the music had stopped inside and that his arm had left her shoulders as some guests were coming out, also seeking air.

She thought she heard him whisper, "Much, much more," as he got to his feet and helped her up, then, holding hands, they mingled with the others and slipped back into the ballroom, where her next partner was waiting to claim her.

Julian watched her take her place in the cotillion that was just beginning, and he seemed to be seeing her for the first time. She was a warm, beautiful young woman, and even Ines, the young Spanish girl he had thought so much about, had never made him feel as he did now—his whole body burning with a need to take her and make wild, passionate love to her, yet at the same time wanting to shield her and protect her from the hurts of a sometimes cruel world.

He sighed heavily. She had certainly responded to his kiss in the most gratifying way, but he was sure she thought of him in much the same way as she did her brother, and was innocently using him to practice on. For a moment he thought of teaching her how to flirt and use more feminine wiles, then decided he had better not, for he could not bear it if she used them to good effect on other men.

He went back outside and leaned against a tree, watching the dancers as they performed the graceful figures and feeling glad that they would be leaving London soon, for the longer they stayed here, the more chance there was of her meeting someone else.

His thoughts went back to the day he and Kenneth, having joined the army, had left for Spain, more than two years ago. He could see her clearly. She had been working with the hawks and was wearing an old, faded cotton gown and serviceable boots, her dark-gold hair trying to escape from the heavy braid she wore down her back.

She dutifully admired their elaborate uniforms and told them, "You've no idea how lucky you are to have been born men instead of women. You would scarcele believe how I envy you your adventures, going off to a strange country and meeting all kinds of people. I hear that Spanish ladies are very beautiful and very, err, romantic."

"I'm sure we'll be far too busy fighting the Frenchies to get into any of that sort of mischief," he had told her, and added, "Now, don't forget you promised to write me, Frankie. I'll expect a letter every week, you know, without fail."

She had teased him, saying, "I'm not quite sure about that. Perhaps once a fortnight if I have the time."

Then he had hugged her and bent to kiss her cheek, but she had turned her head unexpectedly and her lips had touched his, lingering long enough for him to feel an immediate, thrilling response. He had drawn back, as startled as she was, and had touched her cheek gently before moving away.

Even after he and Ken had mounted and ridden off, he had still felt the tingling in his lips.

Her letters had come every week, bright and cheerful messages of hope in an often hot, dreary dust-ridden camp, smelling of sweat and of the blood of the wounded and dying.

Julian caught a glimpse of her elegant lavender gown and walked slowly back into the ballroom. In a few hours it would be over and Kathleen would be officially out. He had thought of taking Francine home instead of letting her brother do so, but now he decided he had best not. In the closeness of the carriage he might get carried away and frighten her before she got used to the idea of seeing him as a suitor and not a brother.

10

W hen Julian came over for the supper dance, Francine remembered his kiss and her cheeks went pink. But he seemed not at all embarrassed and smiled gently as he led her out onto the floor.

Surely he would say something soon, she thought, for they had talked all through the previous dances, but this time he simply whirled her around and around, his gaze warm and tender. Soon she forgot about conversation and gave herself entirely to the joy of the dance and the feel of his arms. She thanked him a little breathlessly when it finally came to an end, and he murmured, "The pleasure was all mine, my dear."

Taking her arm, he guided her into the supper room and to the table that Kenneth and Kathleen were holding for them. Then the men went off to procure refreshments.

"How are you enjoying your big night?" Francine asked quite unnecessarily, for her friend was quite radiant.

"It's like a dream I don't want to awaken from. Your brother is being most attentive, as are a number of other young men, and I believe Kenneth is becoming a little jealous," Kathleen said hopefully.

"You could do much worse than Ken," Francine said, happy at the thought of having Kathleen for a sister-in-law. "But it's better to meet as many eligible young men as possible, in order to make a sensible choice—or so I'm told."

"I know, and though I've been in town only a short time, I've done everything I wanted to do. I have come out properly and been presented, and I've met a lot of people. Now, even if another old uncle or aunt dies, I won't feel so badly about missing everything," Kathleen said reasonably.

"Bite your tongue, young woman," Julian said as he and Kenneth appeared bearing plates of food. "I hope they all live to be a hundred or more, for it's good to see you and Mama in colors once again."

He smiled at Francine, offering a plate of food for her selection. "What can I tempt you with, my lady? A sliver of salmon? A morsel of veal? Or, perhaps, an almond tart?" A roguish gleam came into his eyes, and he turned to Kenneth. "I must say, however, that after the tremendous dinner I watched your sister eat, I'd be amazed if she could do more than nibble on these delicacies."

"The tremendous dinner I ate?" Francine asked, eyes wide with amazement. "I merely tasted a little of everything while you ate as though you'd been starved for a month."

"Don't take any notice of him," Kathleen told her knowingly. "He's just wondering if they perhaps did not bring enough for us all, and doesn't want to have to go back for more and stand in the queue that has formed. My mama is delighted at what she calls his excellent appetite and thinks he's still a growing boy."

"It's a little embarrassing. I'm told it will pass," Kenneth said, "but I'm much the same. It's probably the result of not knowing, for so long, if and when we'd get another meal."

"Excuses, excuses," Kathleen said with a smile. "You two have been so many years together that you automatically stick up for each other."

They ate in comfortable silence, then Kathleen asked, "Are you coming with us when we leave for Yorkshire next week, Francine?"

"Oh, yes." Kenneth looked up. "I've been meaning to ask you about that, Frankie. If you have some reason for leaving at a different time, I will, of course, escort you. However, it would be safer to travel in a larger party, and I'd kind of thought—"

"I came here with Grandpapa's coach and outriders, and was perfectly safe," Francine interrupted. "I can easily go back the same way. You came with the White-heads, Ken, and of course, you wish to return with them, so you needn't worry about me," she assured him. She did, in fact, long to join them but felt that it was up to Lady Whitehead to invite her, not her brother.

"You're not traveling back alone, Frankie," Julian said flatly, much to everyone's surprise. "You know quite well that Mama would not hear of it."

Francine was about to oppose his unasked-for decision when Kathleen broke in. "Julian's right, you know. Mama would be hurt if you traveled alone instead of joining us, and you surely wouldn't want her to feel that way. And what does one more person matter when planning a journey?"

As if by magic, Lady Whitehead appeared at their table, and the matter was settled in less than a minute. "What would your grandpapa think of us if we allowed you to travel home alone, Francine?" she asked. "And it's not even a matter of an extra bedchamber, for you and Kathleen will share, of course."

With the matter settled, Lady Whitehead continued her rounds of the tables, making sure that everyone had everything they needed.

Francine took a tart from the tray and started to nibble it, then looked up to see Julian gazing at her. She smiled, thinking what fun it would be to share his company for the four days or so they would be on the road, for she was sure that Lady Whitehead preferred to travel at a comfortable, leisurely pace.

The dancing was about to commence once more, so they went into the ballroom. Francine saw that Lady Whitehead was just saying her good-byes to Lord and Lady Withers. She hurried to join the group, for she had not seen them all evening.

"There you are, my dear," Lady Whitehead said, putting an arm around Francine's shoulders and drawing her close. "I was just suggesting to Lady Withers that you spend the night here instead of having Kenneth take you back later. If you would like to do so, Kathleen can lend you anything you need, I'm sure," she added.

"What a good idea. If it's no trouble, then I'd be delighted to, my lady," Francine told her, meaning every word, for now she had started to count the hours she would be in Julian's company. And though, as a guest in her grandpapa's house he was always pleasant in the morning, it would be interesting to see if he was a grouchy riser in his own home.

"Run along, then, and tell Kathleen you're staying, for I know she will be delighted. You'll have a rare old time together in the morning talking about everything that happened, while I'll be busy getting the house back in order." Lady Whitehead turned back to the Withers. "We've all been fond of your nephew for a long time, but had no idea what a delight your niece was until just recently."

Lady Withers smiled graciously, as though she alone was responsible, and waited until Francine was out of earshot before remarking, "She was a late bloomer, I'm afraid, for when my own girls had their come-out, I felt it my duty to bring her out at the same time, but she really didn't take."

They said all that was polite about the evening, but left their hostess thinking a little less of Lady Withers for that last remark. She could easily guess why a very young and naive Francine had been included in their daughters' come-out, for no one would willingly bring three young ladies out at the same time unless they were triplets, or in straitened circumstances.

Although she enjoyed the rest of the evening, Francine had already danced her limit of two complete waltzes with Julian, so she had to be content with just remembering. And at the end it was fun to see the last of the guests leave in the early hours of the morning, for she'd never had the chance to do so before, and then crawl, laughing but exhausted, up the stairs on Julian's strong right arm.

She was surprised, however, to find herself alone with Julian in the breakfast room the next morning, and did not, of course, know that he had sat reading in the library for the last hour, waiting for a signal from his valet that she was on her way down.

He rose when she entered, and helped her to a little ham, eggs, and kidneys, before filling his own plate and taking a seat across from her.

"You look quite charming this morning, Frankie, though you cannot have had very much sleep," he said, his smile warm and understanding.

"I suppose I'm really a country girl, for to sleep after eight borders on bone idleness to me. This morning, however, I made myself turn over and go back to sleep again, for four hours was simply not enough. But it was worth it, for it was such fun last night. Do you not agree?" she asked, her eyes sparkling at the recollection.

"Completely," Julian said with a satisfied nod. "We all wanted you to feel it was your party as well, and we succeeded, didn't we?"

She nodded, blinking back tears that threatened, and swallowing hard, for their kindness was a little overwhelming.

"And then you were refusing to travel back to Yorkshire with us," he scolded gently. "Wasn't that a little ungrateful?"

She shook her head vehemently. "I wasn't refusing. I wanted to come," she said emphatically, then added with a shy smile, "but I couldn't accept on my brother's invitation."

"Nor mine either, apparently, until I brought Mama into it." He grinned. "She was standing behind you, listening to us and nodding her agreement."

There was the sound of footsteps outside, and

Kathleen came hurrying in. "So this is where you are," she said. "I went to your chamber looking for you, Frankie, for I thought I was the first up this morning. I'm still so excited about last night that I simply couldn't stay in bed."

Julian had risen on her entrance and held out a chair, but she shook her head.

"I already had something to eat in my chamber, thank you, and I want to steal Frankie now, if you don't mind. I'm just bursting to talk to her again about last night," she said happily.

"Run along, the pair of you," Julian said with a laugh, though he was actually extremely disappointed, for he had particularly wanted to have some time alone with Francine. "I don't think I can stand your vivacity this morning, Kathleen, my love, but I believe Frankie has a stronger constitution than I."

The two girls were the best of friends, and they spent most of the morning together remembering every little incident that had happened the night before, until Francine finally decided she must return to the Withers' house and start preparations for her return home.

The Whiteheads were doing the same thing, and Julian and Kenneth had to take the horses that Kenneth had purchased down to his estate in Sussex, where they spent the night, returning to London the following day.

Two days later, Francine thanked Lord and Lady Withers most sincerely for allowing her to stay with them, for she had become very fond of her aunt and uncle now that she was old enough to understand her aunt's shortcomings. Then she and Dora entered her carriage and drove over to the Whiteheads' home, all ready to start the journey north.

They made a grand procession as they rode through the streets and out of London. The first carriage held Lord and Lady Whitehead, the second one was Sir Godfrey's, carrying Francine and Kathleen. Julian's phaeton was next, with Kenneth riding by his side until they were out of the city, and the fourth vehicle was an

older traveling carriage that held a half-dozen of the
servants inside, while the rest had seats on top of all
three coaches.

Kenneth and Julian would have preferred to ride with
the half-dozen or more outriders, but once they were on
the open road, one of them had to drive the phaeton
while the other could be see most often alongside the
middle coach.

As Francine had anticipated, they traveled
comparatively slowly, stopping at an inn for luncheon
each day and, long before dusk fell, sending a rider
ahead to secure a parlor and rooms for the night.

By the end of the second day they were all becoming
somewhat travel-weary. The only ones not complaining
were Julian and Kenneth, for they had been accustomed
to days of travel much worse than these, and their
young muscles had not yet become city-soft.

As usual, when the carriages stopped, the one riding
alongside dismounted and went to the first two carriages
to help the ladies down. This time Kenneth was driving
the phaeton, so Julian went to Francine's carriage while
Lord Whitehead assisted his wife. A light summer rain
had fallen, leaving puddles everywhere, and he looked
at Kathleen's slippers then put one arm around his
sister's shoulders and another beneath her knees and
carried her across the yard, setting her down just inside
the door of the inn, and she followed her parents farther
inside.

Francine waited for him to return, wondering what he
would do.

"Put your arm around my neck and stop being
missish," he told her when she hesitated. Then she was
in his arms and could actually feel his heart beating
rapidly beneath his jacket, not quite as fast as her own.

"I wasn't being missish," she said indignantly, trying
to hide her delight at such a treat. "I thought that
perhaps you'd need help in carrying someone of my
size."

"If you are insinuating that I'm a weakling, you're

liable to find yourself sitting in a puddle, young lady," he threatened, pretending to let go of her.

When she gave a little gasp and clung to him more tightly, he chuckled. "It works every time," he said, grinning. "It's much more enjoyable than putting a cloak down as Sir Walter Raleigh did. He deserved to lose his head for being such a gallant fool."

Julian set her down when they were inside the door of the inn; then, seeing the crush inside and the men eyeing her, he grasped her hand tightly, remembering how he had once lost her, and almost dragged her through the corridors and to their private parlor. She rubbed her hand when he let go of it, saying crossly, "You need not have been so rough, Julian. I thought you were about to pull my arm off."

"If the coach was still there, I'd take you back to it and let you make your own way here," he snapped, then went over to where Kenneth was pouring ale into tankards.

"There are times when your sister needs putting over a knee and spanking," he he said as he took swig of the cool brew.

"She's probably just weary of traveling. You forget that we're much more used to this than they are. She looks close to tears to me," Kenneth said, and started to go to her, then saw that Kathleen had got there first.

Julian turned, to watch his sister put an arm around her friend and lead her to the fireplace. "What a damned fool I am," he said angrily.

Kenneth put a hand on his shoulder. "Leave it for now," he said. "She'll be all right, and one thing I can say for her, she never holds grudges."

But Julian was determined to make things right between them, and when they took their places at the table, he chose the chair to Francine's left.

She deliberately kept her head averted as she drank a little of the broth that was placed before them, until she felt his warm breath close to her ear and his whispered

"Will you forgive a cross oaf for snarling at you without cause?"

Francine turned an unusually sad face toward him, and he gave her a sheepish grin. "I'll go down on my knees in front of everyone and beg your forgiveness if that's what it takes," he offered, and started to push his chair back.

"Don't," she said in mock alarm, suddenly seeing that he was trying to make amends by teasing her, "or they'll think you've been caught in a parson's mouse-trap."

"Say I'm forgiven or I'll get down there," he smilingly warned.

"It wasn't your fault. I was being bad-tempered and silly," she admitted. "Let's forgive each other and be friends again."

He took her smaller hand in his larger one and held it firmly. "Let not the sun ever go down on our wrath, my love, and we'll always be friends," he said. "Promise?"

"Promise," she said gladly, and was sure she felt his lips touch her ear.

"I think I'm going to suggest to my parents that I take you and Kathleen walking while the coaches are repacked in the morning, and again after luncheon each day, for I think the lack of exercise has much to do with your tiredness," Julian told her seriously. "You're not used to just sitting for days on end."

"That would be very kind of you," Francine said appreciatively.

He patted her hand and gave it back to her, saying, "Try to eat a little more, but don't worry if you can't, for your appetite will return when you're moving around more."

From then on, Francine was never alone with Julian, for he insisted that both she and Kathleen walk with him twice daily and, of course, Kenneth came along also. But he was right, as she knew he would be, for they were not nearly so tired at the end of the next day and, in fact, stayed up after supper for a game of charades.

As they entered Yorkshire and rode passed the coal-fields to the south, Francine started to yearn for Hawk Hall and her grandpapa. She had only been away a couple of months, as before, but the difference was tremendous, for she was returning this time with a new confidence in her appearance and in her ability to attract the opposite sex, but it still seemed that she had as yet failed in her bid to attract the only one she wanted.

Some time in the late afternoon, they entered the dales and then the lane leading to Hawk Hall. As Julian lifted her down from the carriage, she heard her grandpapa's voice greeting Lord and Lady Whitehead.

She stood listening with Julian as the old man persuaded the party to stop for an early supper. "You'll either have to stop at an inn, or eat a cold meal when you get home, and my cook has prepared food enough for all of you, piping hot and ready to serve," he said coaxingly, for he wished to show his appreciation for the care they had taken of his grandchildren.

They needed no further inducement, and Francine hurried indoors to make arrangements her grandpapa would not have thought of, check on supper and add a few more simple dishes, then tidy herself and be ready to act as her grandpapa's hostess. She also changed her gown from the one she had traveled in all day.

When Lady Whitehead and Kathleen entered the house, they were escorted at once to a chamber where bowls of warm water with floating rose petals and lots of linen towels awaited them. A maid helped them off with their outer garments and stood ready to assist in any way.

Similar arrangements had been made for Lord Whitehead and Julian, and within thirty minutes of their arrival they were all sipping sherry in the drawing room.

Lady Whitehead was particularly impressed, for she had seen Francine hurry indoors and knew that she must be responsible for many of the little touches a man would not have known about. She sincerely hoped that her son would one day see what a suitable wife the girl would make, but she knew she must not tell him so.

It had been a welcome relief for them from the fare provided by the inns, but Francine knew better than to try to delay her guests further, for they had another ten miles still to travel that night.

As they walked out to the carriages, Francine thanked the Whiteheads for the hospitality on the journey, told Kathleen she'd see her in a couple of days, then turned to Julian. "I want to thank you for escorting me home in such a grand manner, Julian. I may not always have shown it, but I really appreciate everything you did for my comfort," she began, then felt herself being pulled into his arms and hugged warmly.

"What nonsense is this, thanking me for escorting you?" he asked. "I was glad of the opportunity to do so, and sorry, in fact, that it had to come to an end. It'll take us a few days to get settled in again, but then I'll be over to see you and your grandpapa about some hawks."

A second hug, just as brotherly as the first, almost took her breath away, then he stepped into his phaeton and followed the other coaches.

Francine gave a long sigh. Would he never realize how much he loved her?

She turned and went into the house, joining her grandpapa and Kenneth in the library and having a cup of tea while they sipped a brandy.

"Where was Penelope when we arrived home?" she asked Sir Godfrey. "I know it's past her bedtime, but I kept wondering why she did not come running out to see us when we first reached home, but I did not have time to stop and ask after her."

Her grandpapa sighed heavily. "That little miss is getting a sight too big for her boots," he said. "The servants yield to her every whim, but I'll not have a five-year-old tyrant in my house. I sent her to her room an hour before you arrived and told Nanny she was not to let her out until morning."

Francine looked concerned. "I'll talk to her tomorrow. I'm sure that she's been worse these last few days, knowing that we were on our way here, for she must be as eager to see me as I am to see her again."

Sir Godfrey was looking at the gown she had changed into. "From the cut of the traveling dress you were wearing when you arrived, you found yourself an excellent modiste," he said. "Even after you'd worn it all day it looked better than the one you have on now."

She laughed. "I know. I thought the same thing when I slipped into this one, but at least it is a sight cleaner than the other."

He turned to Kenneth. "Were you surprised when our duckling turned into a swan before your eyes, my boy?" he asked.

"I was very proud of her, Grandpapa," Kenneth said appreciatively, "for she was the talk of London and the envy of all the shorter ladies. The older ones said she looked like our mama, so you must be twice as proud."

"That I am, my boy, that I am," Sir Godfrey said, "in many more ways than one."

11

S ir Godfrey again brought up the subject of little
Penelope the next morning in the dining room.

"She has her breakfast in the nursery with Nanny,"
he told Francine, "and then she's supposed to have an
hour of lessons before coming down for some fresh air.
But it's a rare morning that she isn't down here before
nine o'clock with that cat of hers. And that's another
thing," he said, "the animal's going to drop kittens any
minute, and we'll have to get rid of them right away or
we'll be overrun with cats, and you know how I feel
about them getting into the hawk houses."

"I'll find homes for them, Grandpapa, don't worry.
I've no doubt you have contributed in spoiling her while
I've been away. I'll have my work cut out for a week or
two," Francine said, knowing how fond he always had
been, and still was, of his great-grandchild.

"Perhaps I have, a little, but if you don't bring about
a drastic improvement, I've told her—and I mean it—
she's going over my knee," Sir Godfrey threatened.

Francine was not worried about her grandpapa's
threats, however, for he had brought her and her
brother up and never laid a hand on either one of them,
though there had certainly been times when they had
deserved it.

She had been three and her brother six years of age
when their parents, Sir Godfrey's youngest daughter
and her husband, had died in a boating accident on the
South Coast.

Immediately after the funeral, he had brought them
back to Hawk Hall, his family seat, named for his
ancestors' occupation, which was now his avocation,

since hunting with falcons had become almost a thing of the past.

The grand old weathered stone house that blended so well into the bleak, craggy, moorland setting had been their home ever since.

Kenneth had, of course, inherited his father's title immediately, and much of the property remained in the hands of the executors of the estate until he was twenty-one. The balance would become his when he reached twenty-five. A most competent bailiff and a man of business still kept everything in excellent shape, and Kenneth and Julian had spent several days at his country seat in Sussex each time they had been to London. But for the present, and probably until he married, Hawk Hall was still home to him.

There was a sudden commotion in the hall, and Penelope came running in and flung herself into Francine's open arms.

"You were gone for so long, Frankie, I thought you'd gone and left me," she said tearfully, hugging her cousin as though she'd never let her go.

Francine stroked the little girl's back soothingly, then rose, taking the small hand in hers. "Say good morning to Grandpapa and give him a kiss, and then we'll go up to see Nanny," she said quietly.

"Good morning, Gramps. I'm sorry for being bad yesterday," Penelope said sheepishly before kissing the weatherbeaten cheek he offered. "I'll try to be good today."

He grunted, patted her tiny bottom, then watched her go out of the room holding Francine's hand. He sighed with relief. At his age, a five-year-old was a bit too much to handle. It was time her papa and new stepmother took over.

The next few days sped for Francine as she tried to take care of the multitude of things that had been neglected in her absence, and at the same time keep the little girl occupied, for Nanny was getting a little too old, also, to take care of such an active child.

Kenneth was dining at the Whiteheads', where he had
spent most of the day, and as Francine joined her grandpapa for a glass of sherry before they went in to dinner,
she felt a little uneasy, but put it down to a little too
much work. Things would settle down when she'd been
back a little longer, she told herself.

They had almost finished their meal when Nanny
burst into the room, looked around, then wrung her
hands.

"She's disappeared," she said, almost frantic with
worry. "I put her to bed and was sure she'd gone to
sleep, but then when I checked on her, she wasn't there.
We've gone through every room in the house."

The servants who had apparently been helping her
stood in the doorway.

"What could she be wearing, Nanny?" Francine
asked. "Are her shoes there, her night rail, her dressing
gown?"

Nanny shook her head. "She must be wearing them,
for they're not in her chamber."

The house was searched once more, but there was no
sign of the child, so Francine sent one of the grooms to
the Whiteheads' home with a note to Kenneth to come
back at once. They would have to get the villagers
together to help them start searching the home woods
and the moors.

After more than an hour of inaction, Sir Godfrey
tired of waiting and reached for his outdoor clothes, but
Francine held his arm. "It would be much better if you
stayed here, Grandpapa," she told him. "Kenneth will
be here soon and will organize search parties, I'm sure,
but someone must stay at the house in case she wanders
back here in the darkness."

"I've searched those moors more times than I like to
remember," he began, "and—"

"That's why I don't want you to go. You've done
your share, leave it to the younger ones now. Please,"
she begged.

He might have argued longer, but just then Kenneth

and Julian arrived. "Has she shown up?" Kenneth asked, and when they shook their heads, he said, "If she's hiding somewhere, you'll not save her from a spanking, Frankie."

Francine shook her head. "I don't think she is," she said. "I had a funny feeling even before dinner. I think she's out there on the moors."

Julian came over and put his arm around her shoulders in a reassuring hug. "If she is, we'll find her. We brought some of our men with us, and between yours and the men who've come up from the village, we can search as far as she can possibly have wandered."

"I'll give her a sound thrashing for this night's mischief," Sir Godfrey said. "Men from miles around losing their sleep for one of her pranks."

Francine heard him but knew that he'd do no such thing. He just had to say something that would allay the fear of her not being found. She sat on the steps to the back door, listening, as Kenneth and Julian organized the search parties as though it was a military operation, and soon they set off in three different directions.

There was something vaguely comforting in the sight of the flaming torches they each carried, going back and forth in a planned pattern, the regular calls of the child's name, and the silences as they waited for an answer.

"It looks strange from here, doesn't it?" Her grandpapa's gruff voice came through the darkness. "I've never seen a search from this side of it before. You'd best go inside now, for I'm going to the hawk houses to see if the birds have been disturbed by the commotion."

She sat in the drawing room waiting, and she somehow felt more comfortable because Julian was helping, which was quite unreasonable, for he did not know the moors the way Kenneth and the local men did.

After a while, her grandpapa came back, and she saw the tiredness in his eyes and persuaded him to go to bed for a few hours. "There are at least a dozen women in the kitchen, Grandpapa, making soup and hot toddies for the men when they return, and there's nothing you can do except wait.''

She heard him going up the stairs more slowly than he'd ever climbed them in his life.

Grandpapa was right, Francine thought. It was time Penelope's father came for her, for Aunt Anastasia had told her, just before she left London, that her son's new wife was breeding and a child expected any day. She would miss Penelope terribly, as they all would, but she needed to be cared for in the heart of her own family, and would be excited to find she had a baby brother or sister.

Francine's instincts told her that the child was all right and would be found before the night was out. And though her grandpapa might scold the little girl, he would be too relieved to do anything else, no matter how angry he had been.

Almost instinctively, her thoughts went to the children of her own she might or might not have. She was old enough to have had several by now, and she wondered what the future held for her.

It would be wonderful to have Julian's children. She could almost see them in her mind's eye. And for the first time she realized why she could never marry someone like Charlie, even in desperation, for she simply could not bear to have children like him and his father.

She got up and poked the fire, then placed some more wood upon it to keep it going. Sounds from the kitchen reached her ears occasionally as she waited, for the wives of the searchers who had come with them to help in any way they could were noisier than their own household staff would ever be. It was strangely comforting to hear their voices in the waiting silence of the rest of the house.

Shortly before three o'clock in the morning, she heard the sound of men's voices outside, and Julian walked in carrying the grubby little girl in his arms. Her face was scratched and streaked with dirt and tears, and she was fast asleep.

For once, there was nothing Francine could say, or needed to say, for the relief and gratitude showed in the tears that brimmed in her eyes.

He had sent his men directly to the kitchen, and now Nanny came running. "I'll carry her up while you lead the way," he told her. "I checked her and doubt there's much wrong with her a bath and a night's sleep won't cure."

A maid brought a tray of hot pasties, soup, and toddies to the drawing room, and Francine just stood there, waiting for Julian to come back.

"You'd better sit down before you collapse with exhaustion," Julian told her, steering her to the couch and placing the tray on the table in front of it, before sitting beside her. "I wanted to talk to you about the child, for I heard your grandpapa's threat before I left. I don't believe she was being naughty. Before she fell asleep, she kept crying and saying she couldn't find something and begging me to look for it," he said, worry lines creasing his forehead.

"What did it sound like?" Francine asked. "Kitty, maybe, for I've not seen her cat around all evening."

"No, it was more like little something or other," he said, frowning as he tried to recall the word.

"Little pest," Francine said with a nod. "It's what we used to call her cat when it was young, but I thought she'd forgotten that long ago. But you needn't worry about Grandpapa's threats, for he's an old softy and wouldn't lay a finger on her, I promise, though he might scold her severely."

"Will Lady Whitehead worry as to where you've got to at this hour?" she asked, for she did not know if his parents had been home when the messenger arrived.

"No, she'll not worry, for she knows we came here to help and will probably expect me to stay the night," he said. "I haven't seen you since we brought you back from London. Have you been very busy catching up with your chores?"

She nodded. "There was a great deal to do, of course, for servants, no matter how good, never work as well

for a man on his own as they do when a women is
checking on them. But I'm so glad that Aunt Anastasia
invited me to London just at the time when you and Ken
were going. I've meant to ask, did the two of you have
anything to do with it?''

Julian smiled. "A little, for I could not have enjoyed
myself in London so much if you had been left at home.
I had thought that you would jump at the chance to be
there when we were, but my consequence was
considerably deflated when I heard that your grandpapa
had to almost compel you to join us.''

"I was being silly, wasn't I? But memories of the last
time I was there made me hesitate, I suppose. I'm very
glad now that you all conspired to force me to enjoy
myself,'' she told him, a little ruefully, "for I'll never be
afraid to go there again.''

"I suppose that one of these days Kenneth will open
up the Truesdale's town house,'' Julian remarked. "We
went over to take a look at it while we were there, and it
is a much larger mansion than ours, but it's been closed
up since just after your parents died.''

"It's in Grosvenor Square, isn't it? Why didn't you
take me with you?'' Francine asked, for she had almost
forgotten about the house. "I'll scold Ken for not doing
so, when next I see him, for I would have enjoyed being
in the place where Mama and Papa indulged in a
vertiginous social whirl, as Grandpapa once called it. It
would have been fun to peek under the dust cloths and
see what the furniture was like, and have my ancestors
frowning down upon me from their places on the
walls.''

Julian laughed. "I promise to make him take you
there next year. How's that?''

His arm was around the back of the couch and
Francine laid her head against it. "How long do you
think it will be before Ken and the other men get back?''
she asked sleepily, for the few sips of toddy she had
taken were having their effect.

"It could be several hours. Ken and his group went

off to the east, and the others went in the opposite direction, while I went north, and I didn't dare send anyone on horseback over those moors in the darkness," he said, yawning drowsily, for though he had eaten several pastries, he had also drunk a tankard of the hot toddy. "You go to bed if you like, and I'll wait up for him."

"I'll keep you company a little longer," she murmured, enjoying the feeling of being so close to him, and alone.

They must have fallen asleep almost simultaneously and then crept even closer together, for it was six o'clock when Sir Godfrey came down the stairs and found them fast asleep in each other's arms, Francine's had nestled close to Julian's, his chin against her cheek.

He went out again, then came stamping along the corridor, shouting at imaginary servants who must, he knew, be enjoying a well-deserved sleep by now. When he heard Julian, who as a soldier was used to waking instantly, start to move around, he slipped out of the house so as not to embarrass the young man. There'd be time enough to go into it later if Francine wanted to force the issue.

Back in his own bedchamber, he saw Julian riding in the direction of his home, with a number of his own servants he must have just wakened straggling along behind him.

He waited until later in the morning to approach Francine. She was looking for something in the study when he went in. He perched on the arm of a large chair and looked at her remarkably unconcerned face.

"If you're still in love with Julian and wish to marry him, my dear, you now have the opportunity," he told her, watching her face as he spoke.

"What on earth do you mean, Grandpapa?" she asked. "I don't understand."

"When I came down the stairs this morning and walked into the drawing room, you and he were fast asleep on the sofa with your arms around each other and your head against his cheek. If that is not a compromising position, I don't know what is," he said flatly.

Francine's own cheeks became a rosy pink and she looked embarrassed. "We were just talking, waiting for Kenneth to get in, and I suppose I must have fallen asleep," she said softly. "I was alone when I awoke, though, and I went to my chamber and slept for a few more hours. You didn't say anything to Julian, did you?" she asked in sudden alarm.

He shook his head. "I went out quietly, then came back along the hall, making a lot of noise until I heard him moving around. Then I went outside and around the house, going up the back stairs, and watched him riding away with his servants not long after. What are you going to do?"

"I don't want Julian forced into marriage with me, Grandpapa. You should know me better than that. I want his love more than anything else in the world, but I couldn't bear having him without it." She looked stern. "You must promise that you won't say anything to him about his having compromised me."

"And you should know me better than that, young lady. I'll not interfere in this case, but if he doesn't know his heart soon, I may bang his head against a wall until he sees some sense," he growled.

"I think he's starting to," she said hopefully, then asked, "Have you seen Penelope this morning?"

"No, I peeked in to be sure she had been found, but I did not waken her. However, I have some words to say to her when she does get up," he said sternly.

"Julian says she was looking for Kitty and calling her by the old name we used when she was a kitten, Little Pest."

"That's no excuse for turning the whole countryside upside down looking for her," Sir Godfrey said grimly. "She could have fallen and been killed out there in the darkness."

"I guarantee she's learned her lesson, Grandpapa.

Please don't scold her. I'll talk seriously to her when she's had her sleep out," Francine promised.

"Very well," he said, secretly relieved that she was taking on that responsibility. "Now, be off with you and let me get some work done."

Francine kissed his forehead, then went outdoors to see if she could find out anything about the cat. It should not, of course, have been out of doors at all, for Grandpapa had a constant fear that it would get into the hawk houses one day.

A few inquiries sent her in the direction of the stables, and bunching her skirts as she had when she was a girl, she climbed up into the loft. There, comfortably settled on a bed of straw, lay Kitty with seven tiny pieces of fluff busily feeding their little faces.

There was no sign of anyone having been there, so Francine hurried down the steps and back to the kitchen, where a delighted young maid fetched food, milk, and water and begged to take care of them herself.

After that, Francine went to the hawk houses to check and be sure that her orders had been carried out, for she had not had the time to work with them since her return.

It was there that Julian found her an hour later, and she went with him into the home woods and sat on an old tree stump while he paced back and forth.

"I've just come from your grandpapa, Frankie, and he has given me permission to address you. It is my hope that you will do me the honor of accepting my proposal of marriage," he said seriously.

For a moment Francine was stunned, then she realized that her grandpapa would never have gone back on his word. This was all Julian's idea out of a mistaken sense of duty.

She longed to go away somewhere and cry, for she wanted him more than anything in the world, but she could not, would not take him on these terms.

Her hands were clasped so tightly together that her nails were digging into the flesh as she forced herself to answer him. He waited in silence until she raised her head, then said, quietly but clearly, "Thank you for offering, but I can't marry you, Julian."

His serious face seemed to turn to stone before her eyes and he drew a deep breath before asking coldly, "Do you want time to think about it?"

She shook her head, and he swung around on his heel and strode away. She could see only his blurred outline through the tears that filled her eyes, and when he was almost out of sight, she cradled her head in her arms and sobbed as if her heart would break.

Sir Godfrey found her an hour or more later, just sitting on the tree trunk and she did not even notice him as he walked toward her.

"I did not say one word to him about last night, or rather, early this morning," he told her, and she looked up at him with eyes so filled with misery that he ached for her. "He did not mention it either, but just asked my permission to address you, and I gave him my blessing."

"There was not a smile, not even a glimmer of one, Grandpapa, and he sounded as though he had rehearsed it all the way over here. There was nothing I could do except say no, for I don't want him without his love," she cried, the tears starting up again.

"Come along, sweetheart," he said, putting an arm around her and easing her off her makeshift seat. "It will come out right in the end, you'll see. It's not like you to give up hope after all these years."

She forced a wan smile. "Can we go in the back way? I'd hate anyone to see me looking like this."

"Of course. That's how Kenneth came in last night, by the way. He didn't know anyone was still around, except the women in the kitchen, so he came up the back stairs to his room," he said, more for the sake of saying something, anything, for he knew she wasn't hearing him.

As he left her outside her chamber, she said, "The kittens are in the hayloft, by the way, and you mustn't harm them."

"How many are there?" he asked gruffly.

"Seven," she told him as she closed the door quietly behind her.

Julian had ridden toward home more slowly than usual, his feelings in a state of tumult, for when he had suddenly realized how very much he loved Francine, he had been convinced that she felt the same way about him.

But she had looked at him as if completely shocked and had left him in no doubt as to her decision. She had made it clear that she would not even consider marrying him.

He shook his head in bewilderment, for now nothing would be the same and they could no longer enjoy the friendship that had flourished over the years and, in his case, had grown into a deep, lasting love.

Urging his horse into a gallop, he made for the nearest inn, where he took a room for the night, bought a bottle of brandy, and for the first time in years he drank until he no longer felt the hurt.

12

"Charles Bottomley, you don't have the gumption you were born with," the squire thundered. "That's what came of my marrying a half-wit, and I'll not let you do the same. Francine Truesdale is a sight more quick-witted than you are, and it's her blood we need in my grandchildren to make up for what's missing in yours."

Charlie looked decidedly dismal. "But I don't think we'd rub along at all well, sir," he protested. "She don't like me overmuch, and she's got a sharp tongue when she's riled up."

The squire had been pacing back and forth over the length of the drawing room, but he swung around at his son's words.

"Like you," he roared. "She'd be about in the head if she did. But she'll be on the shelf soon, and Sir Godfrey knows it, so if you put her in a compromising position, he'll make her marry you to save face. I'll be quick to point out, of course, that it's impossible to keep something like that quiet in a house full of servants, and he'll not want his granddaughter disgraced."

"But I did what you told me to do in London, sir, and nothing came of it at all," Charlie said. "She rides better than I do, and it was quite some time before I could get my horse under control, and by then she was halfway back to her aunt's home."

"I told you to make her gallop in the afternoon, you numbskull, not early on a morning when there was no one of any note to see her disgracing herself," his father said scornfully. "Can't you ever do anything right?"

Charlie wanted to tell him that Francine would not ride with him in the afternoon, so he had to go with her in the morning, but he knew it was no use telling his father anything when he was in this mood. He only hoped that, when he finally learned what his father's next plan was, it would not be too difficult, for the easiest-sounding plans always had a way of going wrong when he tried them.

"I happen to know," the squire began, "that Francine enjoys visiting Skipton on market day and browsing through all the stalls. What you're to do is tell her you're going there on Monday and offer to take her in the curricle. If you leave the tiger at home, there'll be plenty of room at the back for her purchases. Then you'll buy her supper at the inn."

His son nodded gravely. "You want us to spend the night there?" he suggested.

"She'll not spend the night there, you shatterbrain," the squire roared, "and you'll have to be very persuasive to get her to stay and have a bite to eat. But you'd better get her there somehow or I'll wring your stupid neck."

He heaved a sigh of despair, then continued. "The thing is to arrange with Joe Higgins, one of the hostlers that works there, to give a little special attention to the curricle while the two of you eat. I'd best take care of that myself, for you're sure to make a mess of it, and I'll slip him a sovereign for his trouble.

"What's he going to do to earn that much money, sir?" Charlie asked, surprised at his father's rare openhandedness.

"He's going to do a little work on one of the wheels, to make sure that it breaks down after you've gone a few miles, simpleton." The squire was fast losing his patience. "Just make sure you take the quieter road back so no one can come along and offer help, then all you've got to do is sit there with her all night and she'll have to marry you."

Charlie looked unhappy. "She's going to be furious

when she finds out what we've done, Father," he said.

The squire gave a snort. "She'll not find out unless you go and tell her, you idiot. She'll think it's just an accident and there's nothing to do but wait for help."

Charlie did not like the scheme at all, but he knew his father well enough to realize it was useless to argue with him, so he had his horse brought around and went over to see Francine.

He found her in the kitchen garden, a basket over her arm, selecting fresh vegetables for Cook to prepare for supper.

"Hello, Charlie," she said, wondering what on earth he was doing dropping by in the middle of the morning, for his calls were usually in the afternoon when he could stuff himself with the dainty cakes and pastries his father's cook seldom baked.

"Good morning, Francine," he began, rather nervously clearing his throat. "I'm going to Skipton market on Monday, in my new curricle, and was wondering if you'd like to come along for the ride."

Francine looked skeptical, for most of Charlie's suggestions originated with his father. However, she had not yet seen his curricle and always enjoyed going to the market. "I have to work with the hawks each morning, Charlie, so I'm afraid it would be too late in the morning before I could get away," she told him, knowing quite well that she could easily have one of the men do her work.

"That's all right," he said with a big smile, for he would not now need to make an excuse for arriving late. "You could take your time looking at the stalls and deciding what to buy, then we could have an early supper at the inn instead of rushing back."

It was what she would probably have done if her brother or anyone else had taken her, so Francine rather reluctantly agreed and arranged the time he was to come for her. She hated to refuse, for she did not dislike the young man when he was away from his father's influence.

Her grandpapa chuckled when she told him of the excursion, and he accused her of wishing to try out the new curricle rather than spend time with its owner.

"You know me too well, Grandpapa," she said with a smile, "but I've no doubt Charlie will be quite cow-handed with the cattle, for he's no horseman."

She was ready and waiting when Charlie came, ten or more minutes late, but she readily excused him when she saw the elegant curricle in a shiny black, trimmed with red, and with bright-red wheels, curricle bar, and center pole. It was drawn by a fine-looking matched pair of grays.

Fortunately, she did not need his assistance to get into the vehicle, for he remained seated holding the horses in check. "Don't you have a tiger to hold the horses, Charlie?" she asked, for it would be a little awkward if she had to climb in with her purchases.

Charlie looked somewhat embarrassed. "I have, but I didn't bring him, for I thought it would be easier to use his seat at the back for anything you buy. When we get to Skipton, I'll leave the curricle at the inn and we'll go around the market on foot. The grays aren't used to being in much traffic."

Francine looked at him rather dubiously, for if the horses were frightened of the traffic of a market town, how would they behave when he took them to London? She gave a little shrug, deciding there was no use in arguing the matter, and sat back to enjoy the ride through the country lanes, secretly glad that Charlie was not much of a conversationalist.

They had started out too late to pass animals being taken to market, but as they neared the town, they could hear the sounds of the cows and sheep, penned on the outskirts, and Charlie had to go more slowly as the road was slippery from the droppings.

They drove into the inn yard and a hostler came hurrying over to hold the horses and allow Charlie to alight first. "Are you Joe Higgins?" he asked the shifty-looking little man, who nodded and waited until Charlie had helped Francine down; then, without a word, the man took the curricle around to the back.

"Let's start down the main street," Francine suggested, "for there's usually a draper halfway down on the left, who has the finest lawn I've seen anywhere."

She found the draper and bought several yards of his lawn, and she also bought some slippers and a pocket-knife for her grandpapa, who was having a birthday soon. A stop was made at the haberdasher and Francine selected ribbons for herself and men's kerchiefs for her brother.

She had known Charlie all her life and had always found him to be a grumbler if he had to wait while others attended to their business, but today she was surprised at his patience as he uncomplainingly carried her packages from stall to stall. She dearly hoped that he was not planning, on the way home, to ask for her hand in marriage, as he had done once before and attempted to again just before the men came back from the wars, for it would account for the absence of the tiger.

"Did you not want to make any purchases, Charlie?" Francine asked as they walked back toward the inn. "If I recall, you said you were coming to the market on your own behalf and asked if I would like to come along for the ride."

He began to stammer, "I was g-going to buy, er, some, er, some horse brasses, and I looked while you were busy with the draper but saw nothing I fancied."

"What a pity your journey was wasted," Francine said with a grin, for she realized that horse brasses was the first thing that came into his head, "but your loss was my gain, for I found everything I wanted. And now we can have a quick supper and be home before dark."

Charlie looked decidedly uncomfortable and could think of nothing to say, so he nodded quickly, then took her arm to guide her across the street and into the inn, where they were escorted immediately to a table in the main dining room.

When the innkeeper came over with a bottle of the finest claret and told Charlie that their dinner would be served in just a moment, Francine became curious. "Did you tell them in advance that we would be coming?" she asked.

Charlie nodded. "My father arranged everything when he was here yesterday," he blurted out, then added, "I mean, I told him I was bringing you and he thought it best to tell them we'd be coming in case Joe, er, that is, the innkeeper, was busy."

"That was very thoughtful of him," Francine said with a decided edge to her voice, for it seemed that the squire was interfering once more. "After all, if he ordered something I don't like, I can always send it back, can't I?"

"Of—of course," Charlie hastened to agree. "J-just say if you want to change anything."

The squire had, however, been most thorough, for the meal of roast duck, asparagus ragout, and Windsor cake for the sweet, was quite delicious and only an ingrate would have complained. Charlie seemed much more at ease, possibly because he had drunk most of the bottle of claret. When he was about to order another Francine put a restraining hand on his arm.

"If I'm not home before it is completely dark, Charlie," she told him, "my grandpapa will send out a search party for us, so I believe we should leave now."

She was not prepared for the startled expression that came over his face. "He will? But surely he lets you stay out late sometimes?" he asked a little belligerently, for the wine was giving him false courage.

"Of course he does when he knows where I am, and that I'm properly chaperoned," Francine told him, rising from the table so that he would have to do so also. "He has always been very protective as far as I am concerned."

"Well, in that case I suppose we'd best get started," Charlie said, his heart leaping at the thought of a rescue.

When they reached the door, the carriage was already waiting for them, and as Charlie handed her up,

Francine suddenly remembered that her grandpapa had gone to dine with his friend and they often played chess until midnight. There was little point in telling Charlie this, however, for she had only mentioned it so that he would leave and not start on a second bottle of wine.

It was a pleasant evening for a drive, and Francine was glad that Charlie had chosen the more quiet road back as she watched the sun draw closer and closer to a distant craggy peak.

Charlie was by no means racing along, as so many young men in curricles were inclined to do. In fact, he was holding the grays back, but it gave Francine a better view of the countryside, so she had no complaints.

She heard the sound of splintering wood before the curricle veered to the right, and she had just enough time to take a firm hold on the side of the coach before it tipped over and was dragged on its side quite a distance by the terrified horses.

When they came to a halt, the coach was hanging halfway into the ditch at the side of the road, and she was not sure if Charlie had bumped his head, for he appeared to be quite dazed.

"Are you hurt, Charlie," she asked with concern, "for, if not, I think we'd better try to get out and see how much damage has been done."

"We'd best stay where we are," Charlie told her, trying to sound firm. "I think I bumped my leg and doubt that I could stand on it. If we wait here, someone's sure to come along."

"There'll be no one coming along this road, for we've not seen a soul since we turned onto it," Francine said firmly. "I'm going to try to climb out while there's enough light to see if either of the horses is hurt."

As she tried to crawl past him, he grabbed her arm. "No, that's not the thing to do at all," he said. "If we stay here, your grandpapa will rescue us if no one else does."

Firmly removing his hand from her arm, Francine climbed over the upturned wheel and dropped lightly to the ground. She went forward to check on the frightened horses, talking soothingly to them as she examined them carefully, and found that one of them seemed to have a bruised hock, for it flinched at her touch, but the other appeared to be unharmed.

"We're very fortunate," she called to Charlie as she started to unharness them. "I'm going to ride this one home, for I don't believe there is anywhere to get help on the way, and I'll send our men back for you."

Charlie started to get up, knowing there was nothing whatever wrong with his leg, but thought better of it and sank back against the carriage. "You mustn't, Francine. You don't know who you might meet on the road, and how can you ride without a saddle?"

"I've done it before, but I must confess it was years ago. Don't worry about me, Charlie. Before you know it, our men will be here to get you home," she said cheerfully as she secured the lap robe to the horse's back with a piece of the harness, then took out the ribbons she had just purchased. Using the heavier ones doubled, she threaded them through the horse's bridle. Then, using the wheel of the curricle as a mounting block, she flung herself onto the horse's back, reached for the pale-pink ribbons, and started out.

Charlie sighed heavily. He knew how angry his father would be when he got home, but what could he have done? Once Francine decided on a course of action, he didn't believe even his father could stop her.

At first, the gray protested, for it was not ridden very often, but Francine talked softly to it and didn't push it hard, for the evening air was pleasant and quite balmy, and within fifteen minutes they were in tune with each other.

By the time she rode into her grandpapa's stables, she knew that her legs and bottom would be stiff for quite some time, but the unexpected ride had been quite exhilarating.

She told Eddie, the head groom, what had happened before she entered the stables, then said, "Go and make

arrangements to rescue Mr. Bottomley, Eddie, and keep
the men inside while I dismount, for there's no way I
can do so gracefully in this gown.''

He hesitated for a moment, then shook his head and
grinned. "If I was you, I'd get close to that bale of hay
and then just let yourself slide down onto it, milady. I'll
not let anyone see you, never fear."

She took his advice, landing softly on the hay and
then climbing off and carefully arranging her skirts.
Then, with hay still clinging to her, she led the gray into
the stables, where preparations were being made for
Charlie's rescue.

"Should I send someone over to the squire's place to
let him know what happened, milady?'' Eddie
suggested.

"I don't believe so, Eddie," Francine said. "You'll
have his son back before he starts to worry about him,
I'm sure. If you can find my purchases, you might bring
them home with you also."

Walking a little stiffly, she entered the house and
made her way upstairs, where an anxious Dora ordered
a hot bath to be brought immediately, and for once
Francine allowed her weary body to be bathed,
massaged, and tucked into her comfortable feather bed
without trying to do anything for herself.

"The saints preserve me from a thankless son,"
Squire Bottomley moaned when Charlie was brought
home in Sir Godfrey's carriage. "How you could botch
up the plan, when everything was done for you and all
you had to do was keep her there, I'll never know."

He stood over Charlie, a disgusted look on his face,
and the young man just looked back at him helplessly.
There was no use in trying to explain what had
happened, for his father would never understand.

"Are you going to arrange for my curricle to be taken
to repair?" he asked. "It's in a ditch on its side with the
wheel snapped clean in two."

"I've already sent grooms over to Hawk Hall to get

both horses, and first thing in the morning I'll arrange for it to be taken to the carriagemaker for repair. Not that you deserve to own a curricle after the mess you just made,'' he asserted, glaring fiercely at his son, ''you should have to use Shanks' nag for a while and see how you like that.''

Charlie wanted to protest that the squire had been the one who deliberately damaged the vehicle, not him, but he had never spoken back to his father in all of his twenty-three years, and it was too late to start now.

The squire suddenly spun around, a look of glee on his face. ''That's it,'' he declared, slamming a large fist on the table at which Charlie was sitting and causing the latter to jump almost out of his skin. ''That's the very thing! The chit is very fond of walking over the moors, if I recall, so you're going to take her for a walk.''

There was a crafty gleam on his father's face that boded trouble for either Francine or himself, Charlie knew, and he waited fearfully to hear the rest of the plan.

''You'll find out which is her favorite long—and I mean very long and lonely—walk on those moors, and you'll ask her to go with you one afternoon.'' He paused, enjoying the beauty of the scheme he had devised. ''Then, the afternoon before, you'll take a spade with you, and you'll take that same walk—don't go on horseback or it might leave hoof marks—and when you reach a likely place, just over a slight rise in the path would be a good one, you'll dig a ditch right across it.''

Charlie looked puzzled. ''A ditch, sir?''

The squire was quite obviously enjoying his son's bewilderment. ''A ditch, not less than a foot and a half deep, I would say, and about the same width, so that she can't stride right over it. Then you'll fill it with heather, or twigs, or whatever is around and put just enough earth back so that it doesn't look obvious.''

''But she might hurt herself,'' his son protested.

''Of course she will,'' Squire Bottomley roared.

"She'll sprain an ankle or perhaps even break it, and either way she'll have to stay there with you."

"But I wouldn't want her to hurt herself, Father. I'd have to go for help and I don't know the moors well enough to find my way after dark." Charlie did not like his father's plan at all.

The squire shook his head. "I thought you'd never take my meaning, but there's hope for you yet. Of course you would not leave her there, but would stay with her all night, if necessary, and then what would the villagers have to say? She'd have to wed you or be disgraced."

"But when she didn't get back, Sir Godfrey would send out a search party for her, like he did when the little girl was lost," Charlie protested. "They found Penelope and had her home in just a few hours."

The squire looked stumped for a moment, and Charlie thought that he'd been successful in stopping this particular scheme, but he was mistaken, for the light came back into the squire's eyes.

"I've got it," he said, "you ask her which walk she prefers, so that's the one she'll say she's taking if anyone asks her, as I'm sure they will. Then, you pick a walk in entirely the opposite direction and dig the ditch in that one."

Charlie looked completely puzzled. "What good will that do if we're taking the other walk?" he asked.

"You bird-brain," the squire said in disgust. "Can't you see that, once you start out, you tell her you've changed your mind and would rather take the one you've dug a hole in."

"But if she knows I've dug a hole in it, she'll not . . ." Charlie started, and then ducked quickly as his father picked up a large book from the table and hurled it at his son, missing him by only a few inches.

"Now," the squire said in a dangerously quiet voice, "let us go over the whole plot again and see if your feeble brain can grasp it this time. You are to . . ."

Once he realized what was required of him, Charlie

argued longer than he had ever dared in the past, to his father's complete amazement, but his protestations were useless against the latter's determination, and in the end Charlie had reluctantly agreed to the plan.

By the time he was allowed to retire for the night, he knew by heart what his father wished him to do.

13

Francine did not dislike Charlie. In fact, she was quite sorry for him at times because no one deserved such an obnoxious father as Squire Bottomley.

She had heard that the latter's attitude toward her grandpapa's grooms, who had rescued a lame Charlie and a lame horse from the broken carriage, had been not at all grateful and almost offensive, and she could not help but feel sorry for the young man.

When he called to see her a few days after the accident, she noticed that he was scarcely limping at all, and she was quite surprised when he asked if he could take her for a walk over the moors the next day.

"Is your leg strong enough?" she asked him with some concern. "You should probably rest it for a little longer before walking so far upon it."

"It was not a sprain at all but was just badly bruised," he told her, knowing full well that she could not ask to see it, "and the doctor assured me that walking would be good for it. Isn't your favorite walk the one that goes past Barrigan's Fell?"

"It's one of my favorites, but I've walked it a lot lately," she told him, not adding, of course, that she did a lot of walking alone when she was as unhappy as she had been feeling these last weeks. "Why don't you pick the one you'd prefer, for I like all of them."

He would have preferred her to name her choice and had to think more quickly than he was accustomed. "How about the path that leads past Jacob's Pillow and on toward Branson," he suggested, after pondering awhile, and she readily agreed.

Charlie had hidden a spade in a ditch before he came

to see Francine, so he left with a heavy heart to retrieve it, then set out along the first-named walk to seek a spot at least a couple of hours away, and do the work his father had told him he must.

He was back, however, at the appointed time the next day, and after starting out, he told her he'd much rather go past Barrigan's Fell. She had walked that way a few days ago and much preferred the walk to Branson and was surprised when Charlie became quite upset.

"I've been looking forward all morning to that walk," he told her, "for you said you really didn't mind which one we took."

It was true, she had told him that, so she said, "Very well, there's little difference between the two, so let's take the one you want to."

The two of them set out at a comfortable pace, conversing little, for Charlie was never much of a talker. Francine was glad of it, for she was enjoying the feel of the wind on her face and the smell of the heather and gorse and wishing so very much that it was Julian by her side instead of Charlie.

After they had walked for about an hour and a half, she insisted that they sit on a boulder for a while to rest Charlie's leg.

"Are you sure you're all right, for we can turn back now if you would rather?" Francine suggested.

Charlie was horrified, of course, for he was sure they had at least another half-hour's walk before they reached the hole he had dug.

"I'm not at all tired," he protested, jumping up right away. "See, my leg's as strong as ever."

He started off again at a fast pace, but had not taken into consideration the fact that they were walking more quickly than he had done the day before when carrying the heavy spade.

Francine did not follow him immediately, for she had heard the distinctive cry of a curlew and was looking around to see where it might be before getting up from the boulder. A moment later she heard a very different cry as Charlie disappeared from sight. She hurried to the top of the slight incline ahead and heard Charlie's moan before she saw him sprawled across the path in front of her.

He had realized what had happened as soon as his foot caught in the trench he had dug, and had somehow managed to cover the hole with his body to prevent Francine becoming suspicious.

"Where do you hurt, Charlie?" she asked as she sank down on the heather in front of him. "Is it your ankle?"

He nodded, wincing with the pain, for he had never been stoic and this time he was really hurt. "My right one."

Francine was used to helping her grandpapa off with his boots at times, and she quickly unlaced Charlie's right one and slid it off the already swelling ankle as gently as she could.

"You can't walk on this," she said with a shake of her head, "and I hesitate to bind it, for it may be a sprain, but then again it could be broken. You should probably not have come for a walk at all, for your bad knee must have given way and let you down."

Charlie smiled wryly despite the pain. This was exactly what he deserved for pretending to be hurt the last time, he decided. Now he really was injured, but at least he'd found something he was good at—he could make a very fine trap. If his father should ever throw him out, he could always get work with a gamekeeper!

"It looks as though you'll have to rescue me again," he said to Francine, hoping she would never find out what he had intended. "If you go right away, you'll be home before dark."

With a last worried look at poor Charlie, Francine turned and hurriedly retraced her steps along the path. It would be dark by the time help could reach him, but there was nothing she could do about that.

Fortunately, when she reached Hawk Hall, Kenneth was home, and it was no time at all before he had rounded up several of the outside staff, including Eddie, the head groom, who brought a lightweight litter from the coach house and several lanterns.

As Kenneth and the men would be taking Charlie back to his own home, Francine asked Mrs. Parsons to keep some food warm for them until they returned. Though any other neighbor would have offered refreshments to the rescuers, she was quite sure that the squire would not.

"I found the oddest thing when we went to get poor Charlie," Kenneth told Francine and their grandpapa some time later. "He didn't trip, as we at first thought. He fell into a big hole, and it's a wonder he didn't hurt more than just his ankle."

"You mean there was a hole in the middle of the path?" Sir Godfrey asked with a frown.

Kenneth nodded. "That's right, a damned big hole about a foot deep right across the path. And what's more, it was freshly dug."

Francine looked puzzled. "How could you tell that, Ken?" she asked. "Surely it was dark when you got there?"

"While the others were making him comfortable on the stretcher, I went back with my lantern, for I had an odd feeling about it and, sure enough, I found the hole. It went right across the footpath, and was filled with heather that had been put there to hide the hole," he told them. "There was a pile of earth that had been dug from it just by the side, and anyone else but Charlie would probably have seen it and been suspicious. But if some idiot is going around digging holes in the paths, you'd best watch your step, Frankie, or you'll be the next one with a broken ankle."

Francine looked thoughtful. She remembered how Charlie had insisted on taking a different path to the one decided upon the day before and he had become flustered and upset when she'd at first objected to the change.

This was the second accident that had occurred when

she and Charlie had been together. Could the curricle have been tampered with? Charlie had been most upset when she had ridden off for help. She wondered, Could Charlie be the idiot who was digging holes on the moors, and if so, for what reason?

She needed to talk to him, and though she was accustomed to going around the village and paying calls unaccompanied, this time she realized that more might be read into it than was intended, for she did not trust the squire.

She had not seen Kathleen since they came back from London, so she sent her a note asking if she could call for her one day this week and take her over to see Charlie.

Instead of answering, Julian and Kathleen rode over together on horseback, arriving before the messenger, who had other calls to make, had returned.

It was the first time Francine had seen Julian since his proposal, and for once, she was completely tongue-tied.

"Good morning, Francine. I came to see Sir Godfrey about procuring some hawks from him, so I brought Kathleen along," he explained.

"Francine?" Kathleen exclaimed, unaware of the tension she was increasing. "When did you start to call her that?"

"Please don't, Julian," Francine asked quietly. "I much prefer being called Frankie."

"Very well, if that's your preference," he agreed curtly.

Kathleen looked at the pair of them, so stiff and formal with each other, and was about to say something, then decided against it.

"Do you want to go see old Charlie before luncheon or afterward? That is, of course, if you are going to invite us to stay," she asked breezily.

"Your manners are sadly wanting, Kathleen." Julian frowned at his sister.

"No they're not, Julian," Francine said softly. "Friends don't have to put on party manners all the time, and we are friends, aren't we?"

He flushed. "Of course," he muttered. "I'll seek out Ken, if he's around, and let you two make your big decision. As long as you don't ask me to accompany you to visit that idiot, I don't care."

When he had gone, Kathleen said bluntly, "I know something has gone wrong between the two of you, and I don't want to make matters worse, but if there is anything I can do at any time, including wringing my brother's neck, don't hesitate to ask."

Before Francine could think of anything to say, Penelope came running into the room and stopped, shyly, when she saw Kathleen.

"You've seen Lady Kathleen before, Penelope. Come and make your curtsy," Francine told her.

As she did so, Kathleen explained. "Only once before, I believe, Frankie, for we became friends in London, and she wasn't allowed down when we brought you home."

"Of cou e, I'd forgotten. I think we'd best go over to Charlie's before luncheon, as it will give us an excuse for not staying long. If you'll excuse me, I'll order the gig around and get my gloves and a wrap."

As she started to leave the room, Penelope asked, careful to be polite, "May I come with you, please?"

Francine was about to refuse, then decided it might be a good idea. "Only if you're going to be on your very best behavior and do exactly what I say," she told her, and as the child ran off to get a coat, she explained to Kathleen. "I want to get Charlie on his own and ask him a few questions that I'll explain later. But I wouldn't want to leave you alone with his awful father, so Penelope can keep you company."

As the three set off for Squire Bottomley's house, Francine explained briefly that Charlie had badly sprained his ankle when out walking with her, and they were ostensibly going to find out how he was coming along.

The squire looked delighted to see the two young ladies and a little less so to see Penelope, but he invited them into the drawing room and offered refreshments.

A few minutes later Charlie came hobbling in on makeshift crutches. He looked pleased to see them, and as they sipped tea, Francine noticed there was a rose garden just beyond the French window.

"Do you think you could manage to show me the garden, Charlie?" she asked.

"Whatever do you want—" Charlie began, but his father interrupted.

"What a good idea. Go along, Charlie, take Lady Francine and show her the roses—show her the whole garden, if you like, while I get to know Lady Kathleen a little better," he insisted.

Penelope was jumping up, for she didn't want to stay with the nasty old man, but Francine shook her head. "You stay here with Lady Kathleen," she said firmly, and Penelope sat down, pouting a little.

It was a slow walk along the narrow path, but eventually they reached the roses and sat on the bench Francine had seen from the window.

"Now, Charlie, I want to talk to you about your accident." She saw him redden and knew she was on the right track. "In fact, about several so-called accidents."

"I don't know what you mean," he said. "I didn't deliberately fall and sprain my ankle on the moors, if that's what you think."

"I never thought you did," Francine told him, watching his flushed face carefully. "But I think it was you who dug the hole you fell into. Did you forget where you'd dug it?"

"No, I just thought . . ." he started to say, then stopped and looked at her shamefaced.

"You just thought what?" she prompted.

He looked down at the path and muttered, "I thought it was a lot farther along."

"And the accident on the road from Skipton? That was planned also, wasn't it?" she asked quietly.

"It wasn't my idea, Frankie, truly it wasn't. My father has the notion that you will marry me if you are compromised, but I know that nothing would make you do that," he blurted out.

Francine had to laugh. "You know me better than your father does, obviously. Why did you go along with his stupid plans? You're lucky that neither of us suffered more than that." She pointed to his ankle.

"He's a very determined man when he gets an idea in his head. He insisted I go to London after you and told me to embarrass you by making you gallop in the park, but it was to have been in the middle of the afternoon, and you wouldn't ride with me then," he tried to explain, looking at her a mite reproachfully.

"So that was intended also," she murmured, "and then there was the curricle accident, and now the accident on the moors. You've got to say no to him, Charlie, for you know I'll not let you succeed."

He became quite agitated. "You don't know what he's like, Frankie," he said. "He says that you've got looks, brains, a title, and a big dowry, and that's what I need or his grandchildren will be as stupid as I am."

Stupidity is not the worst trait the children might be afflicted with, Francine thought, for the squire must be quite mad.

"Well, until your ankle heals, he can't make you do anything," she assured him, "so just concentrate on getting it better, and be glad it was you and not me, for had you deliberately caused me to hurt myself, my grandfather would have horsewhipped you."

She almost felt sorry she said it, for Charlie actually shuddered at the thought.

They walked slowly back to the house, where Penelope was getting most restless, but had steadfastly refused to go and join Francine despite the squire's attempts to persuade her to do so.

Just at that moment, however, the butler announced Dr. David Gardner, who had replaced the village doctor quite recently. He had come to see how his patient, Charlie, was getting along.

He was a tall young man, with reddish hair and a ready smile that probably helped a great deal in his work. From the moment he entered the room he could not take his eyes away from Francine.

"I've been meaning to call on Sir Godfrey Giles," he told her, "just to introduce myself, but there was first an outbreak of measles, then a number of broken limbs, but I'll most certainly stop by and pay my respects very shortly."

They left the good doctor to his work, and when they returned to Hawk Hall, Francine sent Penelope back to Nanny for her luncheon, and she and Kathleen went into the drawing room until theirs was ready. Closing the door so that no one could hear, Francine explained to her friend what the squire had been trying to do.

"But that's terrible," Kathleen said when she had heard it all. "Poor Charlie! We have to try to help him. We must find him a suitable bride."

Francine stared at her, then started to laugh. "You're right, of course, but it never occurred to me to do that, for I don't know many young ladies around here."

"But I know lots of them, for I went to a finishing school not far away," Kathleen told her. "We'll invite him to tea first and make sure there are two or three young ladies present who are more suitable than you are, then see what happens."

"You'd best not ask Kenneth and Julian to come, too, or they'll not give Charlie a second glance," Francine said with a deep chuckle.

"Nor that handsome young doctor we met today," Kathleen said. "He certainly seemed interested in you, Frankie, and I'm sure he'll call here soon with some excuse or other."

Over lunch, they explained to Julian, Kenneth, and Sir Godfrey what they planned to do, though they did not tell them of the dangerous situations in which Charlie had placed Francine.

Sir Godfrey was completely in favor of it, but Julian had some reservations. "It's never a good thing to interfere in someone else's life," he said with a frown, "for you might do more harm than good."

"Oh, Julian," Kathleen scolded, "don't be such a marplot. I don't know what has come over you lately, for you were such fun when you first came back from France, and in London, too, now I come to think about it."

He looked thunderous and started to rise, "Well, if my . . ." he was about to say when Francine began to laugh.

"Children, children," she said, her eyes dancing. "Behave yourselves. You're worse than little Penelope. We're not interfering in Charlie's life, Julian. We're just giving him the opportunity to meet a few more young ladies than he would in the normal way."

Her face was soft and appealing as she tried to explain herself more clearly, and Julian could not resist for long. He sat and listened to the plans, with Kenneth and Sir Godfrey, but when they said that he and Kenneth could not come to the teas, he protested.

"Why should you two have all the fun? I would not at all mind meeting a few of the young ladies of these parts, for I might also find one who interested me," he told them, careful not to look at Francine.

For a moment Kathleen looked shocked, and she dare not look at Francine, for she could see the white of her friend's knuckles as she gripped the edge of the table to stop from shaking. "The thing really is," she went on hurriedly, "the young ladies will not wish to travel far, so the teas must be at our home. Would it be proper for me to sign Francine's name as well as my own on the invitation?"

"Of course it would, you idiot," Kenneth said teasingly, seemingly unaware of the tension in the room. "It's done all the time. The two of you invite him and the other guests, and you give your address. Or at least I hope you do, for I, for one, don't want him here to tea."

Kathleen knew this, of course, but she had just said the first thing that came into her head, and she sighed with relief when Francine's hands relaxed.

"And that reminds me, Frankie, did you tell him that the hole he fell in had been newly dug?" Kenneth asked.

"No, I didn't even think about it, and the result was the same whether he fell into a new hole or an old one," she said quickly, then asked, "Were you able to help Julian with the hawks, Grandpapa?"

"I have the hawks he needs, but you and I will both have to work with him here until he's able to take them and continue the training on his own. I'm delighted you're so interested in it, my boy. He smiled approvingly at Julian. "As you saw today, it's a lot of patient work, but well worth the effort."

"I'm sure it will be, sir," Julian agreed, "and now, I think we should be starting back, Kathleen. Didn't Mama say we were having dinner guests tonight?"

"Oh, dear, I completely forgot. Look, Frankie, just tell me quickly what days would be good for you, and then I'll send Charlie and some of the young ladies invitations. Or perhaps you could write the days down for me in case I forget them."

"That really won't be necessary." Francine grinned ruefully. "We lead a very quite life here and I have no commitments whatever for the next month or more. Just choose the day that is best for you and let me know, that's all."

They left in a hurry, and for the first time that she could ever recall, Francine was glad to see Julian go. It had been embarrassingly uncomfortable for her, but she hoped that it had broken the ice and that future meetings would not be so difficult.

Grandpapa had told Julian that she would be helping train the hawks with him, but if he was as stiff as he'd been today, then it would be a quite impossible situation.

The most dreadful moment had been when he spoke of wishing to meet a girl who interested him, making it perfectly clear that she did not. Kathleen had been a dear to try to bridge the awful silence with the first idiotic statement that she could think of, and fortunately Kenneth didn't even notice it.

Sir Godfrey and Kenneth had walked out to see the

Whiteheads off, and she didn't hear anyone return until she felt her grandpapa's hand on her shoulder.

"If it's any consolation, my dear, he looked as upset as you did after that stupid remark that he made. I'm sure he'd have taken it back if he could, but it was too late then," he said as he cradled her head against his chest. "Don't you lose hope just yet."

"It's going to be very difficult to assist him with his hawks, Grandpapa," she told him. "Must I?"

"It'll help the two of you to break the ice, and it'll relieve my load a little. I know you're not going to refuse, are you, my love?"

When she shook her head, he changed the subject. "That's a very bright idea you girls came up with, to find a wife for old Charlie. Did you think it would kill two birds with one stone?"

Francine smiled. "I didn't think of it at all, it was Kathleen's idea, but I am very enthusiastic if it will stop him asking me to marry him every time I turn around."

"Wonderful creatures, women," he said. "They come up with what sound to be the craziest schemes sometimes, but they often work out very well indeed."

14

K athleen decided that the first attempt to find a wife for Charlie Bottomley should be a picnic rather than inviting him and some single young ladies to tea at her home. That way there would be less danger of Julian joining them and upsetting Francine. She sent a note to her friend, giving her a few days' notice and telling her she must persuade Charlie to go. But it never occurred to her that Charlie would expect to travel alone with Francine, for, after all, they would both be leaving for the same place at about the same time.

Fortunately, Francine did think about it, and she talked her brother into taking her and picking up Charlie on the way. Kathleen was none too pleased when she received the note from Francine explaining this, but she did at least realize the problem.

At precisely twelve o'clock, four carriages converged on the bridge at Linton, and their passengers spilled out and made immediately for the prettiest spot overlooking the river. There was Miss Elizabeth Clayton, Lady Arabella Flint, Miss Caroline Davison and Lady Angela Billings in two of the carriages, Francine, Kenneth and Charlie in another, and to Francine's dismay, Julian was with Kathleen in the last one, an arrangement Kenneth had suggested to his friend.

While some of the Whiteheads' servants began to spread out cloths, napkins, and food, Kathleen proceeded to introduce everyone.

"What lucky gentlemen," Lady Angela remarked archly. "They get two ladies each."

"We're not breaking up into couples," Kathleen was quick to explain. "What we really wanted to do was give poor Charlie a chance to get out a little. Since he hurt his ankle he's been confined to the house a great deal, and we thought he should have a little fun.''

Charlie positively beamed at this, and after Kathleen put a few quiet words into the ear of each young lady, they were soon vying for his attention and sitting in a half-circle around him.

"Where did you manage to find such, er, charming young ladies?'' Julian asked his sister. "Are they all heiresses or something?''

"Yes, all of them," Kathleen assured him, "and now that I see them together, I believe Arabella will be the right one for him. She is not the most beautiful young lady, but she has a very kind heart and her title will impress his father even more than her dowry.''

"May I ask what you said to them that sent them off like bees to a honey pot?'' he asked. "For once in my life I feel slighted.''

"It will do you good," his sister snapped, still rather annoyed that he had insisted on joining them. "And all I said was that he's an only son and his father is fabulously rich.''

Julian chuckled. "If this is your first attempt at matchmaking, I would say you're extremely successful. I don't think I've ever seen that young man looking so happy.''

Despite Kathleen's attempts to get Francine and Julian together again, for this was the reason she had agreed to him coming with her, they showed no desire to do so, and the four of them spent most of the time watching Charlie glowing in the sudden attention he was receiving.

The picnic fare was excellent, and the wine made them all a little drowsy, so that no one had any wish to take one of the pretty walks along the river, although Francine looked toward them longingly. So they sat around lazily making the usual foolish remarks about the weather and the price of lace or other fripperies until it was time for them to leave.

Before the others joined them to climb up the slope to their coaches, Kathleen instructed both Francine and Kenneth to memorize everything Charlie said and to send her a note as soon as they got home.

She was quick to notice that it was Arabella who helped Charlie negotiate the climb, and she felt inordinately pleased with her plan thus far.

Francine sat in silence as they started out for home, remembering how she had once wanted more than a parting hug from Julian, and now even that much would have felt wonderful, provided he meant it, of course.

Kenneth did not fail to notice her silence, but Charlie more than made up for it.

"I've never known such charming young ladies to pay me attention before. Perhaps it was because of my ankle. I wanted to tell them I'd been wounded in the war but thought better of it," he said; then, seeing Kenneth's frown, he hastened to add, "I didn't, Ken. Really I didn't."

"Which one did you like the best, or couldn't you make up your mind?" Kenneth asked. "It was not easy, was it?"

"It was difficult," Charlie admitted, "but I believe Lady Arabella was the nicest. Did you see the way she stayed behind to help me up the slope? She gave me her direction and said I might pay her a call at any time."

"She did seem to be a very nice person," Francine allowed, "and I'm sure she meant it."

Charlie went on in this vein for the whole journey, and when they finally let him out at his home, neither of the Truesdales had the energy to say another word for the remainder of the journey.

As they entered the hall, Kenneth asked, "Are you going to send Kathleen a note, or shall I?"

"I'll send it right away. Then I'm going to rest in the silence of my chamber for a while. He wore me out," she said.

Her brother nodded sympathetically. "Me, too," he

said, then asked abruptly, "What's gone wrong between you and Julian?"

Unable to answer him without crying, Francine looked at him with tear-filled eyes, then shook her head, turned, and ran up the stairs, while Kenneth frowned at her fast-disappearing form in puzzlement.

There was no way, however, that Francine could now avoid seeing Julian, for her grandpapa had insisted that he come every day to work with the birds he would be training and breeding, so that they could get used to him and he would get used to handling them.

Once more, he would be in and out of Hawk Hall as much as if he lived there, but the relationship would not be the same.

"You said that one of your grooms is very interested in working with the hawks, Julian," Sir Godfrey said as the four of them were eating luncheon. "If you are planning to hire a boy also—and you will need at least one—I have a youngster here who is doing very well."

He looked across at Francine and she raised her eyebrows, curious. "Thanks to my granddaughter's kind heart, I took on a lad while you were in London, the brother of her personal maid, and he is a natural handler. He's young, but he seems to have a definite knack for it that you can't teach, it has to be inborn. Talk to him, and if you like the youngster, I'll set him to work handling only your birds."

"He is the little brother of my maid," Francine explained, "and when she told me his alternatives were to work for Squire Bottomley for free until he decided he was trained, or go into the coal mines, I had Grandpapa find work for him here."

"He's a nice, clean-looking youngster, and I believe you'll like him, Julian," her grandpapa added, "but he is only ten years old."

"Isn't he a little young to handle hawks?" Julian asked.

"Francine was handling them at that age, but by choice," her grandpapa said, "not by necessity."

"You mean that youngsters of ten work in the mines?" Julian asked. "They must be old men before they're thirty!"

"If they live that long," Sir Godfrey said. "Take your seat in Parliament and do something about it if you feel so strongly."

"I believe I will before long," was Julian's decisive reply.

"How many hawks is Julian starting with?" Francine asked her grandpapa, bringing them back to the original subject.

"Just two for now, a female shaheen and a peregrine tiercel, then he'll need to hire a man and a boy for every two hawks he adds." He looked at Julian. "You have the knack, also, my boy, as does Francine, but no matter how a man tries, if it's not there, then sooner or later something goes wrong. Kenneth, here, will tell you himself that, though he helps me quite a bit, he's never really comfortable at it. Isn't that so?"

His grandson nodded. "I'd like to be of more help than I am, but I just don't seem to adapt to it," he said.

"It's all in the touch," Sir Godfrey went on. "You must have gentle hands to work with hawks. Any hurried or sudden movement alarms them, and rough treatment of any kind disgusts them and can turn them into enemies," he warned. "And each one is just as different as each human being is, or each dog. You can't treat them alike; you've got to find out their individual moods and fancies.

"Hawks are very aware of sound also, particularly the voice of their falconer. In the old days, you know, a falconer had to have a pair of good lungs to call and cheer the hawk in the air. Wasn't it Juliet who wished for the 'falconer's voice'?" he asked.

"Do you have a hawk house ready for them?" Francine asked Julian.

"No, not yet. Sir Godfrey tells me the best place to put it would be against the conservatory wall so that the warmth from it will help keep out cold and damp. I'll need a loft above for moulting them, and a smaller room to keep all the spare things I don't want in the main room."

"And spotless cleanliness and tidiness, and attention to detail," Francine added. "Is Dora's little brother really old enough to be trusted alone with the hawks?"

"It's not a matter of age, as I said before," Sir Godfrey said. "You worked with me in the hawk house at that age and younger."

Francine smiled. "I did, didn't I? But I would have been forgiven mistakes," she said. She remembered how proud she had been to be helping her grandpapa, and wondered if young Billy felt the same way.

"Well, we'd best get back to them," Sir Godfrey said, rising from the table. "We can't sit here talking all day when there's work to do."

The three men left and a few minutes later Francine left also, for it was past time for the man who picked up mail in the village to return. She went into her grandpapa's study and leafed through the small bundle of letters on his desk. The letter she had expected was not there, but she noticed one for her grandpapa from someone whose name was familiar, for John Anderson was a famous trainer of falcons. Her grandpapa would be pleased to hear from him, she was sure.

On an impulse, she picked up the letter and took it out to the hawk house, where the men were working.

"I was looking for a letter from Aunt Anastasia, and I found this," she told Sir Godfrey, handing the letter to him. "Isn't he the falconer you met years ago when you were in Scotland?"

"That he is, and the best man in the field," Sir Godfrey said, a little puzzled, for the letter did not come from Scotland. He picked up a knife and slit the envelope, then a beam came over his face. "Anderson is shortly journeying back to Scotland and wants to pay me the honor of a visit. That's not what he says, of course, for he's a modest man, but to me it is an honor. What a grand surprise, but he'll be here in a couple of days and the place must be in tip-top condition, for I'll not be shamed in front of him."

"If I can be of service, I'd be glad to do whatever is needed, sir," Julian volunteered, "and will stay over if necessary."

"That's good, Julian, for I'll need all the help I can get. I can bring men in from the stables to help clean everything, but they'll need to be supervised so that the hawks don't become nervous, and that's where you and Francine come in." He looked at them closely. "You may think I'm being fussy, but when you've mixed in hawking circles for a while, you'll realize how important this man is."

Work started immediately, and by the time they went back to the house to change for dinner, Francine was tired but happy. She and Julian had worked together the way they used to, without thinking of anything but the task at hand, and it had been just like old times.

"Thank you, Julian," she said as they entered through the back door and started up the servants' stairs.

"Thank you for what?" he asked, smiling his old, gentle smile.

"For making things like they used to be between us," she said. "I've hated being at odds with you these last few weeks."

They had reached the top of the stairs, and he put his arm around her in the old way, giving her a hug. "Friends again?" he asked.

Relief flooded through her and she nodded. "Friends always," she told him, a little shyly, before slipping away to her chamber to bathe and change.

Now it was a pleasure to have Julian in the house again, and Francine hummed softly to herself as she soaked in the tub that Dora had waiting for her.

"Grandpapa said some very nice things today about your little brother, Dora," she called, and the maid came hurrying over.

"He did, my lady?" she asked. "Then he'll keep him on?"

"Actually he's letting Lord Julian Whitehead have him to help start his own hawk house, but in the meantime he will be working with his hawks here. Will your parents mind him being so far away?" she asked.

"Not if he's doing well, my lady, and getting settled. Everyone says his lordship is good to work for, so I know he'll be happy with him. And we only go home once a week on our half-day off, anyway." Dora looked dreamy. "Soon I'll be able to make plans to get married. It won't make any difference to my work here, will it?" she asked a little anxiously.

"Not until you start having babies," Francine assured her.

"That won't be for a long time," Dora said firmly. "We need to get on our feet before any bairns come along. Which gown do you want to wear tonight, my lady, for you didn't get one out?"

It was, of course, the effect Julian had upon her that had made her so forgetful, she thought. "The yellow one with the brown ribbons, I think."

She was tired, for they had worked hard this afternoon, but the warm water took away the little aches and she looked fresh and charming when she went down to dinner.

Sir Godfrey did not fail to notice the more relaxed manner between the two young people, and he decided to encourage it a little more. "I think I'll set Francine on to watching how you go along and advising you this next day or two, instead of doing it myself," he said to Julian. "It will leave me more time to prepare for John Anderson's visit. If you're willing, you can look to your birds in the mornings, then both of you can give me a hand in the afternoons."

"Is that all right with you, Frankie?" Julian asked.

"Whatever Grandpapa says is fine with me," she said happily, "but I think I'd best not have any more wine or I'll fall asleep at table."

"Don't get too sleepy, young lady," Sir Godfrey said, "for I was hoping for a game of whist afterward."

"Who is partnering me?" she asked, and Julian immediately said, "I am."

After two games they were even, but it was ten o'clock and Sir Godfrey said, "We have to be up and working by six in the morning. I, for one, need to get some sleep. We can continue the game tomorrow night."

Without argument, they all trooped up the stairs, for six o'clock would come all too soon.

The card play had taken away Francine's sleepiness, however, and she lay in her bed for a long time, reliving the nicest day she had known in several weeks. He would be here for at least one more night, she knew, so she had something to look forward to in the morning.

It came sooner than she wished, however, and when the knock sounded on her door, Francine longed to tell them to go away and let her sleep, but she knew she could not.

With eyes only half-open, she watched Julian as he took the recently caught hawk that had been in complete darkness, onto his fist, put on its hood, then lit a candle and searched for its castings, pellets of feathers, and indigestible matter thrown up by the hawk, in the sawdust under the screen perch.

He looked thoroughly; then, sure there was nothing there, he signaled to his man, Arthur Gibbons, who waited nearby, telling him to carry her for a while until she had performed the necessary operation.

In the half-light, Francine nodded her approval, then said sharply to Julian's man, "Always keep a tight hold of the leash with your left hand. When it's just lying there on your palm like that, it could be quickly whipped away if the hawk decided to take flight."

She had never seen the man before, for he was one of Lord Whitehead's servants who said he had been trained with a falconer, but there was something slipshod about his work that she didn't like at all. She glanced across and was surprised to see Gibbons glaring angrily in her direction. She must talk to Julian later, she decided, for her instincts told her this man did not have the right feeling for hawks.

Billy, Dora's little brother, cleaned the sawdust of any other matter and she watched him take it away.

"There," Julian said, "they'll not have to stay in a smelly house."

"It's not the smell that bothers the hawks, for they have no sense of smell at all," Francine told him, "but nonetheless they need the purest possible air to breathe."

Julian smiled and shook his head. "No sense of smell? I am fascinated how very much there is to learn about them."

"I hate to sound like some old schoolmarm," Francine said with a rueful smile, "but I've lived and breathed falconry since I could just about run around the hawk houses, and it's now second nature to me."

Julian's smile was warm. "With your looks and quite delightfully melodious voice, you could never sound like an old schoolmarm, my dear," he said softly.

She looked into his face, trying to read what she hoped to see there, but it was impossible to tell.

She finished her work with Julian, and in the afternoon they, with Kenneth, helped Sir Godfrey in his final preparations for the visiting falconer.

It was a little before teatime, and Sir Godfrey knew that they would be through in good time, so he suggested they all adjourn for a little sustenance. But they had no sooner settled in the dining room with cups of a delicate brew and mouth-watering scones with strawberry jam and fresh cream when Dr. David Gardener was announced.

Sir Godfrey rose. "Glad you took me up on my invitation," he said. "Let me introduce you to my family."

As he approached Francine, Dr. Gardener said, "I have had the pleasure of meeting Lady Francine, and am delighted to do so again."

Francine smiled in acknowledgment, and the good

doctor was introduced to Kenneth and Julian before taking a seat adjacent to his hostess.

"May I say how pleased I am to see you again, my lady," Dr. Gardener said. "I have not been here long enough as yet to meet many of the local gentry, but would prefer to meet them socially rather than for medical reasons."

Francine smiled faintly. "I did not know you were acquainted with my grandpapa, Doctor," she said.

"We met at Mr. Bierley's house when I was attending his housekeeper and Sir Godfrey was enjoying a game of chess. He was kind enough to suggest I call any time I was passing."

"You were fortunate to find us receiving, for we have all been working endlessly in the hawk houses. As we were almost finished, my grandpapa declared a break for tea," she told him.

Suddenly she looked up and saw that Julian was gazing across with a heavy scowl on his face. She had been finding the good-looking doctor a little boring, but now she smiled brilliantly at him. "We would have been sorry to miss you," she told him sweetly.

Out of the corner of her eye she watched Julian's eyes flash as he said something to Kenneth, and suddenly she felt much relieved. Surely he must still have some real feelings for her if he could become so very much annoyed when another man drew her attention.

"I would have been extremely sorry to find you not home," Dr. Gardener said, "but I would, of course, have tried again at some other time."

She leaned over and for a moment wished she had a fan to rap his arm with. "I do appreciate persistence, Doctor," she said loud enough for Julian to hear as she fluttered her eyelashes. "Do stop by any time you are in the vicinity."

Dr. Gardener rose, and as she gave him her hand, he bowed so that his lips almost touched it. She thought she caught a glint of amusement in his eyes, but it was not there when she looked again.

"My lady," he said loudly, "you do not realize how often I am in this vicinity, and I will most certainly take advantage of every occasion."

His back was, of course, to Julian, and Francine was sure the doctor's smile was one of understanding. "And we most certainly hope you will, sir. I meant to ask you. How is your patient, Mr. Charlie Bottomley, coming along?"

"His ankle is mending very nicely," Dr. Gardener assured her, "and he is able to get around just as much, I am sure, as he did before the accident."

"I am so glad, sir," Francine almost gushed.

With a handshake to Sir Godfrey and a nod to Kenneth and to Julian, who glared back at him, Dr. Gardener left the room.

"Hadn't we better finish off before it gets too dark to do anything outside," Julian suggested, and everyone rose immediately. "I must see that everything is all right with my hawks also."

"If you want to help Grandpapa, I'll take care of your birds, Julian," Francine suggested, and he readily agreed.

The three of them went back outside to complete their preparations, and Francine, before coming back inside, slipped in to the hawk house Julian was using and made sure that his hawks were settled down for the night, going over and checking that the leashes were fastened securely as she had been taught to do, then securing the door behind her before going in to dinner.

"That new doctor is certainly silver-tongued," Julian remarked. "For your sake, I hope that he is as good with his ministrations as he is with his bedside manner."

"John Bierley assured me he is extremely well-trained in all the latest methods," Sir Godfrey assured him, "and he should know, for he's the veterinary, and a good one, and the doctor has been treating his housekeeper quite recently."

A grunt was all the response that Julian made.

"I think he's quite charming," Francine said with a

grin. "Much more so than old Dr. Braden was, and his pipe does not smell so vile, either."

"You're outnumbered, Julian, so you'd best give in gracefully," Kenneth said, "and see if you've any better luck at cards when we're through here."

After that, conversation at the dinner table became a little stilted and by no means as friendly as it had been the night before. And afterward, when Sir Godfrey once again suggested that they play whist, Julian showed no desire to partner Francine, but said that he and Kenneth would take on the other two.

To Francine's delight, she and her grandpapa thrashed the two young men soundly, and this time, when she went to bed, she was asleep within minutes and woke to feel refreshed and ready for a new day.

15

Francine had forgotten, yesterday, to mention her doubts about the man Julian was using, but they came back to her this morning when Gibbons came running toward them as they approached the hawk houses.

"My lord," he said to Julian, "the door to the house was left open last night, and the shaheen is gone."

"What are you talking about, fellow?" Sir Godfrey growled. "Even if the door had been left open, the hawk could not have flown if it had been fastened properly to the screen perch. Did you check them last night before we went in to dinner, Julian?"

"No, he did not, Grandpapa," Francine interrupted. "As he was working with you, I told him I would check them, and I did so. Everything was in order, and I did not leave the door open," she said.

"Did you go back later last night?" Julian asked Gibbons.

He shook his head. "No sir. I saw the lady going in there about seven, so I did not think it up to me to go in again," the man said in a surly tone. "After all, she's the one that knows all there is to know about hawks, my lord."

"I should have taken care of it myself, sir," Julian said to Sir Godfrey. "I'll pay you for the shaheen and buy another one from you after Mr. Anderson has been, if I may, then I'll start again. This time I'll be sure to check for myself each night that all is well."

Francine flushed a deep pink, and knowing instinctively that her grandpapa was going to say something, she clutched his arm very tightly until he realized she did not wish him to do so. If Julian believed that servant of his before he believed her, then let him suffer the consequences she decided.

"I have preparations to make regarding Mr. Anderson's accommodations, Grandpapa. I think I'll leave you to finish up out here today," she said, turning on her heel and heading back whence she had come.

There was only one thing that could have happened: Gibbons must have deliberately loosened the leash and then left the door open. The hawk was hooded, but it must have felt the air and flown toward it and out. Poor thing, she thought sadly, they would probably find it lying dead near a tree that it had flown into.

She went into the kitchen, where she knew she would find Mrs. Parsons at this hour having her own breakfast with some of the other staff.

"Did you change your mind, my lady?" the housekeeper asked. "We'll have breakfast for you in a trice in the dining room."

"I'll have it here, Mrs. Parsons," Francine said, "so you needn't set up the dining room until the men come back about nine or so. Just set me a place at this table and I'll have a little something with you."

The rest of the servants seemed to melt away, leaving Francine and the housekeeper to discuss arrangements for Mr. Anderson's accommodations.

When she was finished, Francine asked the astute old lady, "This man of Lord Whitehead's who is helping with the hawks, what do you think of him, Mrs. Parsons?"

"Wouldn't trust 'im as far as I could throw 'im, and that wouldn't be very far, for he's a sight bigger than I am. 'E's one of these who's out to climb over everyone else to get ahead, and 'e'll come a cropper before long," she prophesied.

"My feelings exactly," Francine said. "And I don't think he knows anything at all about hawks."

"That 'e doesn't. For 'e's been asking all Sir Godfrey's men for tips on 'ow to get along. Little Billy knows a lot more than 'e does, but the youngster must be all bruises with the back'anders he's been giving 'im," Mrs. Parsons said.

For a moment, Francine looked horrified, for she'd not thought of that aspect of it, but she knew she must do something at once before more damage to Billy and the hawks was sustained. She hurried out to the hawk houses to find her grandpapa.

He was watching Julian work, as she had done the day before, and she went quietly over to him. Julian looked at her coldly, then continued his work with the peregrine.

"I need to have an urgent word with you, Grandpapa," Francine said, adding, "in private, if you don't mind."

"You're managing all right, Julian," Sir Godfrey said. "I'll be back when I've seen what Francine wants."

They went outside and the old man asked, "What is it, my love? If you want to tell me again that you didn't leave the hawk house open, you've no need to bother, for I'm sure you didn't."

Francine put an arm around him and hugged him close. "I knew you'd have faith in me," she said, kissing his cheek. "But I've just been talking to Mrs. Parsons about Julian's man, Gibbons, and the opinion in the kitchen is that he's a climber who knows nothing whatever about hawks. He's always picking the brains of your men, and he's also beating little Billy when no one's looking."

"Is he, indeed?" Sir Godfrey said, his eyes flashing angrily. "I'll have a word with George Millman. A man who would deliberately endanger that poor shaheen deserves more than just a dismissal. He'll do no more damage around here after George has finished with him."

"Do you think you should talk to Julian about it first?" Francine asked. "After all, it is his father's man."

"That was my hawk before I gave it to Julian, and it is my granddaughter who has been set up to take the blame in a very damaging way," Sir Godfrey said bluntly. "It's high time the two of you got your affairs settled, for I think he's so mixed up about his feelings for you that he doesn't know what he believes and what he doesn't."

"I don't want him if he believes I am a liar," Francine snapped angrily.

"Now stop jumping to conclusions and make sure you take time to make yourself look pretty. The Lord knows you bought enough new gowns in London to keep you in clothes for years," he said, but he grinned and his eyes signaled his approval. He was very proud of her. "What have you planned for dinner tonight?"

"Roast beef and Yorkshire pudding, of course, with the beef on the rib so that we'll have a bone to nibble on when conversation palls. Then there'll be green goose cut in pieces, asparagus soup, carrots and parsnips tossed in butter, and peas fresh from the garden, creamy mashed potatoes with thick beef gravy . . ." She stopped when her grandpapa held up a hand.

"Enough," he said, "you forget we've not yet eaten breakfast. Perhaps you and Julian will breach your differences over ham and eggs and rich coffee."

Francine shook her head. "I'm not at all pleased with Julian right now, and I've already had my breakfast in the kitchen. How do you think I got so much information?"

She kissed his cheek, then swung around and walked jauntily back to the hall with her chin held high and her hips swaying in an unconsciously becoming way. She had enough to do without helping Julian today, for Mr. Anderson would be arriving early in the afternoon.

Mrs. Parsons was waiting for her when she entered the hall, with a number of lists for approval, and after agreeing to all but a few of the housekeeper's suggestions, Francine said, "Sir Godfrey will handle the matter we discussed at breakfast, and I don't believe that the man in question will be any more trouble.''

"That's good, my lady," Mrs. Parsons said with a grim smile, then asked, "Are you expecting anyone else to tea to meet Mr. Anderson?"

"I don't believe anyone else has been invited, but you know that a few people stop by on occasion, so we'd best be prepared for one or two extra," Francine told her, "but I'm sure Cook has lots of cakes, pastries, and biscuits on hand in case they do so."

Francine went about her various chores, enjoying working in the house for once, and was dressed for tea in one of her London gowns long before Mr. Anderson's carriage came in sight. She sent a message to her grandpapa, then went downstairs to greet their guest.

"Good afternoon, sir. I am Francine Truesdale. My grandfather is expecting you, of course, and will be in shortly, but in the meantime, Mr. Anderson, I'll have one of the footmen show you to your room. If there is anything else you need, please do not hesitate to ask for it." She signaled a footman. "Tea will be served in the drawing room at four o'clock, but you'll probably see Grandpapa before then, for he's most anxious to make your stay a pleasant one."

It was almost an hour before tea, and in the normal way Francine would have gone out to the hawk houses in the meantime, but she had no intention of doing so in her green satin afternoon gown. Instead, she went into the back gardens, which led through a wooded area and then out onto the moors, but today she would stay within the garden area in case she might be needed.

She had just settled down on a wooden bench from where she could watch a variety of birds hunting for worms and insects when she saw Gibbons coming toward the house. There was a satisfied expression on his face until he noticed her, and then his expression changed to a sneer as he came closer.

"That's the way, my lady," he said smoothly. "It's what you should be doing instead of interfering in men's work. It was one of your sort poked 'er nose in before, an' I'll not be sent packing this time, so you watch out.''

Francine ignored him, for she had no intention of engaging in an argument with someone of his ilk. He looked about to say something else, equally encroaching, when his expression changed to one of fear.

'' 'Ere now, you don't want to be bothering 'er lady-ship.'' The voice came from behind the bench, and Francine had no need to turn around, for she recognized it as her grandpapa's foreman, George Millman, who she'd known since she was a little girl. "You're just the man I was looking for. I've been 'earing some strange things about you, and I think we'd best take a little walk so as we can talk about 'em in private.'' He grabbed the other man's arm as he tried to move away, then, touching his cap and saying, "Good day, milady,'' he half-walked, half-dragged him toward the woods.

When they were out of sight, Francine rose and went indoors, for the meeting had completely spoiled her pleasure in the outdoors for the moment. She could hear her grandpapa talking to Mr. Anderson in the upstairs hallway, then she caught the sound of Julian's voice also and hastened toward Sir Godfrey's study, where she curled up in one of a pair of big wing chairs and read quietly until the rattle of cups told her that tea was served.

"You wouldn't think so to look at her now, Mr. Anderson, all dressed up in her finery, but my grand-daughter is a most proficient falconer and my right hand here at Hawk Hall," Sir Godfrey boasted. "She has a knack for handling the hawks that is rare in a man, let alone a woman.''

Francine smiled fondly at her grandpapa, knowing he was trying to make up to her for Julian's reserved manner. Despite her hasty retreat, she was also concerned as to what had happened in the woods between Gibbons and George. If the man did malicious damage without being provoked, what might he do after

George had finished with him? Though there were always some of Grandpapa's training staff around the hawk houses, she would feel happier about their safety if one of the family was also keeping a watch.

Her thoughts were interrupted by the unexpected arrival of Lady Kathleen Whitehead.

"I was coming this way and thought I'd best bring Julian some of the mail that has arrived for him," she said brightly. "But if you're serving tea, I'll most certainly stay and have some."

Francine poured and Kenneth was there in an instant to hand it to her, offering her some of the pastries, which she almost pounced upon, for she had tasted Cook's baking before and knew it to be exceptional.

When she was sure that everyone had all they needed, Francine went to sit beside her friend while Sir Godfrey and his guest talked about the feats of famous falcons and Julian listened intently.

"What have you and Julian been up to since I last saw you?" Kathleen asked Francine. "Whatever it was, it has done nothing for my brother's disposition."

"Your brother can take his disposition and—" Francine started to say, but Kathleen stopped her.

"Are you two at loggerheads again?" Kathleen asked softly. "It seems that every time I leave you both alone for two minutes you start to fight. Don't you know that it's much more fun to play than to do battle?" she asked coaxingly.

"Try telling that to your brother," Francine snapped. "He's always ready to believe the worst of me, and I'm not going to let him get away with it this time."

"Just don't let him get away altogether," Kathleen warned, "for I'm sure you would make him a wonderful helpmate. I heard the other day that he had been paying calls upon the Matthews and the Towlers, both good families in our neighborhood with very marriageable daughters."

Francine's heart sank. Even when he was being friendly toward her, he had been visiting other females.

She must have mistaken his friendship for something more than it was.

She decided it would be best to tell Kathleen what had actually happened here, for she might know something about the man whom Julian brought with him.

"Your brother became annoyed when Dr. Gardener came to tea, and would not partner me at whist that night, but Grandpapa and I wiped the floor with the two of them," she said with considerable satisfaction.

"Then, the next morning, your father's man, Gibbons, came over to us and as much as said that I had left the hawk house open the night before. I had to almost break Grandpapa's arm to stop him defending me," Francine told her friend, "and ever since, your brother has looked at me as if I'm a proven criminal."

"He doesn't seem any too pleased to see me either. So I suppose he thinks we're involved in a conspiracy or something," Kathleen declared. "He may be right, for I don't intend to stand by and let anyone put blame on you."

Kenneth, who had wandered over to join in the discussion Sir Godfrey and Mr. Anderson were having, heard the last remark, and glanced over.

"I think I know who you're talking about," Kathleen went on, frowning thoughtfully, "but I'm surprised at Julian taking him, for none of us cared for the man at all. He had a sort of shifty way about him, and I, for one, didn't like the way he looked at me—almost resentfully."

"I understand he convinced Julian that he was quite knowledgeable with regard to hawks, which was probably why he brought him here. In fact, however, he has been getting all his information from my grandpapa's men, then claiming it to be his own experience," Francine told her. "He apparently resents me or, perhaps, all young ladies now, for he came up to me in the garden and said something about someone like me had interfered before. I got the impression he'd been dismissed because of this person. I keep wondering if he has gone, or if he's hanging around to do some serious damage to Grandpapa's hawk houses, for it's so very easy to hurt the birds."

"He'll not try anything until after dark," Kathleen said, drawing on the novels she had read in lieu of experience. "Wouldn't you like me to stay for a few days? One more guest would make little difference, and we could sneak out and keep a watch ourselves."

"Of course you can stay, Kathleen. We'd love to have you here for as long as you wish, but as far as watching at night, if the man is as shifty as you say, we might find ourselves in the middle of something we did not bargain for." Francine rose. "Let me go and tell Mrs. Parsons to prepare a room for you, and then you can write a note whenever you like and send it to your mama."

As she passed her grandpapa's chair, Francine bent down and told him quietly that Kathleen was staying for a few days, and he smiled, pleased that she would have some young female company while he was busy with his guest.

After giving the housekeeper instructions to put Kathleen in the next chamber to her own, Francine started back for the drawing room, but as she entered the hall, the doorbell sounded. She waited a moment for the footman to answer it, then stepped forward with a smile when she saw it was Charlie Bottomley and he had with him Lady Arabella Flint.

"How nice to see you Lady Arabella, Charlie," Francine said, for once truly happy about a visit from the young man. "Do come in and join Lady Kathleen and our guest in the drawing room."

She showed them inside, and as Kenneth performed the introductions, Francine slipped back to the kitchen to ask Cook to send some fresh tea and pastries.

"We just had to come by and thank you for introducing us," Lady Arabella gushed. "Charlie brought me to meet his dear papa today, and now he and my father are to get together next week, and you know what that means," she said archly. "It's so very exciting and it's all because of you, my dear Francine."

"Not really," Francine said modestly. "It was, in fact, Lady Kathleen's idea, for she knew that Charlie had little chance to meet young ladies in this quiet community."

"Oh, yes, so very kind of her also, but it was you who brought Charlie along in your carriage when he'd injured his poor ankle. What a lucky break that was." Lady Arabella tittered. "I just made a joke! Charlie, dear, I just made a joke. I must tell it to Mama and Papa when I get home."

Kenneth had pulled his chair closer to Kathleen's shortly after she arrived, for the other three gentlemen, after greeting the guests, were committing the dreadful faux pas of discussing something serious over afternoon tea.

"So you met Squire Bottomley for the first time today," Francine remarked. "And you got along with him right away, I am sure."

"A charming gentleman, my dear, quite charming." Lady Arabella seemed about to swoon at the memory. "I knew that dear Charlie just had to have a papa like himself—gentle, kind and helpful—but I was agreeably surprised to find that he was all that and much, much more."

Francine silently wished Lady Arabella might never find out what a mistake she had made in the father, if not the son. Personally, she had always found him dominating, overbearing, and after her series of near accidents, dangerous, but it was, after all, a matter of personal judgment.

"What delicious almond tarts! You must ask your cook to give me the recipe, for ours always makes them too dry," Lady Arabella went on. "It's so important to have them a little moist or much of the flavor is lost."

"Of course," Francine murmured. "I'll send it over to you in the morning."

Charlie looked blissfully happy, even though he had not spoken a word since he entered the room. This young lady was probably the best thing that had happened to him in a long time.

Francine glanced over to where Kathleen and Kenneth were in a friendly discussion on the works of Sir Walter Scott, a favorite of Kenneth's, but she knew that Kathleen found Byron more to her taste. Her brother looked completely charmed by her, and her friend was looking up at him with such a happy glow on her face that for a moment Francine felt a pang of something resembling jealousy. It was gone in a moment, but she inwardly scolded herself severely. She was at odds once more with Julian, but that should not make her envious of anyone else's happiness.

As she thought of him, she looked over to where Julian sat, listening more than joining in the discussion between her grandpapa and Mr. Anderson. He looked across, as though he had felt her eyes upon him, and he seemed about to smile until he remembered he was angry with her.

With a shrug she turned back to her guests. Charlie and Lady Arabella were just leaving, and she walked with them to the door.

"It was so nice of you to call," she told them, "and I will send that recipe to you, as I promised, Lady Arabella. Give my best wishes to your father, Charlie."

As the door closed behind them, she sighed. At least that was one problem taken care of, thanks to her good friend Kathleen.

"They're perfect for each other," Kathleen said when Francine returned to the drawing room, "for he seems to be content just listening to her going on and on, and smiling his agreement to everything she says. I found her to be garrulous but without malice in school, but it will be bellows to mend if she ever realizes Squire Bottomley's odiously encroaching ways."

"I'm sure he'll not do anything to endanger the match, for he must be eager to get his hands upon her dowry. He has probably mapped out a campaign to ingratiate himself with her family also, so I need not worry further in that regard,'' Francine said happily.

"Which leaves the way clear to start a campaign against my brother,'' Kathleen said, dimpling mischievously. "Invincible indeed! The men in his regiment will have to eat their words if I have anything to do with it. You did know that was what they called him, didn't you?''

"Ken said something about it a long time ago,'' Francine told her airily, "and if Julian wishes to live up to that reputation, it's all right as far as I am concerned.''

"He's making a complete cake of himself, glaring at you across the room in that way, and I shall tell him so as soon as I get the oppportunity,'' Kathleen said firmly. "If he didn't love you at least a little, he'd not bother to notice you at all.''

Although she realized there might easily be something in what Kathleen said, and felt a little better because of it, Francine still determined not to make the first move toward a resumption of their relationship, such as it was.

"I'm glad you came by,'' she said to her friend, "for I was becoming as cross as crabs about the whole thing, and now I believe I can put it more into perspective. He is behaving more like a little boy than anything else, and I should treat him as I would Penelope.''

"I don't think he would allow you to smack his bottom and put him to bed.'' Kathleen chuckled. "But if you should decide to try, I beg to be allowed to watch.''

Francine's grin was infectious. "You shall have a seat in the front row, I promise, so that you can catch me when he sends me flying for cover.''

"What are you two chuckling about over here?'' Kenneth had abandoned Sir Godfrey once more and come to try some lighter entertainment. "I may be a slow top as far as falconry is concerned, but I can still enjoy a good joke.''

"Kathleen was just entertaining me with a strictly feminine anecdote,'' Francine told him. "Do join us, though, for we feel a distinct lack of masculine company at this end of the room.''

"They'll be going out to the hawk houses soon, for I can see Mr. Anderson positively itching to get out there and see whether my grandpapa is exaggerating in his descriptions of them,'' he said with a knowing smile. "Was I mistaken or did Charlie say he was finally getting leg-shackled?''

"It wasn't Charlie, for he hardly said a word, but Lady Arabella all but asked us to wish her happy, so I think the knot will soon be tied,'' Francine confirmed, "and the sooner the better as far as I am concerned.''

"You mean you don't feel as though you've been jilted?'' Kenneth teased, and Francine aimed a playful punch at her brother's chin while Julian, looking up at that moment, frowned darkly.

16

Kenneth and Kathleen had gone for a stroll in the garden after tea, and Francine was just about to make her escape also when her grandpapa said quietly, "I want you to come out to the hawk houses with Mr. Anderson, Julian, and me, Francine, and I won't take any excuses."

When he used that tone of voice, Francine knew not to argue with him. "I'll go and change into something more suitable," she said, "and join you in a few minutes."

"We'll wait for you, so don't be all day about it," he said sharply.

There was no way out of it, so she changed as quickly as she could and joined the three men.

"My granddaughter is a falconer in her own right, John," Sir Godfrey said proudly. "What she lacks in strength, she more than makes up for in her natural aptitude. She is unusually neat and tidy, and she is never careless in her habits. If she is the last one in a house at night, you can always be sure that all the leashes are fastened properly and all the doors are locked behind her." He turned to look at Julian as he made the last statement, and the younger man had the grace to flush in embarrassment.

"Has the shaheen been found?" Francine asked quietly.

Sir Godfrey nodded. "One of my men came a few minutes ago to let me know."

Julian gave him a questioning glance, but realized that it was not a matter Sir Godfrey wanted to discuss in front of his guest, so he let it rest for now.

They went slowly through the first hawk house, which was certainly a credit to Sir Godfrey, for everything was spotless and the hawks looked in excellent condition.

The next two houses were as good, if not better, and Mr. Anderson turned to Sir Godfrey and said, "Rarely have I had the privilege of seeing hawk houses in such shape." He swung around to Julian. "You probably don't realize how unusual this place is, for falconers don't always take the care they used to when the sport was more popular. As a result, the hawks catch chills, pick up diseases sometimes, and suffer at the hands of inexperienced trainers."

They were walking toward the last house when a man came running toward them closely followed by another, who stood back a little and waited for Sir Godfrey's orders.

Francine thought at first that it was some beggar or tramp who had trespassed onto the property, then gasped as she realized it was Gibbons. He had obviously received a severe thrashing, for his face was swollen and his eyes almost were closed.

"I've come to you for protection, my lord, for this man caught me unawares and started beating and kicking me for no apparent reason. He threw me off the property, but I am in your employ and not Sir Godfrey's, and I'm not leaving without my few personal things," he blustered.

"Good God, man, what is this all about?" Julian asked.

"Come over here, George, and tell Sir Julian what you found out," Sir Godfrey ordered. "This is my chief trainer, George Millman," he explained.

"I'm sorry to tell you, sir, but young Billy's in worse shape than this fellow is. Apparently the youngster saw 'im go back in after Lady Francine left 'is lordship's 'awk house last night." George Millman looked at the other man with contempt. "The lad didn't know what this fellow was doing there, but when 'e 'eard 'er ladyship was being accused of carelessness, 'e spoke up.

As soon as 'e got the lad on 'is own, this one beat the 'ell out of the little fellow—beggin' your pardon, milady. I 'ad a couple of men take the lad to the doctor, and then me and Joe Berkitt took care of this one, but it was mostly me.''

Sir Godfrey looked stern. ''What shape is young Billy in?'' he asked. ''Did they take him in the gig?''

''Yes, sir, they did. Aside from some real nasty cuts about the face, and bruises all over, 'is arm was broken in two places and 'is shoulder dislocated, but I daren't put it back in case I did damage,'' George told him.

''It's all her fault. She did it,'' Gibbons started to shout, and suddenly lunged toward Francine.

Three men started forward, but Julian was the fastest. Grasping Gibbons' shoulder, he swung him around and delivered a smashing blow to the man's chin and was about to haul him upright and repeat the action when Sir Godfrey stopped him.

''I want some answers from him. George can lock him in an empty shed until I'm ready,'' the older man said. ''You'd best send a note to your father so he'll not get his old job back. And now Mr. Anderson would appreciate an explanation, and I'm sure you would like to see for yourself that, thanks to you, Francine was not hurt.''

The two older men continued the way they had been going, and Julian stared for a moment at a rather shaky Francine, then took her by the arm and led her toward the home woods.

They walked in silence until they reached a secluded spot, then Julian turned to Francine and asked, ''Why didn't you deny it last night when Gibbons said you were the last person in the house?''

''There was no need for me to do so,'' Francine said snapped. ''I had already said that the hawk was leashed and the door fastened when I left. Why repeat myself, for if you preferred to believe him, you were perfectly free to do so.'' Her voice was a little shaky but there was no doubt about her meaning.

Julian looked down, watching the movement as he kicked at a clump of grass. She had every right to be angry with him, he knew, for there was no doubt that he had thought she was not telling the truth.

As though she read his thoughts, Francine said, "I don't lie, Julian, but I know that it is possible for me to make a mistake, despite Grandpapa's confidence in me. I try very hard not to make a mistake where the hawks are concerned, though, for the smallest one can do a lot of damage, as you found out today."

"That was no mistake. It was done deliberately to discredit you, but I cannot for the life of me understand why." He turned her to face him and lifted her chin so that he could see her expression as he asked, "Am I forgiven for not having complete faith in you? I give you my word that it will never happen again."

His sincerity was her undoing. Tears suddenly filled her eyes and one rolled slowly down her cheek. Julian caught it with one finger, then licked the salty moisture from it, never once taking his eyes from Francine's.

"Of course you are," she said brokenly. "It's been such a horrid day with you either ignoring me or, worse, glaring at me as though I were a monster."

He pressed her close, cradling her head against his chest and stroking her golden hair with a tender touch. She could feel his heart thump-thumping against one ear, while his fingers were getting close enough to the other to make her feel strangely excited.

Then his next words brought her to her senses with a jolt.

"It was ridiculous of me to believe another and not you, for you have been like a sister to me for some eight or more years, and I know full well that you do not lie," he said softly.

With a tremendous effort, Francine drew her head away and moved until his arm was still around her waist, but they were side by side. He still thought of her as a sister and not a woman, after all she had been through to convince him otherwise!

She took a deep breath and after a moment said with remarkable calmness, considering the despair she felt, "I can't stay here any longer, for we're having a very special dinner tonight in honor of grandpapa's guest, so we'll have to go and dress shortly, but first I want to find out how Billy is."

"I want to see him also. I cannot recall ever being so thoroughly disgusted with anyone in my life. For a grown man to vent his anger on a little boy who had done nothing wrong is unthinkable," Julian said bitterly. "Where will we find him?"

"I'll go and ask in the kitchen, but I can promise you one thing: he will not be in the room above the stables, but will have been quietly assigned a room in the house by our kindhearted housekeeper, until he is completely well again," Francine assured him. "Mrs. Parsons told me earlier in the day that Billy was constantly receiving bruises from your man."

"If you had come to tell me, he wouldn't be lying injured now, Francine," he said in exasperation. "Surely you were not afraid to do so, for you've faced me in a far worse temper than I was in today."

"But then Grandpapa was not there to help me out," she said pointedly. "That was why I came into your hawk house this morning and pulled Grandpapa away for a few minutes. He said he would have George take care of it, but apparently he was not in time."

They had reached the back door and went directly into the kitchen, where Mrs. Parsons told them which room Billy was in. "His sister is with him now, for the little chap's had a hard time of it," she added.

Billy was normally a good-looking little boy, with big blue eyes and jet-black hair, but now his eyes could scarcely be seen for the purple bruises around them, and his lips were cut and swollen. His right arm and shoulder was swathed in bandages, but when he saw who his visitors were, surprise still registered on his battered face and he tried to get out of bed, but Dora pushed him back firmly.

Julian went to sit at the side of the bed while Francine stood at the front.

"You have nothing to fear from that bully anymore, Billy," he assured the boy, "and if anyone starts to do anything of this sort to you again, you're to come to me at once. Remember now!"

"Yes, milord," Billy mumbled. Then he said proudly, "The doctor said I was very brave 'cos I didn't make a sound when he fixed my shoulder and set my arm."

"I'm sure you were, Billy," Francine said with a smile. "And Dora, here, is taking good care of you, I know."

Despite his bravado he looked a little pale and they did not stay long, but Julian determined to come back in the morning and check on him.

Julian was in a quandary. As he dressed for dinner, he could not decide what to do, and he was not one to discuss his problems with others.

His love for Frankie had only become more intense since the night that young Penelope had been lost, though one might have thought the blunt refusal he had received to his offer of marriage would have had a dampening effect upon it. Where was his pride? Now he was even allowing it to interfere with his normal reasoning to such an extent that he must do something one way or the other about it.

Today had been filled with so many conflicting emotions that he had made an extremely bad judgment in believing a servant of his father's whom he did not even know well and had never very much cared for. The only reason he had brought him here was because of the man's supposed knowledge of hawking, and he should have realized that was nonexistent the first time he worked with him.

He had very nearly made an utter fool of himself when he saw Frankie's tears, but realized in time that she had had a very trying day, including an attack upon her person when she could have been seriously harmed had he not been close by at the time.

With a sigh of disgust, he made another adjustment to his cravat before he was completely satisfied with it, and checked to be sure the back of his hair was arranged as perfectly as it was in the front.

Suddenly, he remembered the morning in London when they were riding in the park and he had the audacity to complain about women fussing over their appearance. He could see it as clearly as if it had been this very morning. She had teased him unmercifully, about the care he took over his cravat and his boots, and he could see her sparkling green eyes, her lovely laughing mouth, and her bright red lips as she asked, "Did you not spend at least fifteen minutes or more waiting until every hair on your head was arranged in a perfect windswept style?"

Somewhere along the line, he realized he had made a mess of things, and he dearly wished that he could go back in time and do better on the second try. Was it really too late? he wondered as he went down to the drawing room for a much-needed glass of sherry.

Frankie had not yet come down, and after greeting his host, Julian turned toward his sister, who looked quite dazzling in a blue silk gown that he knew to be one of her own.

"You didn't, by any chance, leave home planning to spend the night here, did you?" he asked with a hint of reproof.

"No, of course I did no such thing," Kathleen said impatiently. "Sometimes brothers can be quite impossible! When Mama received my message, she had the forethought to delay the man I sent until she packed a couple of gowns and things."

He touched her cheek lightly. "Sorry, Sis," he said affectionately. "I was being a little big brotherly, wasn't I?"

"It's all right doing it with me, but I wish you'd stop being like a brother to Frankie. If Ken behaved to me the way you behave to Frankie, I'd be furious," she said, feeling the time was right to say something to him.

"Why?" Julian asked. "I've always treated her that way."

"That's the whole point. She is not your sister and, I am sure, would much rather you found her attractive as a woman," she said urgently.

"Has she told you as much?" Julian was trying not to show how interested he was in the subject . . . and how hopeful.

Kathleen hesitated. "Not in so many words," she admitted, "but I do know she feels that way."

Just then, Francine came hurrying into the room, dropping a curtsy to her grandpapa and his guest. "Please forgive me for being late," she begged charmingly. "For some reason Penelope was reluctant to let me go tonight. And she seemed a little hot so I'll check on her after dinner. I hope she isn't sickening."

"Francine is referring to my great-grandchild, whom you have not yet met, John, but I am sure the little imp will remedy that tomorrow. She has been remarkably healthy, Francine, so I very much doubt there's anything wrong. But check by all means if it will set your mind at rest," Sir Godfrey said, his eyes twinkling.

She smiled. "I'm sure you're right, Grandpapa. Have I time for sherry?"

As if in answer Julian appeared at her side and placed a glass of the golden wine in her hand. She thanked him prettily, while wondering to herself what was different about him. His hair was arranged in a perfect windswept, as usual, and the folds of his cravat formed a meticulous waterfall. He had often looked admiringly at her new gowns, but tonight there was an odd look in his eyes. One she could not recall ever having seen before.

"A perfect windswept," she repeated aloud, but very softly, "and a meticulous waterfall. Do you remember that day in the park. . . ?" She stopped in midsentence, her lips parted and her eyes bright with the recollection of the happy occasion.

"It's strange that you should think of it now, for it

came back to me this evening just before I left my bed-chamber," he said wonderingly. "How roundly you teased me for my uncalled-for criticism of women and their propensity to fuss over their appearance."

"We laughed all the way home, as I recall," Francine told him, "and Lady Withers couldn't understand what was the matter with me when I entered the dining room with a laugh still on my lips." And with joy in my heart, she added silently.

"I wish I could make you so light-hearted always, Frankie, instead of scolding you without cause and making you sad," he murmured almost to himself. "Your laughter is one of the loveliest, most joyful sounds I have ever heard."

He was about to say more, but then Kenneth came over to them, for Sir Godfrey had captured Kathleen's attention. "What are you two looking so secretive about?" he asked. "Anything you can tell me?"

Julian shook his head. "Just recalling some of the happy times in London last month. I've been there on many occasions, but I simply do not remember having enjoyed it half so much as I did this year."

"Neither do I," Kenneth said, "but of course, we'd been away for more than two years, so it was like seeing it through new eyes."

"You're neither of you old enough yet to go around wearing that infuriating look of detached boredom that most of the roués have," Francine informed them, her eyes dancing. "I watched some of their carefully cultivated mannerisms and felt vastly relieved that I had you two to laugh and cry with, and to keep me away from those wolves." She paused, serious now. "If I didn't say thank you properly at the time, I'd like to do so now."

"Frankie." Julian put a finger under her chin and tilted her face so that he could see her grateful expression. "You don't have to thank either one of us. It was probably more of a pleasure for me than for your brother, but I wouldn't have missed this Season with you for anything."

He looked tenderly into her eyes, and Francine's pulse quickened involuntarily. Sensing something very personal passing between them, Kenneth moved quietly away.

"This is not the time, nor the place, I know, but I have the strongest desire to kiss you until those green eyes become glazed with passion and those lips become even rosier red. Can you understand that, Frankie?" Julian asked, his voice barely a whisper.

"Yes," she murmured, scarcely daring to breathe in case the moment disappeared as so many of them had before.

"Perhaps not tonight, for it will seem strange if we try to sneak away, but soon I intend to give in to that desire," he told her.

A discreet cough sounded close by. Mrs. Parsons had been trying to get Francine's attention for some minutes without success.

"I'd like to start serving dinner, my lady," the housekeeper said, "for I wouldn't like the Yorkshire pudding to go sad."

"Thank you, Mrs. Parsons. We'll come through to the dining room right away." Francine looked at Julian and raised her dark eyebrows.

With a deep chuckle he placed her hand upon his arm and they led the way.

17

There were four men to two ladies at the dinner table, so Francine had arranged for the men to sit at the ends of the table, and she and Kathleen facing each other in the center of each long side.

One last-minute change by Francine had been to place Julian on Kathleen's left, for, with conversation general, she preferred to be able to look at him across the table.

She kept wondering what it would have been like had they been able to slip out of doors into the soft night air, for she had never felt so close to him before, nor known him in so romantic a mood. Was he finally starting to feel for her the way she felt about him?

Cook had outdone herself. The beef was roasted to perfection, almost melting in the mouth, and the Yorkshire pudding was not sad, but just right, crisp on the outside but light as a feather within.

When the last spoonful of Nottingham pudding had disappeared, Francine and Kathleen rose and went into the drawing room.

"What's this about Gibbons trying to attack you, Frankie?" Kathleen asked. "Ken said he wasn't there himself, but heard that although there were three men to protect you, it was Julian who handled the matter by grabbing the wretch before he could do you any harm."

"I was very lucky that your brother was close and moved so quickly," Francine said, with a slight shudder, "for although Grandpapa taught me ways to protect myself many years ago, I just froze when the man flung himself toward me and tried to grab me by the shoulders."

"Wasn't it exciting, though, when Julian charged to

your rescue?'' Kathleen asked, eagerly, "like a real-life hero?''

"You've been reading too many romances, young lady," Francine remarked, "and as for your brother, he makes me feel as though I'm on a seesaw. One minute I'm up and in favor, and the next one I'm down and he's glaring at me and snapping my head off. Dont you dare tell him I said so, though, for I'm up very high right now, and I'd like it to stay that way.''

"You know I wouldn't," Kathleen began, "but I'd love to have . . .'' she began, but just then the gentlemen came in to join them and she never finished her remark, for Julian came over to sit beside them.

He smiled warmly at Francine. "That was one of the finest dinners I've ever had," he told her. "You are not only a gracious hostess, but a considerate one also, to plan a meal that both a hungry man and a more delicate lady could enjoy.''

Francine's cheeks turned a deep pink at the compliment, and she murmured, "Thank you, Julian, but I couldn't have done it if Grandpapa did not have such an excellent cook.''

Kathleen looked at her brother with a knowing smile on her face, and he turned and frowned at her. "Don't you agree with me, little sister?'' he demanded.

"Of course, my dear brother''—she leaned forward and placed a hand on his arm—"but you put me to shame, for I forgot Frankie was my hostess and thus also forgot my manners," Kathleen said with mock formality. "There were other more interesting things I wanted to discuss with her, and my chance came when we left you gentlemen to your port.''

"Just watch how you behave, young lady," he growled, though his eyes twinkled. "You came unexpectedly to tea, then invited yourself to stay for a few days. Because I practically live here does not give you freedom to come and go as you please.''

"Perhaps not, Julian," Francine said, "but being just about my only real friend does.''

Julian made a long face. "I'm deeply hurt," he said with mock reproach, placing a hand over his heart, "for I've counted myself your friend for some eight years and in the space of only one minute you absolutely deny the relationship."

"But I place you in a special category. If I name her my only real woman friend, will that make you feel better?" Francine asked, her eyes dancing with merriment.

He nodded. "I just made a complete recovery. All is forgiven."

"How many glasses of port or brandy did you have after we left you?" Kathleen asked suspiciously. "You're in a merry mood tonight."

"Watch it, little sister," Julian warned, smiling dangerously. "You're not too big to go over my knee." He frowned and held out his hands as though measuring, then added, "On second thoughts, however, perhaps you are, for you have long legs and it would be dashed uncomfortable for both of us. Should I answer her very sisterly question?" he asked Francine.

"Why not?" Francine asked with amusement.

"Why not indeed?" He nodded in agreement. "I had one small port, ladies, and if you don't believe me, you can ask Ken."

"Do I hear my name spoken in vain?" Kenneth said, appearing at Julian's elbow. "You youngsters seem to be having a good time, judging by the laughter coming from this corner. May I join in?" He pulled up a chair without waiting for an answer.

"Glad to have some male support, for you wouldn't believe how these young ladies were insulting me," Julian told him. "Tell us why you deserted your grandpapa in his time of need."

"I didn't really," Kenneth told them, "but I don't think I can stand to hear about one more remarkable, famous, or distinguished hawk. Grandpapa, on the other hand, is having a wonderful time, and I'm happy he finally has someone who can speak his language."

"Of course he is," Francine cut in. "It's good to see him so much in his element."

"I say, Frankie," Kenneth remarked, "that was an outstanding meal you planned. Couldn't have done better if I'd picked it out myself."

Francine smiled. "That was because it was very much a man's kind of dinner, good simple, English food."

"What we'd have given for it only six months ago," Julian said, a faraway look in his eyes. "Do you remember how, whenever anyone managed to get meat, it was always bacon or pork, Ken? We were usually so hungry by the time we got it that we were grateful, but how we dreamed of a good piece of beef."

"And as for Yorkshire pudding, only a Yorkshire woman can make it properly," Kenneth added, "though its name has been used for some of the most atrocious, soggy pieces of dough I've ever had the good sense to leave on my plate untouched. We didn't expect to find it in Spain or France, of course, but at some of the banquets in London it was completely unrecognizable."

"If we don't stop flattering her, Frankie won't be able to get her bonnet to fit her head, she'll be so puffed up with pride," Julian avowed. "It's a good thing my sister had no part in the planning of that meal, or we'd never have heard the end of it. She'd still be bragging about it two years from now."

There was a discreet cough.

"If I may interrupt you children for a moment," Sir Godfrey said sarcastically, "Mr. Anderson and I are going to take a walk around the hawk houses just to be sure everything is in order. Afterward, my guest will have an early night, for he is travel-weary, and I will challenge any one or all of you to a game of whist."

"Oh, dear," Francine said when the two older gentlemen had left the room. "Poor Grandpapa! We've been laughing so much we must have made an awful racket."

"He didn't look at all worried to me," Julian said firmly. "He and Mr. Anderson were so intent in their discussion that I don't believe he heard us at all. And if he did, he'd be glad to see you enjoying yourselves."

"He'll be even more glad when he and I trounce you soundly at whist," Francine said airily.

Julian's eye gleamed. "You think so? I'll be happy to take you both up on that when he returns. Will you partner me, Ken?"

Kenneth readily agreed, for he knew that Julian was an excellent player and he wanted to be on the winning side for a change.

But this was not the night for changes. Sir Godfrey and Francine played even better than usual, and the two young men did not stand a chance. It was a lot of fun, however, and Francine went to bed feeling pleased with the way things were going.

The next morning, Sir Godfrey and Julian went to pick out another shaheen for him to start training anew, and while they were busy, Francine decided to clean the hawk house Julian was using, as Billy was not yet able to get out of bed, let alone perform his duties.

It was messy work, but she was used to doing it, and she wanted to leave Kathleen and Kenneth alone together as much as possible. She entered the hawk house in her usual quiet manner and went to gather the equipment she needed from one of the hooks on the wall; she was so intent on what she was doing that she did not hear someone enter and come up behind her.

As she reached for the pan, her right hand was grasped from behind and twisted behind her back, then her left hand was grabbed and she felt a searing pain in her wrists as a leather leash was bound so tightly around them as to cut deeply into the flesh. Not a word had been spoken, but she could hear her captor's heavy breathing and she could smell the most atrocious odor emanating from him.

"Now we'll see how much you know about a few other things, my fine lady." The words were breathed on the back of her neck, rather than spoken out loud, and the smell intensified. But what was much worse was that she recognized the voice. It was Julian's man, Gibbons, seeking revenge for what some other lady had done to him years ago, and for the ill-treatment he felt he had received at Hawk Hall because of Francine.

He started to push her toward the back of the hawk house, and when she stumbled, he jerked on the cords, causing agonizing pains in the muscles of her arms and shoulders.

When they reached the back of the interior, he swung her around to face him and plunged his hand into the front of her dress. As Francine heard the old cotton garment start to rip, she lifted her head, trying to struggle, then saw to her relief that John Anderson was creeping quietly toward them with a spade raised in readiness.

Everything happened very quickly then as the spade caught the man on the back of the head, sending him to the ground, while the hand grasping her gown clenched, ripping the fabric from neck to waist as he fell.

Suddenly the hawk house was filled with people as Julian and Sir Godfrey came running in, followed by several of the assistants.

Unable to even hold her gown together, Francine turned her back to them and called, "Will someone please unfasten my hands?"

Julian got to her first and tried to turn her, but she resisted firmly.

"Unfasten my hands, please," she begged.

As he glanced over her shoulder, he saw the torn gown and her beautiful white breasts clearly visible. He took out a pocketknife and cut the bonds, then removed his jacket and put it around her, fastening the buttons to cover her completely. When he felt her tremble, he put his arms around her and held her close. "It's all right, my love," he murmured. "I believe John Anderson got here just in time, didn't he? Are you hurt anywhere?"

She shook her head. "Thank God someone saw him follow me in here. He must have been in hiding, waiting for his chance."

Sir Godfrey looked at the man, who was just beginning to come around, then he came over to his granddaughter. "Are you all right?" he asked, his gruff voice hiding his concern, and when she nodded, he said to Julian, "Take her back to the house, will you? I'll see to things here."

"I'd like to get my hands on him, sir," Julian said grimly, but Sir Godfrey shook his head.

"I'm going to press charges this time. He'll either be hanged or deported for attempted assault on a lady," he said.

"Either one is too good for him," Julian grumbled, but he took Francine gently by the arm and led her back to Hawk Hall.

"I'm sure you'd like to lie down and rest for a while, so I'll ecort you to your chamber and then get my sister to come and sit with you," he murmured.

"Please don't disturb her, Julian," Francine said quickly. "I'll ring for my maid to help me change and then I'll join you in the drawing room, if you don't mind."

"Are you sure?" Julian was surprised, expecting her to show signs of actute distress, but was delighted that she did not.

Though her smile was a little forced, she manged one nonetheless. "See, I'm not shaking anymore," she told him, and held out her hand to show him.

He looked at the bruises forming on her wrist where the leash had been bound so cruelly tight, and swore softly under his breath.

"I cannot imagine why he should hate me so, for at our first meeting I was only showing him how to go along," she said, frowning in puzzlement. "When he approached me in the garden he said something about one of my sort poking her nose in once before, and that he wasn't going to be sent packing again."

"It's not you personally, I'm sure. But some men cannot abide a woman doing anything better than they can, and it sounds as if you are too much like a previous employer who turned him off." Julian opened the door and gently pushed her inside her chamber, then stepped back. "I'll wait for you in the drawing room."

Once inside her chamber, with the door closed behind her, Francine went over to the bellpull and gave it the required number of tugs. Then she went to the armoire and took out a morning gown.

Dora was there in just a few minutes, and her questioning look turned to one of shock when she helped her mistress off with Julian's jacket. "Whatever happened, milady?" she asked.

"I met up again with that awful man who hurt your brother so badly," Francine said by way of explanation. "Bring a bowl of warm, perfumed water, for I must thoroughly wash myself where that smelly creature touched me."

The warm water felt good, and Dora came back with some ointment, for she noticed that his nails must have scratched her mistress's soft skin.

"There, milady," she said when she was finished. "You're as good as new again. Did you want to rest awhile before getting into your fresh gown?"

"No, I've no time for such indulgence, Dora," she said. "Help me into the gown and fix my hair, for I'm keeping our guest waiting downstairs."

Looking no worse for her misadventure, she went down the stairs, hoping to spend a little while with the man she loved so very much and who had seemed last night as though he felt the same way. She was surprised, however, to hear strange voices as she approached the drawing-room door.

Julian rose when she entered. "I understand it has been some time since you met your cousin, Lord Gerald Withers, and this is his wife, Lady Veronica," he said gently.

Francine went icy cold inside, for she guessed at once what they had come for. She forced a semblance of a smile. "It must be all of ten years since last we met, Gerald, and I am delighted that you have brought your wife to meet us," she said brightly. "But you must be exhausted from your journey. Let me send for some refreshments and I'll have a room prepared right away."

"You're very kind, Cousin Francine, but the purpose of our journey is to take my little daughter back to our home, so I do not believe we should stay the night," her cousin said a little stiffly. "Some refreshment would be very welcome, however."

It was what Francine had been anticipating for some time, but now that it had come she felt sick at heart. As he had not even visited the little girl in the more than two years she had been with them, it would be very difficult for Penelope to feel that he really was her father.

Francine could see Mrs. Parsons hovering in the hall and she went out to ask for something light to be prepared so as not to spoil their appetites for luncheon. She also requested that someone be sent to fetch her grandpapa.

Sir Godfrey did not look very pleased to see his grandson, for he also immediately realized the purpose of the visit, and though he knew, as did Francine, that it was the best thing for the child, he would have liked some time to prepare her for the upheaval. He did not let this interfere with his duties as host, however, and opened a bottle of his finest sherry with which to toast his grandsons's newborn heir, who had, of course, been left at home.

By the time luncheon was ready, the atmosphere was considerably warmer in the room. Nanny brought Penelope down to join them for the meal, and she looked adorable in her prettiest dress.

"This is your papa," Francine told her. "Do you remember him?"

"No, I don't," Penelope said frankly if a little disappointingly. She bent her knee and did a rather clumsy curtsy, then turned and made a better curtsy to Lady Veronica, but spoiled it by asking, "Who are you?"

"I'm your new mama, Penelope, and we're going to

become the best of friends," Lady Veronica told her with a kindly smile.

Francine was dismayed, for she had hoped they would wait until after luncheon, when Penelope was a little more used to them, before telling the child why they were here."

"Are you going to live with us, then?" Penelope asked, her eyes wide with curiosity.

"No, you're going to live with us, Penelope," her father told her, smiling stiffly. "We're taking you home today."

Suddenly Penelope looked afraid. "I don't want to go with you," she said firmly, shaking her head. "I want to stay here with Frankie and Grampa."

"We know you do," Lady Veronica said soothingly, "but we want to share you with them. You'll be able to come back and visit them later."

A look of horror came over the child's face, and she stamped her feet, crying, "No, I'm not going with them. I won't. I'm staying with you, Frankie." With tears pouring down her face she threw herself upon Francine, crying, "Please let me stay. I'll be good, I promise."

Francine stroked the little girl's shoulders gently and suggested to her cousin, "Why don't I take her upstairs to Nanny while we have luncheon, and give her time to get used to the idea?"

Gerald looked relieved, for he'd never liked screaming children. He nodded. "Go ahead, Francine," he said, "and we'll give her plenty of time to get over her crying, for I don't want a screaming brat for company in the carriage."

"Really, Gerald," Lady Veronica scolded as Francine took Penelope out of the room, "that's not very kind. Of course she's upset at the thought of leaving the people she loves, but she'll soon find out that we love her also."

"Hope you're not making a mistake," he muttered, but his wife hushed him.

Luncheon was a little subdued, but the wine Sir

Godfrey opened soon had the desired effect of lightening the atmosphere. Directly afterward the men all went outdoors, for Gerald expressed an interest in seeing the hawk houses while he was here, and Lady Veronica stayed behind with Francine and Kathleen.

"I know you're going to miss her terribly at first," Lady Veronica said, "but she has been away from her own family for far too long, and I promise I will take good care of her. Having a little baby brother to look after may help her get used to being with us."

"I'm so happy for you, my lady," Francine said, finding to her surprise that she meant it. "Ought you to be traveling so soon?"

Lady Veronica nodded. "I have a wet nurse for my son, and have felt completely well both during and since his birth. You are, of course, most welcome to visit us at any time."

"Thank you, you're very kind," Francine murmured, though inwardly wanting to hate her for taking Penelope away from them. "I'm glad she's going to someone as patient and understanding as you appear to be."

"And I do apologize for not giving you any warning of our visit, but Gerald is so very impulsive, you know," Lady Veronica told her.

Francine could not imagine for a moment that her stiff, stolid cousin could be even mildly impulsive, but she gave what she hoped was an understanding smile.

As soon as the men returned, Gerald said that they must be going, and he asked Francine to bring his daughter down again. And as Francine got up to do as he wished, Lady Veronica rose also.

"I left something in the carriage that I bought especially for Penelope. Do you think you could show me where to find it?" Veronica asked Francine, who took her out to the carriage and waited, curious to see what she had bought.

Lady Veronica reached inside and came out holding a lovely baby doll, dressed in the most exquisite silks and laces. "Do you think she will like it?" she asked.

"Of course, she'll adore it," Francine told her. "You obviously know the way to a little girl's heart. Do you wish to come with me to get her?"

"I think that might upset her. I'll wait at the foot of the stairs," Veronica said with a rather shy smile.

This time they were more successful. As soon as Penelope saw the doll, she held out her arms, and Veronica gently placed it in them, kissing the little girl's cheek. "I thought she might be company for you on the ride home," she said.

There were just a few inevitable tears as they said their good-byes. The doll appeared to have done the trick, and Penelope was about to step into the carriage when she suddenly let out a loud scream.

"Kitty. I can't go without Kitty," she cried, and ran to where Francine and her grandpapa waited.

Cousin Gerald looked exasperated, but Veronica came back to see what was the matter.

"It is her own cat," Francine explained. "It came with her as a kitten when Lady Withers brought her more than two years ago, and though it had kittens recently, they have all now been given good homes."

"Then, if it is hers, we must take it with us," Veronica said firmly, despite her husband's frown. "Do you know where it might be, or do we have to search for it?" she asked with a hint of amusement in her voice.

Francine smiled. "I think it will be in the kitchen. Shall we go and look, Penelope?"

A few minutes later, they came back complete with Kitty and a basket with a pillow inside. While Gerald watched, his wife settled Penelope, her doll, and Kitty comfortably inside the carriage, then leaned out. "We're ready now, my dear," she said to Gerald, "and there's plenty of room for you."

A little gingerly, he stepped inside, the door was closed, and they were off once more.

As soon as she and Sir Godfrey returned to the house, Francine said, "I'm going to ask you to excuse me for an hour or two. This has been a very difficult day and I believe that now I will lie down for a while."

   She climbed the stairs wearily, then slowly walked along to her chamber, feeling as though she had just aged ten years. Once in her room, she flung herself on the bed and sobbed her heart out for the child she felt she had just lost, and for the ones she feared she might never know.

18

F rancine could not remember when she had last felt so melancholy. The house seemed empty without Penelope's childish voice echoing through it, her pranks and her natural delight in the simplest of things.

She had spent the remainder of the day, after Penelope had left, resting in her bedchamber, a most unusual thing for her to do at any time, but she had felt she needed a little while to become accustomed to the child's absence before facing her guests.

Later that afternoon Kathleen had knocked on the door and asked if she might see her for a few minutes, and it was then that she told Francine that Julian was taking her home, and he would return in a day or so after checking as to how his own hawk house was progressing.

"Julian thinks that we should leave you on your own for a few days. We both know how fond you are of the little girl, and to lose her on the same day that you were so viciously attacked is enough to send even the strongest constitution into a decline," Kathleen said. "I'm not sure exactly what he meant, but he also said something about not wishing to upset you by pressing the matter you talked about last evening."

Francine looked puzzled, and Kathleen went on to say, "When leaving for Scotland, Mr. Anderson said you were not to be disturbed, but to tell you how very much he has enjoyed his stay here and to thank you for your hospitality. Julian said that he had nothing but the highest praise for Sir Godfrey's excellent standards as a falconer, and your grandpapa was, of course, quite puffed up about it."

"Oh, dear," Francine said, "I cannot lie abed in this way. I must get up to see him leave, or Grandpapa will be cross."

"Sir Godfrey said that on no account were you to get up, and in any case, Mr. Anderson has already left, so it wouldn't do any good," Kathleen told her. "And now I'm leaving also, but I'll be back within the week to see how you're getting along and to make sure Ken has not forgotten his promise, for he said that he would let me see the planets through his telescope."

She left then, and Francine tried to remember what Julian's message about the night before had really meant. Was he once again regretting what he had said to her? All she could do was wait until he returned and see what his attitude was then.

Deciding it was nonsense to stay in bed moping, she rose for supper, but though her grandpapa tried to cheer her up as much as possible, she was glad to accept his suggestion of an early night. To her amazement, she slept right through until morning and woke feeling quite refreshed.

It was no surprise to her to find that Kenneth also seemed at a loose end, and Francine could not help wondering if, perhaps, he was becoming fond of Kathleen, who she knew was already half in love with her brother. Far from forgetting his promise to Kathleen, he spent much of the next day in the sitting room off his bedchamber getting his telescopes focused correctly.

As Sir Godfrey stayed most of the day in the hawk houses, Francine busied herself around the hall, which was very quiet because, now that Penelope was gone, Grandpapa had sent Nanny off on a week's holiday to visit her family. With all the guests departed, the house somewhat resembled a mausoleum, Francine decided.

It was with feelings much resembling relief, therefore, that Francine observed through the window Dr. David Gardener step out of his carriage. He would, she was sure, take her mind away from her own depressing thoughts for a while.

"Dr. Gardener." Francine smiled a warm welcome. "How very nice of you to call."

"Well, you know how quickly the servants pass information around," he said. "I heard that you had been attacked by some rogue a few days ago, and when I did not receive a call for my services, I assumed you were uninjured. However, I thought it best to make sure."

Kenneth joined them just as a maid placed a tray of tea before her, and Francine pushed up her sleeves and held out her hands to show the bruises on her wrists left by the tight bonds. "I think this was the extent of the damage, Doctor," she told him, "but I appreciate your concern."

He took her hands in his, turning them to see the black-and-purple marks on both sides. "How long were the bonds in place?" he asked.

"Not more than five minutes, I would say," she told him, "for Mr. Anderson saw him follow me into the hawk house, sent word to Grandpapa, and came himself immediately."

"You were fortunate, my dear, for had they remained there so very tightly secured for several hours, the circulation could have been completely cut off, with possible permanent impairment of movement."

"Then I am indeed in Mr. Anderson's debt," Francine said while Kenneth echoed her sentiments.

She handed their guest a cup of tea and proffered a plate of Cook's special saffron cake.

"Do you share your sister's and grandfather's passion for hawks, my lord?" he asked Kenneth.

Kenneth smiled ruefully. "Much to their disappointment I really do not have their enthusiasm, but of course, I know enough about them to give a hand when needed. I have much loftier interests, I'm afraid."

Dr. Gardener raised his eyebrows. "Indeed? I had not thought it possible to get much higher than the peregrine flies, unless you are, perhaps, a balloonist?"

"I am an astronomer," Kenneth told him. "I was engaged in advanced study of celestial bodies at

Cambridge, and am planning to build an observatory when I finally return to my estates in Sussex."

"How very interesting," the other man observed. "I suppose the information did not filter through the grapevine because the servants probably do not understand what it is."

"We astronomers are considered to be a little strange," Kenneth admitted. "However, it has a great deal more to offer than falconry, for the latter is, after all, a thing of the past, whereas I believe that we will one day travel to observe and perhaps even land upon some of the planets."

The doctor was much impressed. "Do you really think we might land upon the sun?"

Kenneth gave a dry laugh. "No, sir, that is out of the question because of the heat that emanates from it, but I do think we might possibly visit the moon someday."

Just then there was a brisk step in the hall and Francine's heart skipped a beat as Julian walked into the room. "Just in time for tea, I see," he said with a warm smile in Francine's direction, then he noticed Dr. Gardener and he no longer appeared pleased.

Dr. Gardener returned Julian's brief nod, then remarked, "Lord Truesdale was just telling me of his interest in astronomy, my lord. Do you share this interest or does yours lie in some other direction?"

"I studied only enough astronomy to prevent me making a fool of myself when I'm with some of my friend's colleagues," Julian drawled. "As I will one day be responsible for considerables estates and the people who make a living on them, my inclination lies in learning the latest agricultural practices, such as new breeds of cows and sheep, improved land-drainage methods, and ways to keep farm workers here instead of trying their hands in the factories of the fast-growing industrial towns."

Dr. Gardener had been standing with a teacup and saucer in one hand and a plate of pastries in the other, but as Francine sat down before a low table, he moved to take a seat close to her.

Julian's brows drew together in a black scowl, for it was the seat he had been planning to take but had been too busy answering the doctor's question. He sat down across from them and helped himself to the cakes Francine offered.

"What can a small place like this offer for a young and presumably ambitious doctor?" Julian asked.

"When taking over the practice of a retiring doctor, it can offer steady work," Dr. Gardener said. "In the cities all the wealthier patients already have their favorite practitioners, who they frequently forget to pay, and a doctor could starve to death with his poorer patients."

Julian raised an eyebrow. "How things have changed from the time of dedicated doctors. Now the first consideration is that of the patient's ability to pay, and I had thought it a noble profession," he said disdainfully.

Dr. Gardener flushed and Francine looked across at Julian with surprise. It was unlike him to be rude to anyone in his own house, never mind in someone else's.

"Has Mr. Charles Bottomley now fully recovered from his accident?" she asked, changing the subject.

He nodded. "Completely. In fact, since he met the charming Lady Arabella he has almost forgotten there is anything wrong with his ankle. It is wonderful how you ladies distract us at times," Dr. Gardener said softly, but just loud enough for Julian to hear and scowl once more.

"But to get back to your last remark, my lord," Dr. Gardener continued, "it is easy to speak of dedication in medicine when a doctor receives a salary from a hospital or, in the case of research, from a university. But general practitioners in the field of medicine make up the vast majority of doctors, and unfortunately they have to eat also."

Julian nodded, but his frown remained.

Noticing this, Francine deliberately leaned toward the doctor, smiling. "Sometimes gentlemen need distraction from the pressure of their work," she said with a twinkle in her eyes. "Whenever you find the need of someone to talk to and understand your problems, you must not hesitate to come here, Doctor."

"David, please," he requested firmly.

"Of course, David, if you prefer it, and you must call me Francine," she told him invitingly.

"Do you specialize in anything, Doctor?" Julian almost shouted in his effort to take the man's attention off Francine. "Aside, of course, from holding the hands of your female patients suffering from neglectful husbands." He withdrew a handkerchief from his pocket and mopped his brow as though he was feeling unduly warm.

Dr. Gardener appeared to have got a crumb stuck in his throat, for he started to cough and had to take several sips of tea before he could respond to Julian's question. He did not appear to have noticed the intended slur upon his character.

"I have made quite a study of apoplexy and have observed that it most frequently affects gentlemen who are inclined to become very easy aggravated and over-heated," he remarked mildly, although Francine was sure he saw his mouth twitch at the corners. "Gout also interests me in that most gentlemen who indulge in rich foods and imbibe wines and brandy to excess seem to suffer from it eventually."

"In other words," Kenneth interposed, "we bring about our own infirmities."

"To a large extent," Dr. Gardener agreed, then turned to Francine, who was looking at Julian, for she had seldom seen him appear quite so angry as he was now—not even when he was scolding her for galloping in the park.

She suddenly realized that the doctor had asked her a question, and feeling someone had to agree with him, she nodded and murmured, "Of course."

To her complete surprise, Dr. Gardener gave her a winning smile and rose to his feet prepared to leave. "Thank you, my dear Francine. I'll call for you at two o'clock tomorrow, then, and will think of little else in the meantime."

He bowed low over her hand, and for a moment she thought she heard a chuckle, but his face was quite serious when he raised it once more and she decided she must have been mistaken.

As he headed toward the door, Julian rose also and, without a word, strode out after the doctor.

"What did I agree to, Ken?" Francine asked, but found herself speaking to an empty room, for her brother had raced out after Julian to prevent anything untoward happening between the two men. He had seen the murderous look on his friend's face.

Because of Julian's bad mood and rude remarks, it had been an exhausting hour, and Francine had no desire to see him and have to put up with more of his bad temper. A walk on the moors was just the thing to clear the blue devils away, she decided.

Five minutes later, wearing a cloak over her gown, a bonnet on her head, and a pair of leather boots for walking, she set out at a fast pace through the copse and onto her beloved moors. She strode along swinging her arms and taking big gulps of the fresh air as she went, following a familiar path and not looking back even once to see what, if anything, the men were up to.

She had covered quite a considerable distance when, suddenly, one of her arms was grasped firmly and she was swung around and slammed against a strong, broad chest. For a moment she felt afraid, remembering the attack upon her yesterday, but once her senses took over, she knew without a doubt that it was Julian, and though he was even more angry than before, her fear turned into fury.

"Just what do you think you're doing, Julian Whitehead?" Francine shouted, intent on getting in the first word. "How dare you grab me in this rough way? I'm not one of your ladybirds that you can treat any way you have the urge."

"No, you're not," Julian angrily agreed. "But you seem pretty anxious to become one of the good doctor's," he thundered. " 'Of course I'll go driving with you, David,' " he mimicked in falsetto tones.

"I did nothing of the . . ." Francine began, and stopped. Was that what she had agreed to? "I'll go driving with whoever I want to, whenever I wish," she snapped to cover her confusion. "It's none of your business who I go out with anyway.

"And how dare you insult guests in Grandpapa's house? You're nothing but a smug, conceited, pompous old crosspatch," she shouted, and stamped her foot in aggravation.

"Ouch, you little vixen," Julian yelled, for she had, this time completely by chance, come down hard on Julian's left foot. As he grasped her shoulders, quite prepared to shake some sense into her, she saw all the birds around take flight and suddenly realized how odd they must both appear to the poor creatures.

She started to laugh at their own foolishness, and suddenly they were both laughing helplessly, all anger forgotten.

As Francine tried to catch her breath, Julian's lips captured hers in a bruising, passionate kiss, and then all conherent thoughts left her as she allowed the powerful emotions surging through her to take over completely. She clung to him, her head swimming but not willing to stop these wonderful sensations, completely unaware that her body was shamelessly and urgently pressing of its own volition against his. Her lips were parted and his tongue was tasting her sweetness to the fullest extent and eagerly asking for more.

Finally he raised his head and gazed down at her bee-stung lips and glazed eyes, a question in his own. "Have you, by any chance, been wanting this as much as I have?" he asked softly.

"For years," she moaned, "but I thought you would never come to realize it."

He looked puzzled. "But I don't understand. Why did you refuse to marry me?"

"Because you didn't mean it then." Francine's voice was muffled, for her face was pressed against his crumpled cravat. "You were being noble because you had spent part of the night in my company."

Julian shook his head slowly. "I was doing no such thing. Don't you know that I'm never noble, you little idiot? I had just realized how I felt about you, and I couldn't imagine that you did not feel the same way," he told her. "When you turned me down so decidedly I was too crushed to try to explain."

She lifted her face so that her lips brushed his as she murmured regretfully, "I am so very sorry, darling. I thought you were just doing the right thing, for Grandpapa had already asked me if I wanted him to speak to you.

"What fools we have been . . ." she began to say, but she did not finish for her lips were captured in another long, lingering kiss, and when he released her once more, she rested her head against his shoulder.

They wended their way slowly back across the moors toward Hawk Hall, taking an amazingly long time to traverse such a short distance, but they were greatly hampered by the fact that the footpath had never been intended for two people to walk with their arms around each other.

When they reached the home woods and Julian saw the exact spot where he had proposed, he stopped, flopped her unceremoniously upon the tree trunk where she had sat not so very long ago, then went down upon one knee.

"Lady Francine," he began, trying to school his features into a serious expression, "will you do me the honor of accepting my proposal of marriage—this time?"

She looked at him with eyes filled with love and laughter, then her brows drew together in a scowl. "Well, I'm not sure whether I will or not," she said, trying to keep her lips from quivering. "What are your future prospects? Can you look after me in the manner to which I am accustomed?"

"I believe so," Julian said, appearing to consider the matter. "I will allow you to work with my hawks, even letting you clean out the houses, as you seem to enjoy it so much. I'll provide you with a gig, for I know you would find my phaeton a little beyond your driving skills,'' he said, keeping a straight face even when she threatened him with her fist.

"You'll remain a lady, I hope, or at least as a viscountess you will keep the title, though I pray that it will be many years before you become a countess,'' he said on a serious note.

"So do I, for the only reason I am accepting your offer is, of course, because I adore your mama and papa,'' she said with a grin, "and I'm fond of your sister also.''

"I'm not sure that I can afford the cost of your expensive modiste, but as the gowns have achieved their objective, perhaps Madame Eloise's creations would suffice. Certainly when you become . . .'' he paused, seeing Francine's face suffuse with color. "I think that is something we must talk about seriously, is it not, my love, when I am in a more comfortable pose, for you have accepted my offer, have you not?''

"Of course I have, silly. Get up, for goodness' sake, before your knee locks in that position and you have to ask David Gardener to come back and help you,'' Francine teased.

He sprang to his feet, clasped her hand, and pulled her to hers. "That's something else we have to talk about, young lady,'' he said firmly.

"You didn't get into a fight with him, did you?'' Francine asked, looking worried.

"Not yet,'' Julian said on a note of warning, "but if you allow him to take you driving tomorrow, I very well may.''

"I didn't know that I had agreed to do so,'' Francine explained, "for you were disagreeing so very much with every remark he made that I said, 'Of course,' when in fact I had not heard his question.''

He drew her into his arms, and her heart started to beat rapidly in anticipation. "You're not going to let him take you out, are you?'' he asked, and when she shook her head, then lifted it for his kiss, he captured her lips with an intensity that surprised them both and left Francine trembling with emotions she did not completely understand as yet.

"Let's go in the back way and through to the sun room," she suggested.

Julian nodded. "Just for a few minutes," he agreed, "for once your grandpapa knows we are to be wed, he'll see that we're chaperoned constantly, I've no doubt." They were in luck, for no one was around when they entered the house and made their way to the seldom-used room.

Francine sat down on the sofa and Julian joined her, slipping an arm around her shoulders and turning her toward him so that he could see her face.

"I've always wanted to have at least four children," he began quietly, searching her face for her instinctive reaction. The radiant smile that broke over it told him better than any words could. "But that is only if you are able to have them without damage to your health."

"But I've always been healthy, and you must know that I want at least four, if not more," Francine protested, then asked, tongue in cheek, "But how will you feel if David Gardener delivers them?"

"That brings up another question, love. Where would you want to live? I would prefer to be as much alone as possible, and there is a dower house in the grounds of ours, but it is somewhat small," he said. Then he added with a laugh, "Particularly for us and at least four children."

"Do we have to decide right away?" Francine asked.

"I'll live wherever you want to, I promise. But Grandpapa has always said that Hawk Hall will be mine when he passes on. And he's a great deal older than your mama and papa. If he asks us, could you bear to live here with him?"

"I think so, for he likes his privacy himself and would give us ours, I'm sure, without question. And, of course, before long, Ken will have to go and take care of his Sussex estates. Let's leave that question up in the air for now, shall we? Do you know you have twenty-three freckles around your nose?'' Julian asked, drawing her closer to get a better count, then even closer still.

Kenneth had been sitting near the drawing-room window and gazing out over the moors while his grandpapa caught up on the unread newspapers, when he saw two obvious lovers come from the home woods and approach the house. Before he saw their faces, he recognized the blue gown Francine had been wearing.

"Aha," he said with considerable glee. "If my eyes do not deceive me, I believe I can safely say that the good viscount is no longer invincible."

His grandpapa looked up from his copy of the *Times* and glanced out, a satisfied smile upon his face. "They'll have many a tiff yet before the knot is tied, for they're both too volatile for their own good," he said. "But it looks as though you're right. I don't hear anyone in the hall, so they must have come in the back way."

He rang for the housekeeper, and when she presented herself a few minutes later, he asked, "Do we have any champagne in the ice house?"

"Of course, Sir Godfrey," she told him. "Will you have some before dinner?"

"I believe so. You may bring it in here and leave it on the sideboard with four glasses until we're ready," he told her, and when she went out, he turned to his grandson. "If I was a betting man, I'd gamble on their coming in here within ten minutes, but you know Julian's sense of honor better than I."

Kenneth nodded. "I'll wager a pony that they're here in five minutes or less," he said, taking out his pocket watch and looking at it.

Two minutes later there was the sound of footsteps coming slowly along the hall, and a ruffled but radiant Francine entered, closely followed by Julian, whose necktie was still rumpled despite hasty attention to it.

Sir Godfrey and Kenneth rose as Julian cleared his

throat. "I have the greatest pleasure in telling you both that Frankie has just agreed to become my wife," he told them as Francine gazed up at him lovingly.

"I say, shouldn't you have asked Grandpapa's permission, Julian? Surely that's the way it's done in the best of circles," Kenneth suggested with a grin.

"But he did, some weeks ago, my boy," Sir Godfrey told him, "and it seems it's taken my granddaughter all this time to make up her mind. I'm delighted, of course. Shall we?" He gestured toward the sideboard where the champagne sat in a silver bucket.

Kenneth went over to do the honors while Francine looked at her grandpapa in amazement. "How did you know?" she asked.

Sir Godfrey and Kenneth exchanged glances, then said in unison, "We'll never tell."